PRAISE FOR CANDY HALLIDAY'S PREVIOUS NOVEL
DREAM GUY

"A fun romp."

—*Publishers Weekly*

"FOUR STARS! Laugh-out-loud funny . . . a fast-moving romance . . . an appealing story that is fun without being silly."

—*Romantic Times BOOKclub Magazine*

"A lighthearted, contemporary war of the sexes using technology to further the skirmishes . . . Fans will enjoy this fun tale that is one click away from providing the *Dream Guy*."

—*Midwest Book Review*

Also by Candy Halliday

Dream Guy

MR. DESTINY

CANDY HALLIDAY

WARNER
FOREVER

NEW YORK   BOSTON

Book design by Giorgetta Bell McRee

Warner Books

Time Warner Book Group
1271 Avenue of the Americas
New York, NY 10020
Visit our Web site at www.twbookmark.com

Printed in the United States of America

First Paperback Printing: November 2005

10 9 8 7 6 5 4 3 2 1

For Shelli and Tracy—truly destined to be together.

Acknowledgments

Special thanks always to Jenny Bent, agent extraordinaire. Extreme thanks to Karen Kosztolnyik, editor incredible. Thank you always, Blue, for putting up with me. Quint and Caroline—you make my life complete.

MR. DESTINY

CHAPTER 1

~~~

Kate Anderson flashed hot all over.

The summer heat wave assaulting New York City had nothing to do with it.

Here she was, Miss Efficient Art Gallery Manager, overseeing the annual "Art in Central Park" outdoor exhibit cosponsored by the Metropolitan Museum of Art. Yet, what was she doing? She was fantasizing about the handsome mounted patrol officer galloping up the path in her direction.

Fantasizing about him *naked*, to be exact.

Prewedding jitters Kate assured herself.

That, and her pesky subconscious trying to challenge her belief that size didn't matter.

Size didn't matter.

Not to Kate.

Not if you were a prominent corporate attorney with a no-nonsense outlook on life that would finally bring focus and clarity to her life.

She'd met Harold Trent Wellington shortly after her time-to-grow-up-now thirtieth birthday. From their first date, Kate had known Harold was exactly the type of man she needed to keep her grounded. Harold was handsome by any woman's standards—tall, lean, a touch of distinguished-looking premature gray at his temples. He was older and settled, another plus. They shared the same interests: opera, art, the finer things in life.

Maybe Harold was a neat-freak and a tad bit anal. Maybe they had a nonexistent sex life at the moment, but they were working through Harold's feelings of inadequacy in the bedroom with a reputable couple's therapist. The main thing was, Harold had been a calming and positive influence over her life from the moment they started seeing each other.

Proof being, overseeing today's outdoor art exhibit; a responsibility her still-in-her-irresponsible-twenties self wouldn't have been able to handle in her *pre-Harold* days.

So size didn't matter at all.

Kate simply wouldn't allow size to matter.

She blinked twice, willing the officer's naked image to go away. It didn't. Her fantasy was still nude, rippling muscles everywhere, begging to be touched.

The total opposite of Harold, Kate thought briefly.

Harold's only interest had been in passing the bar, not in pumping one.

But yikes!

Now the police officer was staring back at her just as intently.

Oh God.

Had he read her mind?

Of course not.

That was impossible.

There was no way the officer could have known what

she'd been thinking. Still, the look on his face was more than just perplexed. He looked shocked. As if he couldn't quite believe what he was seeing.

Kate sent a nervous look around her, pleased to see the crowd of people milling in and around the exhibit couldn't have been more orderly. There were a few couples, several small groups, one or two lone art admirers. Many of them were regular customers she recognized, politely showing their support for Anderson Gallery of Fine Arts. Everyone was even speaking in hushed tones, as if the exhibit were being held inside at her grandmother's prestigious art gallery in SoHo, one of the most notable art galleries in the city.

No, nothing was amiss with the crowd.

Nor would he find anything wrong with her paperwork, if that was the reason for the concerned look on the officer's face. She had a permit and everything else in order right there on her clipboard.

But wait.

Was he looking at her?

Or was he staring at the painting beside her?

Kate glanced at the oil painting sitting on an easel to her right. She'd never cared for the artist who called himself "Apocalypse." His paintings were usually dark and violent. But there was nothing offensive about this painting. Who could possibly be offended by a painting of the Madonna and Child?

She squared her shoulders when the officer pulled on the reins, bringing his mount to a stop a short distance away from her. He slid one leg easily over the back of the horse. The second his shiny black boots hit the ground her fantasizing stopped.

Thank God.

He was fully clothed again.

He walked up and stopped in front of her, the name on his badge announcing he was Officer Anthony Petrocelli.

An Italian on a stallion, Kate thought.

No wonder her libido had kicked into overdrive the minute she saw him.

She followed his gaze to the painting. "From your expression, I can't tell if you like this painting, or if it disturbs you," she said. "And that's a first for me. I can usually read people pretty well."

His sexy grin caught her off guard.

Kate tensed.

She was *not* going to let her gaze drift any lower than his chin—even if he held his gun to her head.

He didn't reach for his revolver. Instead, he unsnapped his chin strap and took off his helmet.

Mercy.

He was all male and even more handsome than she'd imagined. Sexy brown eyes. Chiseled features. Olive skin. Just a hint of a five-o'clock shadow running along his strong angular jaw.

Maybe it was the contrast between this guy and Harold, Kate decided, that made him so appealing to her. He had that reckless unrefined edginess about him—something calm, cool, and always collected Harold didn't have.

He ran a hand through his short black hair and hit her with another grin. "I don't know how to tell you this," he said, "but you and I were destined to be together."

What?

The fantasizing was definitely over.

After an idiotic statement like that one, he could have

been stark naked with a willy the size of Texas, and she still wouldn't have been interested in Officer Anthony Petrocelli.

Kate sent him a bored look. "That has to be the corniest pickup line I've ever heard."

"I'm not trying to pick you up," he said quickly. "If you'll let me explain, I think you'll understand why I had to stop and talk to you."

"Not interested," Kate told him.

His challenging look called her a liar. "A total stranger walks up to you. He tells you the two of you are destined to be together. And you aren't the least bit interested in why a guy would be willing to make a complete fool of himself with a statement like that?"

"Not in the least," Kate said.

Of course she was curious.

But she wasn't going to *tell* him that.

For all she knew he could be some weirdo pervert who was only impersonating a police officer. Except for the horse, she decided, glancing past him for a second. She doubted even a pervert would go to the trouble of rounding up a horse. Plus, this was one *fine*-looking weirdo pervert, if he was one. One she doubted had any trouble whatsoever when it came to picking up women.

"*I'm* interested in why you would make a complete fool of yourself with a statement like that one."

Kate turned around to find Alexis Graham, a.k.a. best friend, standing behind her. The best friend who was *supposed* to have arrived at the exhibit hours ago to lend support. *And* the best friend who was also camping out on Kate's sofa at the moment, thanks to the current squabble Alex was having with her husband.

Alex was dressed for success as usual—a power suit befitting her important AT&T executive title. Her signature short dark hair was heavily moussed and slicked back dramatically—manly almost. Except there had never been anything *manly* about Alexis Graham. Not her seductive grin. Not her flirtatious personality. Definitely not her dynamite all-woman figure.

"Oh, come on, Kate," she said. "Let the officer tell us his story." She ignored Kate's stern look, stepped forward, and thrust out her hand. "Alex Graham, best friend." She looked back at Kate. "This is Kate Anderson."

He smiled. "Are you the artist, Kate?"

Kate missed the question.

Her mind was wandering back in the naked direction again. It made no sense, but now that she knew he wasn't trying to pick her up, it was safe to fantasize about him. Besides, fantasizing was harmless. Her thoughts were her own. It wasn't anybody's business if standing this close to a man with such raw sex appeal made her want to . . .

Alex punched Kate with her elbow.

"What?" Kate said when Alex sent her a what's-wrong-with-you look.

Alex looked back at the officer. "No, Kate isn't the artist," she said. "Kate's grandmother owns the gallery hosting this exhibit. Kate is the manager of Anderson Gallery of Fine Arts."

Damn!

Her best friend was giving her fantasy way too much information.

Alex ignored Kate's frown and smiled at him.

When he happily smiled back, Kate's eyes betrayed her and moved slowly down from his chin. Lower, lower . . .

"It's ironic you should bring up the subject of grand-mothers," he said. "My grandmother is the reason I'm standing here now."

Forget grandmothers!

Grandmothers had no place in the middle of her fantasy.

He pointed to his name tag. "Petrocelli. Think big, med-dlesome, Italian family. That would be mine. Think an adorable but eccentric grandmother from the old country. That also would be mine. A grandmother who reads tea leaves for the male members of the family on their sixteenth birthdays so she can make a marriage prediction."

"Fascinating," Alex said.

Kate was still only half-listening. Her gaze kept wan-dering back to his mouth. He had the most incredible lips. Full, yet firm. The kind of lips that would . . .

He laughed, snapping her back to the conversation.

"I'm glad you think tea-leaf reading is fascinating, Alex," he said. "I call it ridiculous."

"I'd say ridiculous is a fair description of this whole situation," Kate said, and Alex quickly shushed her.

He said, "Twenty years ago my grandmother read *my* tea leaves. She predicted I wouldn't marry until I was thirty-six years old. That I would marry a beautiful blonde with green eyes. And . . ."

"Oh, please," Kate said, and "pop" went her fantasy bubble again.

"*And*," he repeated, "my grandmother said I would meet this woman in Central Park, standing beside the Vir-gin Mary."

Alex gasped.

All three of them automatically looked at the painting sitting on the easel directly beside Kate.

"Unlike the rest of my crazy family," he said, "I've never had a superstitious bone in my body. Tony, I told myself, a blonde with green eyes? Maybe. But the Virgin Mary hanging out in Central Park? Forgetaboutit."

"Until today," Alex spoke up. "When you came riding through Central Park and saw Kate standing beside this painting."

"Exactly," he said. "And since I just turned thirty-six a few weeks ago and I'm still not married, the *Twilight Zone* music definitely kicked in for a second."

"And who could blame you?" Alex said. "Right, Kate?"

All Kate said was, "Wrong blonde." She held her left hand up, hoping the sizable bling bling on her finger would snap both of them back to reality. "I'm already engaged. I'm getting married in two months."

Alex nodded—sadly, Kate noticed—confirming everything she'd just said.

She felt like slapping Alex. And she definitely didn't like the way *he* was staring at her now—searching her face—as if he sensed that whether she was getting married in two months or not, she'd been fantasizing about the naughty things she'd like to do to him from the moment he'd come trotting up the trail.

"Well, there you go," he finally said, impaling her with one last look. "So much for destiny."

"And such a pity," Alex said.

This time Kate gave *Alex* an elbow-to-the-ribs punch.

He snapped on his helmet. "Thank you, ladies. For listening to my story."

"Our pleasure," Alex said with a wistful sigh.

"And thank you, Kate, for finally putting my grandmother's prediction to rest."

Kate's nod was cordial.

Almost.

She wanted him gone. On his way and out of her face. She was an engaged woman. Soon to be married. The last thing she needed was some gorgeous and overly congenial hunk like this one showing up to remind her that if she did marry reserved and marginally stuffy Harold, she might be getting the short end of the stick—in more ways than one.

Good. He's leaving.

He sent both of them a friendly salute, then turned and walked back to his horse. After slipping a boot into the stirrup, he pulled himself effortlessly up on the back of his horse, rode off down the path, and never looked back.

Alex immediately sent her the perturbed look Kate was expecting. "You dummy. He was gorgeous. He had a great sense of humor. He even got a little misty-eyed talking about his grandmother, for Christ's sake. How could you let a romantic guy like him ride out of your life like that?"

Kate rolled her eyes. "You tell me, Alex. Why do *you* think I wasn't interested in some misty-eyed cop with a crazy story about his tea-leaf-reading grandmother? Aside from the fact that I'm already engaged. Because I *am* going to marry Harold, Alex. You can boycott my wedding. You can even keep pulling stunts like the one you pulled just now, trying to fix me up with random guys on the street. But it isn't going to work. I'm interested in Harold. And *only* Harold."

Alex snorted. "Oh, come on, Kate. The only reason you've ever been interested in Harold is because you've always been a sucker for a sad story."

"A sad story?" Kate shook her head in protest. "Harold doesn't have a sad story. He's smart. He's successful. He . . ."

"He has a gherkin instead of a dill?" Alex said. "And that's pretty damn sad if you ask me."

Kate frowned. "I never should have told you his ex-girlfriend made some ego-shattering comment that Harold's still trying to overcome."

"And I still can't believe Harold told *you* his french fry was a tad short of a Happy Meal. What kind of a man would admit that? Unless, like I said, he was trying to play on your sympathy?"

"He didn't just walk up to me and say, 'Hi, I'm Harold Wellington, and I have a small penis,' Alex. Harold's intimacy problem is a mental issue, and you know it. You were the one who suggested we should see a couple's therapist so Harold could get his confidence back in the bedroom."

"And how's that going for you?"

When Kate frowned again, Alex said, "I'm boycotting your wedding because I don't trust him, Kate. You're my dearest and closest friend. It worries me that Harold has been rushing you to the altar from the first night he met you. What's the big hurry? You've only known him six months."

"Eight months," Kate corrected. "Long enough to know Harold is the most charming man I've ever met. Plus he adores me. Tell me how being married to a successful and charming man who adores you can be a bad thing."

"He's nauseatingly charming to you, Kate," Alex said, "but he's an arrogant prick to everyone else." She thought for a second, and said, "No, make that an arrogant *unresponsive* prick, since that's more appropriate for Harold and his limp Wellington."

"Alex!" Kate scolded, looking around them. "Clean up your language, or at least keep your voice down."

Alex grinned, leaned forward, and whispered, "I bet there's nothing *limp* about Officer Petrocelli. And from the way he was looking at you earlier, I'd say he'd be more than willing to prove it to you."

"Not interested," Kate said, and it was true, now that temptation had finally ridden off down the path and out of her sight.

"Liar," Alex said with a smirk. "I saw the way you were ogling the guy before he even stopped to talk to you. Admit it. Why do you think you didn't even realize I was here?"

Kate's cheeks flushed. "Okay! I admit it. I was attracted to the guy the second I saw him. It was all I could do to keep from dragging him into the bushes and demanding that he frisk me. But that still doesn't change a thing."

"How do you know? If he'd frisked your brains out, you might have come to your senses and called off the wedding."

"See!" Kate said. "There's just no winning with you, Alex."

Alex reached out and put a supportive arm around Kate's shoulder. "Hey, there's no reason to feel guilty about being attracted to a good-looking guy. Especially with your hopeless celibacy situation. What bothers me is that I've never once seen you look at Harold the way I just saw you look at the man who could very well be your Mr. Destiny."

Again, Kate blushed at the truth.

She pushed Alex away, and said, "I'd be worrying about my own celibacy situation, if I were you."

There.

She could give back as good as Alex could send.

Alex only sent her a sympathetic look. "At least I know my celibacy situation is only because I'm being too stubborn to go home right now."

"Don't lecture me, Alex."

"Don't mess with destiny, Kate."

Alex's warning made her shiver.

She'd had her own premonition moments earlier as she'd watched him ride away. Something told Kate she hadn't seen the last of Officer Anthony Petrocelli.

"Well, I just took stupidity to a whole new level," Tony said aloud, when he was safely out of hearing range of the two women who had just witnessed him making a complete fool of himself.

Skyscraper shook his head up and down several times, pulling his bridle from Tony's hand. "Hey!" Tony said. "That wasn't a cue for you to agree with me."

The horse's ears pricked for a second, then relaxed, signaling to Tony that even his horse wasn't going to argue that moot point. Except *stupidity* didn't accurately describe the stunt he'd just pulled.

Insanity would be a better word.

Only a crazy person would have walked up to a total stranger and spent five full minutes telling her about the idiotic marriage prediction his grandmother had made twenty years earlier—especially when she'd told him up front that she wasn't interested in anything he had to say.

Of course, then her take-charge best friend had butted in and opened the door so he could prove without a doubt that he really was too stupid to live.

Tony shook his head disgustedly.

Skyscraper did the same.

He shifted in the saddle slightly, making Skyscraper's ears twitch impatiently at his restlessness. But even after he'd settled back into a comfortable riding position, he couldn't stop thinking about how Kate Anderson had looked when he rounded the curve and saw her standing there on the path.

The late-afternoon sun had been at her back, shining through the flimsy material of her free-flowing dress, and giving him a silhouette peek at luscious curves he wouldn't have had the privilege of seeing otherwise. The sexiness of her stance alone had set his head reeling.

His gaze had drifted up from her shapely legs to her beautiful face. High cheekbones. Perfect mouth. The sexy way she was nibbling at her bottom lip. That's when his heart had picked up more than a few extra beats.

And the real clincher?

Without a doubt, that long straight hair of hers, shining like spun gold against her slender shoulders.

He'd been awestruck at the mere sight of her.

That had been before he'd even noticed the painting of the Blessed Virgin sitting on the easel beside her. *Or* before he'd gotten close enough to determine the color of her eyes.

Yet once he did get closer, those moss green eyes had drawn him in like a magnet. For one brief second, he'd even had the audacity to think, *This woman is my destiny.*

"*Idiot*," Tony said aloud, and Skyscraper came to an abrupt halt. Tony nudged the horse gently in the sides with his knees. "I meant me, dammit. Not you."

Skyscraper snorted, then moved forward again.

A green-eyed blonde standing beside the Virgin Mary. He still couldn't believe it.

Nonna's twenty-year-old prediction had come back to haunt him for real.

In fact, Nonna's prediction had been all everyone in his large family—from his parents to his tongue-in-cheek brothers-in-law—had been talking about since his thirty-sixth birthday party a few weeks ago. Crazy people. All of them. Even crazier was the family legend that Nonna had never been wrong about one of her sainted marriage predictions.

Not that he hadn't voiced his own unpopular opinion on the subject the night of his birthday party, because he had. He'd patiently pointed out that it had been the generic nature of Nonna's predictions, not destiny, that had fulfilled the marriage prophecy for the four Petrocelli men preceding him. His own father's tea-leaf prediction being one of them—whether his mother wanted to believe it or not.

So maybe his parents had met on the subway. What New Yorker didn't ride the subway? And maybe his mother had been wearing a coat with a fur collar and a pair of red high heels. There had to be thousands of women in the city, even today, who had fur-collar coats and red high heels in their closets. Believing his grandmother could actually predict the future was nothing short of ludicrous.

Almost as ludicrous as finding a green-eyed blonde standing beside the Virgin Mary in Central Park.

Tony let out a deep sigh.

Skyscraper responded with a horse-type version of the same, forcing air though his muzzle so it came out in a long, loud pffffft.

"Would you just focus on the trail?" Tony said, which was another stupid thing to say because Skyscraper knew their routine as well, if not better, than Tony did himself.

As proof, Skyscraper left the path without even being prompted. Heading, Tony knew, for one of their first favorite afternoon stops. A particular shaded park bench located at this end of the park near the Met. A park bench where summer days like this one would find Solomon Stein, a rather stooped elderly Jewish man, working the daily crossword puzzle in the *New York Times* and feeding the pigeons.

Sol looked over the top of his wire-rimmed reading glasses when Skyscraper came to an automatic stop by his park bench. "I'm stumped again," he said, reaching out to give the horse a fond rub down the full length of his nose. "Ten-letter word that means carefree. Begins with 'i.'"

Tony thought for a second. "Insouciant."

Sol penciled in the word with a frown on his face.

"You're welcome," Tony said.

Sol only grunted. "I say this every time you give me a split-second answer to a word that's had me stumped for hours. What a waste of a good Princeton education."

Tony laughed. "And every time you say that, I remind you that *no* education is a waste. *And*, that after spending two miserable years sitting behind a desk on Wall Street, I finally pulled my head out of my MBA ass and headed straight for the Police Academy."

Sol shook his gray head. "A cop with a Princeton education. What's wrong with that picture?"

"Nothing," Tony said. "It's who I am. It's what I do. Get over it."

"Only if you'll admit you have that photographic memory I've always suspected," Sol said, reaching into the paper sack sitting on the bench beside him. "Which, aside from being a Princeton man, is the only explanation I have for why I've never been able to stump you with a crossword answer yet."

"We all have photographic memories, Sol," Tony said, grinning. "Some of us just don't have enough film."

Sol looked over at Skyscraper. "A wise man and a wise*ass*. A deadly combination." He slipped the horse the apple wedge he'd taken from the sack, then waved impatiently, motioning them forward. "Get your smart-mouth partner out of here," he said to Skyscraper. "He's breaking my concentration."

As if the horse understood, Skyscraper headed back to the trail, leaving Sol with his pencil already poised back over his crossword puzzle again.

But Sol hadn't been the first to question why Tony had decided "to protect and to serve" rather than continue his uptown life and his coveted spot on Wall Street. He'd surprised everyone when he'd taken an unexpected turn during his late twenties. Still, that didn't mean he'd let his experience on Wall Street *or* his fine Princeton education go to waste.

He'd invested wisely in the stock market.

Because he had invested wisely, he'd been able to purchase an apartment building not far from his parents' Italian restaurant—Mama Gina's—in Queens. He'd bought the building from a money-grubbing slumlord who hadn't cared about the living conditions or the safety of his tenants. He'd turned the building back into the type of residence people wanted to call home.

Tony was proud of that.

He lived in the building himself.

When a tourist family of four began waving in his direction, Tony pulled on the reins and brought Skyscraper to a stop. Looking at their smiling faces reminded him exactly why he wasn't still sitting behind a desk in some stuffy office on Wall Street. He liked the flexibility of his shift schedule. He also liked the freedom of being outside—almost as much as he loved the opportunity to mingle with the people.

That's what had drawn him to the police force.

And the biggest reward of all?

His opportunity to serve as a goodwill ambassador for the greatest city on earth.

"Could you pose for a picture with the kids?" Mr. Tourist called out.

"Sure," Tony called back. "Skyscraper is a real ham when it comes to posing for pictures." Though Skyscraper was as gentle as he could be stubborn, Tony still bent down and gave the horse a few reassuring pats on the neck when the kids started in their direction.

The little girl, Tony guessed, was around eight years old. She eagerly sprinted forward, a big grin on her freckled face and her red pigtails bouncing up and down as she skipped in their direction. Her too-cool older brother, however, was more reserved. The teenager jerked the bill of his New York Yankees' ball cap farther down on his forehead and took his time sidling up beside them. He did a few major eye rolls as his father snapped the shutter several times.

"You're a Yankee fan?" Tony asked, trying to ease the kid's embarrassment at finding himself in a situation too humiliating for his age.

The kid looked up at him. "Isn't everybody?"

"Right answer," Tony said, and the kid grinned.

When the family went on their way, Tony nudged Skyscraper forward. But as they plodded along on their regular park patrol, he couldn't keep his mind from wandering right back to the woman who had been wearing a rock on her finger so large it was borderline tacky.

That's what bothered him.

His gut instinct about people was usually correct.

Kate Anderson didn't strike him as one of those all-about-money-and-prestige social climbers. She just didn't give off those all-about-me vibes. Nor did she strike him as the type who would be engaged to a man who obviously felt the need to flaunt his success by giving her a showy top-this diamond.

In fact, had she been standing in a would-you-date-her lineup instead of beside the Virgin Mary in Central Park, he would have still picked her out for himself in a heartbeat.

Until he saw the engagement ring.

The ring said it all.

She was marrying an uptown man.

He'd turned his back on uptown long ago.

Still, Tony couldn't shake off the feeling that something wasn't quite right there. He hadn't missed her wooden response when she'd held up her hand and announced she was getting married in two months. There'd been no sparkle in her eyes. No lilt to her voice. No excitement that she would soon be marrying the man of her dreams.

Were those the actions of a typical bride?

Hardly.

Being the oldest child born to Mario and Gina Petrocelli, and the only brother to five younger sisters, he'd gone through five big fat Italian family weddings. Typical brides? He could write a book about them. Kate Anderson was *not* your typical bride.

He hadn't missed the best friend's expression at the mention of the wedding, either. He was, after all, a cop, trained to read between the lines when it came to dealing with people.

Yup. There is definitely a problem in paradise.

Just not his problem.

His problem was going to be breaking it to his family during their weekly Friday night dinner at his parents' restaurant that Nonna had lost her touch. Maybe then everyone would cut him some slack and stop asking every five minutes if he'd met the green-eyed blonde.

Oh, I've met her, all right, Tony thought sadly.

Forgetting her—that was going to be the problem.

CHAPTER 2

Kate took her place in line at Mr. Woo's, her usual Chinese take-out stop, less than a block away from her Midtown apartment building. She never saw Harold on Friday nights unless some special function required their attendance. Friday nights were what Harold referred to as his "wind-down" time. He spent his Friday evenings at a private men's club with a massage and sauna ritual that supposedly helped him rejuvenate from his hectic workweek schedule.

The rest of the weekend, Harold reserved for what he called "quality time." Quality time was spent with her and with his widowed mother, whom Kate, surprisingly, adored completely. In fact, Alex often accused her of liking Margaret Wellington much better than she liked Harold.

Never one to keep her opinions to herself, Alex had also warned her not to expect Harold's routines to change after they were married. Kate suspected Alex was right about that prediction. But it didn't matter. It was the order and consistency he demanded in his life that had drawn her to Harold in the first place.

Life with Harold was guaranteed to be simple and uncomplicated. What could be better than simple and uncomplicated?

"Hot and spicy," someone yelled out.

Kate blushed, thinking about the cop.

It took her a second to realize the guy at the head of the long waiting line was only giving instructions on how to prepare his food.

Damn Alex.

It was just like Alex to come sneaking up behind her when she was ogling the cop.

At least when she got home, she knew she could count on Eve to back her up when Alex started ranting about why she hadn't been interested in the cop's destined-to-be-together story. Eve Thornton was her other roommate—like Alex, another best friend from their Wells College days. Eve was a real sweetie. Plus, Eve actually liked Harold.

Sad story, the voice inside her head jeered, reminding Kate of Alex's *sucker* accusation earlier in the park.

I was a sucker for Eve's sad story.

She'd admit it.

She had felt sorry for Eve when her worthless snake of a fiancé dumped her two days before their wedding. Eve had already given up her apartment and moved in with the snake, so she really had noplace else to go. Unless she wanted to move down to Miami and move in with her parents, who lived in a retirement community—which certainly hadn't been an option.

What good friend wouldn't have offered Eve a shoulder to cry on and a place to land until she sorted things out?

Only weeks had turned into months, and months had turned into over a year, with Eve going from being depressed into a full-blown case of what her physician had diagnosed as social anxiety disorder. Eve never left the apartment, much less the building—she had an overwhelming fear that the first person she would run into was her ex with his *latest* fiancée.

She and Alex had both tried to convince Eve that running into her ex was highly unlikely, since Eve was living in Manhattan, and the snake had moved his latest victim into the house he'd supposedly bought for Eve on Staten Island. But Eve kept insisting she just couldn't take that chance—not until she'd had sufficient time to get over the snake completely.

The only good thing, Kate supposed, was Eve's career. Being a freelance Web designer meant Eve still had the ability to support herself. But Kate did wish sometimes that Eve had the type of job that required her showing up at the office every day. Eve's ability to work from home had only made her exit from society that much easier.

Kate jumped when the counter clerk snapped his fingers and motioned in her direction. She stepped forward and gave him her order. A few minutes later, she scooped up the white paper sacks and headed home. But as she walked the short distance to her building, she did wonder if Eve had kept her promise and at least made it out of the apartment and to the corner and back today.

In a two short months, Eve was going to be on her own again whether she was ready or not. Eve wouldn't be able to rely on her for daily shopping and errand running. After the wedding, Kate would be living with Harold in his ritzy Upper East Side penthouse, with a full-time maid and a chauffeur doing *her* shopping and running *her* errands for a change.

A life of leisure, Kate thought, trying to get excited at the prospect of being waited on hand and foot for the rest of her life.

She pushed that thought to the back of her mind, then hurried up the steps to her apartment building. She smiled when her building's "honorary" doorman opened the door for her so she didn't have to fumble around looking for her key.

A Santa Claus physique and no hair whatsoever, Mr. Womack had the type of rosy cheeks that just begged to be tweaked. Alex called him an old snoop, but he was a lovable old snoop who Kate suspected preferred sitting in the lobby watching people come and go to sitting upstairs alone with no human contact to help pass the time.

"Again? You girls are staying in on Friday night with takeout?" He clucked his tongue disapprovingly. "Please, Katie. Take an old bachelor's advice. Get out and live a little before it's too late."

Kate laughed. "Good advice, Mr. Womack."

She called this back over her shoulder, then headed for the elevator. But as she rode up to her sixth-floor apartment, Kate couldn't help but worry about Eve, about Alex and John, and about her own true feelings for Harold.

Could she finally force Eve back into the world of the living in the short time she had left before the wedding? Would Alex and John finally reach a compromise over their squabble because just-turned-forty John wanted to start a family now, and close-to-getting-the-promotion-of-a-lifetime Alex felt now wasn't the right time for her?

Most importantly, *was* Harold just another sad story she hadn't been able to resist?

No. I feel comfortable with Harold.

Comfortable wasn't everything, true.

But nobody got *everything* when it came to marriage. Did they?

Kate opened the door to her apartment in time to hear Eve say, "How romantic to have a total stranger walk up to you and claim you were destined to be together."

Frick.

So much for Eve taking her side.

Alex had already won Eve over.

Kate dumped her keys and her purse on the table by the door. As she started for the living room, she heard Alex say, "Romantic is only half of it, Eve. This guy was hot. Picture every hot Italian actor you can think of, and I'm not kidding. This guy was triple times hotter than anyone you can come up with."

"De Niro?"

"Younger," Alex said.

"DiCaprio?"

Alex sighed. "Not that young, Eve."

"Armand Assante?"

"Eve! I didn't mean it literally. I didn't mean you should think of *every* Italian actor on the planet. I just meant this guy has that whole Italian thing going for him. You know? Sexy as all hell and then some?"

"Wait. I've got it. A cross between a young Al Pacino and an even *younger* Sylvester Stallone."

"Whatever!" Alex said, but she groaned loudly after she said it.

I'd better get in there before Alex goes postal, Kate

thought, and marched down the hallway and into the living room. She didn't see the object propped up in the middle of her sofa until Eve and Alex both turned around to look at her.

"Alex!" Kate scolded. "I told you when you insisted on buying that painting to leave it at your office. I *don't* want it here."

Alex looked over at Eve. "Is that any way for a bride to talk about an expensive wedding present from a best friend?"

The expression in Eve's big blue eyes told Kate she wasn't sure what she was supposed to say, but that she definitely didn't want to take sides.

But that was Eve's personality in general. Passive. Easily confused. Almost mousy, except for her pretty face and a halo of shiny auburn curls befitting one of those cute angelic cherubs. *Cherubesque,* in fact, best described everything about Eve. Her tiny, barely five-foot frame. Her perfect cherry red bow lips. Even the pleasingly plump curves that made any man's mouth water.

"You have to admit, it is a beautiful painting, Kate," Eve finally said, when Alex kept glaring at her.

Kate looked from one to the other. "Great friends the two of you turned out to be. One's a traitor. The other one's a big bully."

She placed the take-out sacks on the coffee table, picked up the oil painting of the Madonna and Child, and marched back to the front hallway closet. Kate even slammed the closet door for effect.

She didn't want the Virgin Mary staring out at her from some painting, watching her every move. She didn't want to think about the Italian on the stallion, either. Or the fact that he most definitely had that *Italian* thing going for him that was sexy as all hell and then some.

What she wanted to do was eat her Moo Goo Gai Pan before it got cold. She wanted to relax and watch whatever movie the girls had decided on for the evening—as long as there was *no* hot Italian actor in the starring role. *And,* she wanted to go to bed early and get a restful good night's sleep.

Then, she'd be able to drag herself out of bed at the crack of dawn the next morning. Harold wouldn't be upset, because she wouldn't be running late as usual. And they could make their weekly trip to Bridgehampton to spend the rest of the weekend with Margaret.

Kate let out a sigh, thinking how know-it-all Alex also couldn't resist pointing out how devoted-son Harold had been using the need-to-spend-the-weekend-with-Mother excuse from the moment Kate had met him. Rather, of course, Alex insisted, than risk Kate spending the weekend alone with him at the penthouse, where getting-more-sexually-frustrated-by-the-minute Kate could have possibly challenged Harold to demonstrate exactly how well those therapy sessions were really helping with his penile dysfunction disorder.

Penile dysfunction disorder.

Did it get any sadder than that?

Stop it!

She had to stop obsessing over Harold's penis.

Or the lack thereof, as the case might be.

Harold adored her.

He was also perfect husband material.

Her grandmother certainly thought so. And no one's opinion mattered more to Kate than that of Grace Anderson.

Sad story.

No!

She wasn't going to let Alex's accusation creep into her mind where her grandmother was concerned.

Of course, her widowed grandmother had been devastated when her only child—the son who had won notable acclaim for his photography—suddenly ran off with the promising young artist Grace had personally taken under her wing. Her grandmother had been betrayed by both of Kate's parents when they declared themselves antiestablishment and headed off to California, wandering aimlessly from one commune to another in search of the true meaning of life.

Kate hadn't even met her grandmother until she was twelve years old. She probably wouldn't have met Grace then had her parents not decided to live in the not-exactly-safe jungles of South America for a year so her father could photograph the quickly disappearing rain forests for *National Geographic.*

Grace had agreed to take her in, and once she'd arrived in New York City and had a taste of a conventional lifestyle, Kate had known living with her grandmother was where she wanted to stay. It was the one time in her life that having free-spirit parents actually paid off. Her parents both agreed it was her decision to make. They allowed her to stay with Grace when they returned from South America.

Alex claimed she'd been trying to fill the void her father had left in Grace's life all these years, and maybe she had. But she had done so out of love, certainly not out of *pity* for her grandmother. That notion was as silly as Alex's claim that marrying Harold was just another way of proving she was nothing at all like her bohemian parents.

Alex and her damn executive opinions.

But still thinking about her beautiful and always gracious grandmother, she did wonder what Grace was doing at that very moment in gay Paree. Last year, Grace never would have taken a buying trip to Paris and left her in charge of the gallery for a whole month.

Even Alex can't argue with that fact.

Last year, she'd been doing what most twentysomethings in New York City were still doing every night of the week. She'd been cruising the night spots with her friends. Living it up. Holding on to that last bit of youth before life dictated that thirty had arrived and it was time to straighten up, fly right, and act like a reasonably responsible adult.

She'd turned thirty in January, right after she'd met Harold. The fact that Harold was older (he'd be thirty-eight in November) had made it much easier to settle down than she'd ever imagined.

So, forget Alex.

Whether Alex believed it or not, she was perfectly satisfied being a responsible thirty-year-old who was now settled down. She was extremely fond of feeling blissfully comfortable with Harold, instead of being stuck on a bad-date merry-go-round playing the same sad song. *And* she was going to be wonderfully happy and delightfully content being married to comfortable, settled, organized Harold—who adored her completely.

Amen.

"Kate," Alex yelled out. "Stop analyzing your entire life and come eat. Your food's getting cold."

"I'm not analyzing my entire life," Kate yelled back, aware that Alex and Eve both knew she was lying through her teeth.

She'd always been a master analyzer.

The problem was, the more she analyzed the situation, the more confused she usually became—paralysis by analysis, her friends called it.

Like her relationship with Harold, for instance. She'd given up on love long before she'd even met Harold. Not because she hadn't had her fair share of random boyfriends, because she had. She'd just never felt that zoom, bam, bop, knock-you-right-out connection Alex was always talking about.

Not with any man.

Ever.

Maybe Harold *had* more or less steamrolled right over her from the very beginning. Maybe there had also been plenty of red flags waving in the back of her mind over the fact that there was no real physical attraction between them. The simple fact was, she and Harold were both ready for marriage. They were compatible. And they'd talked at length about what it really took for a marriage to be successful.

Commitment.

Respect.

Devotion.

Physical attraction would be nice, but . . .

"Kate!"

"I'm coming," Kate yelled back.

Frack.

Sometimes best friends could be a real pain in the ass.

Yet, Kate couldn't imagine her life without Alex and Eve in it.

Besides, this time Alex was right.

There was a carton of yummy Moo Goo waiting in the living room with her name on it. She could hear the music gearing up on the television, indicating the feature presentation was getting ready to start. And though she sometimes felt like strangling Eve—and she *always* felt like strangling Alex—spending Friday nights staying in with takeout and her two best friends had definitely become the highlight of her week.

Any further life-analyzing moments could be saved for later. Later, when she'd most likely be lying in her bed all alone staring at her bedroom ceiling. Trying *not* to fantasize about a certain superhunky cop who claimed that *he,* not Harold, was supposed to be her freaking destiny.

Tony waited until stomachs were full, and the conversation around the large family table at the back of his parents' restaurant had died down to a dull roar. Then he tapped his knife against his wineglass, signaling that he had an important announcement to make.

On Friday nights the restaurant employees attended to the customers so Mama and Papa Petrocelli could enjoy quality family time with their sizable brood. Tony looked around the table at the people waiting to hear whatever he had to say.

Papa was sitting at the opposite end of the table in the place of authority—Mama in her usual seat to his right. Papa was still handsome, silver sprinkled throughout his dark hair, his bushy eyebrows, and his thick mustache. Mama was still beautiful, no gray showing in her thick, ink black hair. But her body was round and full now, thanks to bringing six children into the world. Also thanks to the rich Italian dishes she not only loved to cook but loved to eat—the same dishes that had made the family restaurant so popular.

His five sisters were there, all of them young and pretty. They were seated down both sides of the long table with their husbands, all of whom Tony liked. His nieces and nephews, eight of them ranging in ages from three to ten, were running freely around their grandparents' restaurant. No one seemed concerned that the kids might be terrorizing customers who had been brave enough to come to Mama Gina's on a family Friday night.

In other words, everything was normal—chaos as usual.

With the exception that one very important family member was missing.

His grandmother lived in New Jersey with her oldest son, his uncle Vinny. Nonna's absence was the main reason Tony had decided to make his announcement about meeting Kate Anderson to the family tonight. Whether he believed in his grandmother's ability to predict the future or not, he would never do anything to insult her or hurt her feelings.

"Well?" Papa boomed from the head of the table. "Were you pounding on your wineglass because you wanted more Chianti? Or do you have something important you wanted to say?"

Everyone laughed.

Tony took a deep breath and forced himself to say, "Today I met the blonde with green eyes in Central Park. She was even standing beside an oil painting of the Madonna and Child."

No one said a word.

Then everyone started talking at once.

His mother even had her hands clasped over her full-figured bosom, her eyes cast upward to the ceiling as she said a prayer of thanks.

Shit.

Tony banged against his glass again.

When everyone settled back down, he said, "Don't get so excited. I'm afraid meeting the blonde is as far as Nonna's prediction goes."

A stream of questions came at him from every direction, again all at once.

"Yes," Tony said, answering his sister Theresa who was sitting closest to him. "Like a complete fool, I did stop and talk to her. I even told her all about Nonna's prediction. And it took her less than two seconds to inform me that she's already engaged and her wedding is only two months away."

"What?" His mother's expression was wide-eyed with concern. "But your destiny with this woman is written in the stars, Anthony! Did you not explain this to her?"

Tony groaned inwardly. "Mama. What was there to explain? *I* told her about Nonna's prediction. *She* told me I had the wrong blonde. There was nothing more to say."

"Nothing more to say?" Mama's usually smiling face was now screwed up in a worried frown—not a good sign. "Don't be ridiculous, Anthony. You must go see her again and tell her to postpone her wedding. Make her understand *you* are the man she was meant to marry."

Tony was dumbfounded.

When two of his sisters actually nodded in agreement, Tony threw his hands up in the air.

"Oh, come on, Mama. I thought *you* would be pleased that this woman is already engaged. If I remember right, you cried for days after my sixteenth birthday. I thought it had always been your dream that your only son would marry a nice *Italian* girl. Not some green-eyed blonde."

His mother waved away his comment. "That was then. This is now. Times have changed, and so have I." She looked around the table. "Not one of your sisters married an Italian man. Does it matter? No. Family is family. This is the new mill-en-i-dome," she said, sounding out the word carefully. "A smart boy like you should know that."

Millennium, Mama, Tony thought, but he knew better than to correct her. Besides, everything his mother said was true.

Theresa had married her romantic French-Canadian philosophy professor. Maria was married to a somewhat reserved Brit in the import/export business. Angelina's husband was an entrepreneuring Cuban-American, determined to make a success of his trucking business. Elaina had married a slightly overbearing German who was a big-deal architectural consultant. The baby of the family, Carlina, had somehow run across a Cajun straight from the swamps of Louisiana—the kid was currently working for the Sanitation Department and seemed to be taking big-city life in stride.

When he thought about it, they could hold a damn United Nations meeting sitting right there at the family table. That thought gave Tony one more glimmer of hope.

"I doubt this woman is Catholic, either, Mama," he threw out, clearly grasping at straws now.

Again, his mother waved away his comment. "I

decided long ago I was leaving religion to God to worry about. All I can do is pray for all of you."

"Mama, please," Tony said, trying to keep his temper in check. "Do you really expect me to go find a woman who has already told me to buzz off? And then demand she postpone her wedding because *I'm* the man she's supposed to marry?"

"Why, yes," she said, as if she couldn't believe her son was asking such a stupid question. "What other choice do you have?"

Jesus, Mary, and Joseph!

Tony looked at his father for help, but his mother reached out and took her husband's hand. "Tell him, Mario. Tell your son how important it is to follow his destiny, just as you and his uncles before him have done."

"Mama," Tony pleaded. "I already know all the stories. I've heard them all my life. But this is one time Nonna was *wrong.*"

Damn. Did I really say wrong?

Judging from the gasps at the table that sucked most of the air out of the room, he had.

His mother even paled to the point that his father reached out and placed an arm around her shoulder to steady her.

"*Wrong* wasn't a good choice of words," Tony said, backtracking as fast as possible. "I meant Nonna's prediction for me is obviously *different* from the others. Maybe we should let Nonna read my tea leaves again," he added, hoping to appease the angry looks coming from Mama and his frowning sisters. "Like you said, Mama, times change. People change."

"No," she said flatly. "You have accused your grandmother of being wrong. The only way to prove it is for you to bring the blonde here, to the restaurant. We won't tell Nonna you've already met her in the park standing beside the Blessed Virgin. If she is the one you're supposed to marry, Nonna will know it the minute she takes the blonde's hand."

"I'm done here," Tony said, throwing his napkin down on the table. "And I am *not* going to go find the blonde."

Forget keeping his temper in check.

There was no reasoning with these people.

He pushed his chair back.

When he stood up to leave, his mother pointed a finger at him the way she used to do when he was a kid. The stern expression on her face froze Tony right where he stood.

"Then you leave *me* no choice," she said, standing up from the table herself. "I will go pray now."

Everyone sent Tony you're-in-deep-shit-now looks.

"Mama, please don't do this."

She ignored him and pointed to the ceiling. "To the Saints in Heaven above I will pray. Day and night I will pray. Until you bring the blonde to meet Nonna." She said this, being dramatic as only his mother could be. "But you have my word, Anthony." She pointed her finger at him again. "If Nonna doesn't sense that the blonde is the woman you're supposed to marry, I'll accept it. You have my word about that."

Before Tony could argue, his mother left the table.

His poor father hurried after her, a terrified look on his ashen face. "Gina, my little dove, be reasonable," he called out.

As soon as his father was out of sight, everyone at the table burst out laughing.

Except Tony.

"I guess you'd better go find that blonde," Angelina said between giggles.

"Arrest her if you have to, Tony," Maria teased. "You know how stubborn Mama gets when she's praying."

Everyone laughed again.

"This *isn't* funny," Tony said. "Maybe if you girls had lived with one of Nonna's marriage predictions, you might have a little more sympathy for me."

"Don't blame us," Maria said, "we didn't make the rule that Nonna's predictions were restricted for her precious sons and her only grandson."

"I wasn't *blaming* you," Tony began, "I just meant . . ."

Carlina interrupted him. "Remember the last time Mama locked herself in her bedroom to pray?" She looked around the table for an answer.

"Two years ago," Elaina said. "When Papa refused to fire that hot little waitress whose skirts were so short you could see her kooch every time she bent over to place a plate on the table."

Everybody laughed.

"Mama's no fool," Theresa said. "She caught Papa looking at that hot little kooch one time too many."

"Poor Papa," Maria said. "He only held out two days."

"Yes, but he moped around the restaurant for a solid month after he fired that girl," Angelina said, and everyone laughed again.

"Well, in case none of you have noticed," Tony told his snickering siblings and their spouses, "*I'm* not Papa. This time, Mama has met her match."

"I'll bet five hundred dollars on Mama Gina right now," Horst, Elaina's big blond German husband announced.

Tony flipped him the finger.

Everyone howled even louder.

"Go ahead. Knock yourselves out laughing," Tony said. "Just don't expect me to stand here and take it."

He turned and headed for the door.

"I hope you were smart enough to get the blonde's name," Theresa called out after him. "Because you will have to find her, Tony. Mama will see to it."

They were all still laughing when Tony walked out of the restaurant.

Crazy idiots.

But he really couldn't blame his family for having their fun at his expense. Had the shoe been on someone else's foot, he would have been laughing just as loudly and instigating mischief exactly the way everyone else was doing with him.

Pray to the Saints in Heaven above.

Well, he had news for Mama.

Her prayer threat wasn't going to work with him.

The only reason his mother always won her black-mailing prayer scam anyway was because his father couldn't hold up under the pressure. Well, *he* wasn't Papa, just like he'd told the laughing hyenas back at the table.

Laughing hyenas.

Maybe hyenas laugh because they know what's coming next.

Tony pushed that thought aside and kept on walking.

He headed down Thirtieth Avenue, both hands jammed in the pockets of his jeans. Weather permitting, he always walked the five blocks from his apartment building to the restaurant on Friday night. It gave him a chance to scope

out the neighborhood, keep his thumb on the pulse of
what was really happening on the streets of Astoria.

Old habits die hard.

Serving at least five years on a regular beat was one of
the requirements a candidate had to meet before applying
for a position as a mounted patrol officer. He'd paid his
dues. He'd maintained an exemplary record as a patrol officer. He'd finally reached his goal and been accepted by
a mounted patrol unit. But he never intended to lose his
streetwise edge.

Was I smart enough to get the blonde's name?

Who was Theresa kidding?

He'd gotten her name and more.

Anderson Gallery of Fine Arts.

Yeah, she'd be easy enough to track down.

Not that he was even considering tracking her down.

Hell no!

He was a cop, dammit. He was trained to listen and remember even the smallest of details. If he had to, he
could close his eyes and give a sketch artist a perfect description of Kate Anderson in two seconds flat. Right
down to the sexy Cindy Crawford type beauty mark on
her left cheek.

Forgetaboutit already!

The woman was history.

Keep it that way.

When his apartment building came into view, Tony let
out a frustrated sigh and looked down at his watch. It was
only nine-thirty. He was restless, to say the least. Just not
restless enough to head off to one of his regular haunts
and look up some of his buddies for a few games of pool
and a couple of beers.

No, maybe he would head over to the Red Bull for a few beers, Tony decided. It would sure beat going home to an empty apartment, where he had nothing else to think about but pretty *engaged* green-eyed blondes.

He briefly even thought about turning around and heading back to the restaurant to talk some sense into his mother, but the sound of squealing tires turning the corner slowed his pace. When he saw the yellow chopped low-ride cruiser slow to a stop in front of his building, the muscle in his jaw twitched instinctively.

Tony knew the car.

He also knew the driver and his cronies.

A bad bunch of punks in anybody's book. If any of them lived to see their twenty-first birthdays, Tony suspected they'd probably do their celebrating somewhere behind bars.

He picked up his pace again.

He swore when he saw Joey Caborelli open the front door of the building and head down the steps.

Joey was a good kid, barely sixteen. The son of one of his tenants, Rose Caborelli, a struggling single mom nurse who worked the night shift. Joey was good kid headed for a bad ending if those punks were reeling him in.

Without a second thought, Tony put his fingers to his lips. His loud whistle jerked Joey's head in his direction. When the kid saw Tony walking toward him, he quickly waved the car away.

The driver peeled rubber, then slowed down defiantly. Tony stared the jeering faces down as the car eased past him. One of the punks in the backseat spat out the window and called him a foul name. They all laughed before the driver peeled rubber again, then roared off into the night.

Tony glanced back toward the building.

Joey was still standing on the sidewalk.

He was dressed like the young punks who had just driven away—sleeveless tank top, baggy jeans worn low on his hips, a do-rag tied around his head to hold down a matted mess of dreadlocks. Despite the surly smirk on his lips, Tony suspected Joey's desire to become a gang member was nothing more than a need to belong.

The kid's staying behind had been his first clue.

His actions told Tony that the last thing the boy wanted was the resident cop mentioning something about his choice of friends to his mother later on.

"Friends of yours?" Tony asked, when he walked up and stopped beside the kid.

"Nah," Joey said, avoiding his gaze. "Never saw them before."

"They're a bad bunch, Joey," Tony said.

Joey still wouldn't look at him. He kicked at the concrete with the toe of his unlaced tennis shoe, instead.

I'm wasting my breath.

Tony had one of two choices, and he knew it.

He could continue to give Joey a long lecture that would go straight in one ear and right out the other. Or, he could go one step further and make an impact on the kid that would hopefully last him a lifetime.

Tony reached out and put his arm around the kid's shoulder, then began dragging Joey with him off the curb and across the street. He was pleased when he felt Joey tremble slightly.

Fear was an excellent motivator.

Before the night was over, Tony intended to scare the living crap out of Joey Caborelli.

They stopped in front of the shiny new black GTO coupe that Tony hadn't been able to resist ordering the minute he saw the car featured in *Road & Track* magazine.

"Sweet ride," Joey said, trying to wiggle out of his grasp.

"The most powerful GTO ever made," Tony said, still holding on to his squirming captive. "Zero to sixty in 5.3 seconds flat. Since you seem to be in the mood for cruising tonight, why don't you and I go take it for a spin?"

Joey sent him a nervous look when Tony finally let go of him. "Hey, I told you, I don't know those guys. I'd better get back inside," he said, his voice cracking now. "Ma don't like me going out without asking."

Tony took his car keys from his jeans pocket. The door locks clicked, and the lights flashed when he hit the button. He wasted no time opening the passenger-side door.

"Buckle up," he told Joey as he pushed him down onto the passenger seat. "I'll make things right with your mom."

Tony headed for the driver's side, thinking how hard Rose struggled just to make ends meet. He knew Joey's deadbeat dad never contributed financial or emotional support for the kid. He'd seen too many good kids from broken homes slip through the cracks while society turned its head.

Joey wasn't going be one of them.

Not if he could help it.

His unwilling passenger didn't know it yet, but he was getting ready to go on a tour straight through the bowels of hell. The same tour of the city morgue Tony's retired police captain Uncle Vinny had given him when he'd been a brainless sixteen-year-old kid headed in the wrong direction.

Tony slid behind the wheel, turned on the ignition, and revved up the GTO's engine.

"Where are we going?" Joey was brave enough to ask.

Tony's reply was simple. "We're going where you'll end up, Joey. If you keep hanging out with those punks you say you've never seen before."

CHAPTER 3

Kate stood at the front window of the posh bridal shop on Grand Street, just around the corner from the gallery on Broadway. She was waiting for Alex and Eve to meet her there.

She was also irritated with herself for allowing Alex to bully Eve into coming. It was true. Eve *had* been making considerable progress over the last two weeks.

She and Alex had even coerced Eve into having dinner with them in a public restaurant two Friday nights in a row. And what a big surprise. They hadn't bumped into the snake and his new fiancée once.

Eve had even made a joke about how silly she'd been herself—another huge step in the right direction.

Still, Kate couldn't help but worry that finding herself surrounded by a shop filled with wedding dresses might cause Eve to suffer a setback. Eve's I-want-to-be-there-for-you declaration only made her feel worse. Her goal had always been to help Eve get back on her feet. The last thing she wanted was Eve trying to prove her loyalty and ending up in a tailspin again.

At least Thursday afternoons were routinely slow for all of the shop owners in SoHo, Kate reminded herself. Which was why she had chosen four o'clock for Alex and Eve to meet her at the bridal shop. Not that Alex hadn't protested. Alex couldn't believe she'd turned down Grace's offer to bring back some noteworthy designer creation directly from Paris.

Alex could complain all she wanted, but Kate's immunity to *designeritis* as Alex called it, wasn't apt to change. Nor was her not-a-bit-pretentious personality apt to change, which was something Harold (also a big fan of designer everything) was going to have to accept after they were married.

Besides, selecting her wedding attire was her choice to make, and Kate had her own agenda.

The bridal shop's owner, Diane, was an attractive brunette in her fifties who had always been faithful about sending customers around the corner to the gallery to browse. Kate appreciated those referrals. She intended to return that favor by giving Diane her own patronage.

She glanced around the shop again, pleased to see that this Thursday afternoon wasn't any different from most Thursday afternoons. Other than Diane, she and a sales-clerk were the only people in the shop.

Good.

She had Eve's crowd phobia under control.

Now, if she could usher Eve past the rows of wedding dresses fast enough . . .

Kate stepped closer to the window.

A taxi had pulled up and stopped in front of the shop. She waved supportively when Eve left the taxi first.

But she didn't miss the fact that Alex had to practically push Eve through the door.

"Are you sure you want to do this, Eve?" Kate asked, ignoring the don't-sympathize-with-her look coming from watchdog Alex.

Maybe Alex's no-nonsense approach *had* been responsible for forcing Eve back into a normal routine over the last two weeks. But Alex had the tendency to push too far, too fast. Besides, a *little* sympathy every now and then never hurt anybody.

Eve nodded, and Kate said, "This won't take long, sweetie." She didn't care whether Alex liked her protective attitude or not.

Only Alex was too busy looking around the shop with her nose in the air to notice. "I still can't believe you prefer buying off the rack to having Grace bring you a designer dress from Paris."

"That's exactly what Harold said," Kate told Alex, knowing suggesting Alex had anything at all in common with Harold would annoy her to the core.

Alex's beady-eyed frown proved her right.

"And," Kate added, "I'll tell you exactly what I told Harold. Off the rack will suit me just fine."

" 'Off the rack will suit me just fine,' " Alex mimicked.

Kate ignored her and turned back to Eve, who, unfortunately, was looking shakier by the minute.

"I'm really glad you're here, Eve. I didn't want to make my final choice without including my two best friends." She gave Eve a quick hug. "But Gram and I did narrow my choices down to three bridal suits before she left for Paris. This won't take long. I promise."

Eve smiled. Weakly, Kate noticed.

But Alex frowned.

"Bridal *suits*? Excuse me? You've been talking about the type of wedding dress you wanted from the moment Eve and I met you. A bridal suit is *not* the vivid description I remember listening to over and over and over again through four years of college."

Kate put her hands on her hips. "Well, excuse me for obviously boring you with that description over and over and over again." She stared Alex down. "You're right. I never imagined wearing a suit to my wedding. But a suit is more practical than a wedding dress for a short ceremony in a judge's chamber."

Alex rolled her eyes. "A short ceremony in a judge's chamber isn't the vivid description I remember of the wedding you wanted, either."

"Only because I had no idea I'd be marrying an attorney whose mentor since his father died just happens to be a judge."

"And who probably really wants a short ceremony in his mentor's chamber because he's afraid his bride's quirky parents will show up stark naked from their latest new adventure, the happy camper nudist colony."

"*Not* funny," Kate said. "My parents were invited to the wedding, and you know it. You also know they politely declined, rather than have *me* stressed out over their long-standing feud with Grace. They'll be holding their own ceremony in my honor on my wedding day, thank you very much."

"Right. I forgot," Alex said. "The naked zenfest. Maybe I should go to that one."

"Maybe you should," Kate said. "Since you're still boycotting the ceremony I'm having here."

"I'm boycotting the *groom*," Alex corrected. "Not the ceremony."

"Girls. Please," Eve finally said. "All of this arguing is making me queasy."

Kate glanced in Eve's direction.

The poor dear was starting to look a tad green.

She sent Alex a see-what-you've-done-now look.

Kate took Eve by the arm, led her past the rows of wedding dresses that were also possibly making her queasy, and directed her to the back section of the shop. When they reached the area with the customary viewing platform, a huge three-sided mirror, and several complimentary chairs, Eve didn't protest when Kate gently pushed her down to sit on one of the chair's lush cushions.

"No more arguing, Eve, I promise," Kate said, before Alex caught up with them. "I've already taken the suits to the dressing room. This will be quick and easy."

"Wait," Alex called out.

She hurried toward them, a vision from heaven on the hanger in her hand and poor Diane hurrying right along behind her.

"If you aren't going to wear a wedding dress, at least try this one on for us," Alex said. "I swear, this dress is so close to what I remember you describing, you could have designed the thing yourself."

Diane sent Alex a murderous glare, then forced Alex's hand upward to keep the hem of the dress from touching the carpet. But when she looked back at Kate, Diane smiled, and said, "This is a Vera Wang creation, Kate. It's a perfect choice for any bride. *Off the rack* or not."

Dammit, Alex, Kate thought. *Do you always have to put your foot in your mouth?*

She sent Alex a stern look.

Alex mouthed "be-otch" behind Diane's back.

Eve, on the other hand, was genuinely smiling for the first time since she'd walked into the shop.

"It really is a beautiful dress, Kate," Eve said. "Please? At least try it on for us."

Diane wrestled the hanger away from Alex, then held the dress out for Kate's inspection. Heart-shaped bodice completely covered in sequins. Tiny strings of pearls for the t-straps. A tight-fitting waist, giving way to a clinging satin straight skirt. A front cutaway extending from the hem to slightly above the knee.

Diane turned the dress around, and Kate's breath caught in her throat. The all-pearl straps crisscrossed above the sexy plunging v-shape back, just like she'd always wanted.

Alex hadn't been kidding.

She really could have designed the dress herself.

Kate started to reach for the hanger, but stopped herself. "No. I shouldn't. Harold and I have already agreed a bridal suit would be more practical than a wedding dress."

"Then let Harold wear the bridal suit of his choice," Alex snipped.

Kate hesitated. "I guess it wouldn't hurt to try it on." But she looked directly at Alex when she added, "Just as long as you realize you are *not* going to talk me out of my decision to wear a suit."

Alex shrugged. "You're the bride. Brides should wear whatever they want. Maybe you should remind *Harold* of that fact."

"I'll put the dress in the dressing room for you with the other things you've picked out, Kate," Diane said politely. "If you need any help . . ."

"That's what *we're* here for," Alex broke in.

Diane sent Alex another frosty look, then disappeared with the dress.

"Do you always have to be so confrontational?" Kate scolded.

Alex waited until Diane came out of the dressing room and headed back to the front of the store before she said, "Me? Bitchzilla was the one being confrontational. Didn't you see the way she snatched that dress out of my hand?"

Kate rolled her eyes.

Arguing with Alex was as effective as tunneling through a mountain of granite with a freaking mascara wand.

However.

All was forgotten when Kate stepped out of the dressing room and up onto the platform a few minutes later. Both of her best friends rushed to her side. All three of them just stood there, looking at Kate's reflection in the three-sided mirror.

This would be the one, Kate thought. *If I were wearing a dress at my wedding, this dress would be the one.*

"Wow, Kate," Alex said. "You look absolutely . . ."

"Beautiful," a voice said before Alex could finish.

Startled, Kate whirled around.

She would have fallen backward off the platform, had Alex not reached out and grabbed her arm to steady her.

Oh. My. God.

This couldn't be happening.

She was staring straight at the last person Kate ever expected to see again—much less find standing in the middle of a bridal shop.

The surprised look on Kate's face was nothing compared to the shock Tony felt when he made his way to the back of the bridal shop and found her standing on that platform. The sight of her in a wedding dress straight out of some fairy tale completely overwhelmed him. For one brief moment, Tony wished Nonna's prediction had been more than just a cruel joke.

As for the speech he'd been rehearsing since he'd received the panicked phone call from his father that morning, those words escaped Tony faster than a crook with a head start in a high-speed car chase.

All he could do was stand there and stare.

He didn't snap out of his trance until Kate pushed her friend Alex aside and picked up the folds of her dress.

"Wait," Tony called out, as she hurried from the platform. "Please. I need to talk to you for a minute."

"Go away," she yelled back over her shoulder. "We have nothing to talk about." She disappeared through an archway and out of sight.

Alex grinned when Tony walked in her direction. "Kate won't be hard to find," she said, motioning toward the archway. "Don't worry, it's safe. She's the only one in the dressing room."

"Thanks," Tony said.

Alex put her hands on the woman's shoulders standing next to her, then started pushing the petite redhead toward the front of the store. The redhead kept looking back over her shoulder at him. Tony heard her say "Jack Scalia but ten times better."

Her comment made no sense at all to him.

But it made Alex throw her head back and laugh.

Dammit!

This was not working out the way he'd planned.

He hadn't planned to interrupt Kate. Or to ruin some special moment she was having with her friends, which is pretty much what he suspected he had done. What he'd planned to do, when he finally tracked her down at the bridal shop, was simply to take a second of her time, ask for her help, and hopefully walk away with her agreeing to a quick trip to Queens on Friday night.

But his potential accomplice had fled the scene.

And he had the entrance to the women's dressing room secured as if he were on some high-profile stakeout.

To hell with that.

Tony took a deep breath and stepped through the entrance to no-man's-land. A quick look up and down the narrow space told him where he'd find her.

"Kate," he said, rapping lightly on the only closed door in the dressing room. "I apologize for disturbing you here. But I need your help. Please. Would you just hear me out for a second?"

She didn't answer.

Nor did she open the dressing room door.

Tony stood there for a few more embarrassing moments before he said, "Look. I don't blame you if you already think I'm certifiable. I won't even blame you if you decide not to help me. But I do have a problem. And believe it or not, you really are the only person who can help me."

Still no response.

"Okay, you're right," he said. "It was wrong of me to barge in on you here at the bridal shop."

She jerked the door open.

Tony jumped back.

"That's the first intelligent thing I've heard you say," she said, her green eyes flashing.

Hell.

She was still wearing the dress.

Mouth in gear.

Brain stuck in park.

All Tony could think to say was, "You really do look beautiful in that dress."

"Congratulations," she said. "That has to be the *second* corniest pickup line I've ever heard."

She tried slamming the dressing room door.

Tony reached out and caught it in time.

"I swear. I am *not* trying to hit on you."

She raised an eyebrow. "Says the cop to the victim he's obviously stalking."

"Let me prove it," Tony said. "If you agree to help me out, I'll buy your wedding dress for you. Think about it. Would a guy who was trying to pick you up buy the dress you were going to wear when you marry another man?"

She let go of the door.

She sent him a smug look when she reached for the price tag attached to the front of the dress and flipped it over.

Tony didn't even blink.

"Believe me. That's a bargain for the jam I'm in. Say you'll help me. I'll pay for the dress right now."

She *did* blink.

Several times.

"You *are* certifiable," she said. "How did you even find me here?"

"Jason? Your assistant at the gallery?" Tony said. "He told me where to find you."

When she frowned, Tony said, "But don't give the guy a hard time for cooperating with a policeman in uniform. I told him I needed more information from you about some weird guy who was bothering you at the exhibit in Central Park a few weeks ago. I just didn't tell him that the weird guy was me."

He tried smiling.

The expression in her eyes softened a little.

Tony decided begging might work even better.

"Please? Would you just hear me out?"

"Okay," she said, tossing her long, silky hair back over one shoulder. "Let's hear it. Tell me what's so important that you would lie to my assistant, track me down at a bridal shop, follow me all the way into the women's dressing room, and offer to buy me a wedding dress if I helped you."

Sad story, Kate thought, when he finished explaining his problem.

He grinned, and said, "I'm sure you're thinking how relieved you are that we *aren't* destined to be together. I doubt there's a woman alive who would want to get mixed up with a crazy family like mine."

No, what she was thinking was that his little-boy grin looked out of place on a big, strong policeman—which only made the grin ten times more irresistible. And she was also thinking that he was obviously a man devoted to his family whether they were crazy or not, or he wouldn't be standing there in a women's dressing room.

Be careful.

He's getting to you.

Too late.

Especially when he kept looking at her so intently Kate had the uneasy feeling that there really was some kind of special connection between them.

Don't be an idiot.

You can't get involved.

Kate said, "And you really expect me to believe your mother will stay locked in her bedroom praying until I come to the restaurant and prove I'm not the woman you're supposed to marry?"

He shrugged. "Hey, no one is more surprised than I am that my mother has held out for almost three weeks praying. She's a very stubborn woman. What can I say?"

Kate didn't have an answer.

"I know this isn't your problem," he said.

"You're right. It isn't my problem," Kate told him.

If she had any sense, she would send him on his way. *Now!*

Still, she couldn't keep from feeling a little bit sorry for him. With a grin like his? And when—amazingly enough—she really was the only person who could help him with the problem he was having with his mother?

"Let's say I did show up at your parents' restaurant," Kate said. "And let's say your mother keeps her word and doesn't tell your grandmother we've already met. Don't you think when you introduce your grandmother to a green-eyed blonde she might just put two and two together?"

He shook his head. "Not possible. My grandmother has been blind since birth."

"Oh, God," Kate said. "I'm so sorry. I didn't know."

The grandmother was blind, too?

Had Alex called this guy and told him every one of her sympathy buttons to push?

"There's no need to apologize," he said. "But my grandmother's being blind is the main reason my family believes she has the ability to predict the future. They believe it's God's way of compensating her for the loss of her eyesight."

There was that grin again.

Damn.

"Wait a minute," Kate said. "If your grandmother has been blind since birth, how does she *read* those tea leaves?"

He laughed. "Braille-like, I guess you'd call it. She puts her hand over the cup, and . . ."

"Forget I asked," Kate broke in.

She shook her head, trying to clear it.

The conversation was getting more bizarre by the minute.

"Look," he said, his expression turning serious, "I know everything I've told you sounds like an episode straight from the files of *Ripley's Believe It or Not*. But I swear, the last thing I ever intended to do was bother you again. I truly believed if I told my family you were already engaged, they'd forget the whole thing."

Great.

His sincerity was even more disarming than his grin.

"So, that's it," he said, still holding her gaze with those dark brown eyes that seemed to look into her very soul. "I've told you everything I came to say. And whether you decide to help me or not, I'll never bother you again."

Dammit, why did you have to come along now?

It just wasn't fair.

Kate truly liked everything about him.

His devotion to his wacky family alone was enough to win any woman's heart.

Then there were those tiny laugh lines at the corner of his eyes that crinkled when he grinned, proof that he laughed much more often than he frowned. She was a sucker for his voice, too—deep and sexy. Even the way he was standing turned her on—confident, sure of himself, yet not the least bit cocky.

You don't even realize how gorgeous you are.

Which only made him that much more adorable.

She needed to get this guy out of her life.

Pronto!

"You promise," Kate said. "One quick trip to your parents' restaurant tomorrow night to meet your grandmother, and you'll never bother me again?"

"Cross my heart," he said, and made the motion over his chest. "You can even bring your fiancé with you."

When Kate hesitated, he said, "But you don't have to tell him anything about my grandmother's prediction, if you think it would make him jealous. Just show up at the restaurant. You can excuse yourself to go to the restroom for a second. I'll take you on a quick detour to meet my grandmother. And then you and your fiancé can enjoy a great meal without any further interruptions. On the house, of course," he added. "How does that sound?"

"I don't keep secrets from my fiancé," Kate said. "I told him about you the day after I met you in the park."

What she *didn't* say, was that when she did tell Harold about him, instead of being jealous, Harold had laughed in her face.

"How embarrassing for you, darling," he'd said. "Like *you* would be interested in some blue-collar cop."

She hadn't cared for Harold's snotty attitude, and she'd told him so right in front of his mother while they were having dinner that night at the country club in Bridgehampton. But being the charming man that he was, Harold had managed to turn her reprimand around to his own advantage.

"See why I'm so crazy about this woman?" he'd said to his mother before sending Kate an adoring smile. "Kate's a genuinely caring woman. Just like you've always been, Mother."

Caring?

Or gullible?

She'd sure been gullible enough to believe a couple's therapist could help Harold with his impotence problem.

No!

She couldn't let her mind drift in a penis direction.

Not now.

Not with *him* standing right in front of her.

Not with those fabulous lips holding her attention while he kept talking, talking, talking—when all she could think about was grabbing the lapels of his uniform jacket, jerking him inside the dressing room with her, slamming the door shut behind them, and . . .

"I'm glad your fiancé knows the whole story," he said.

The word *fiancé* snapped Kate back to the conversation.

"I'd like to thank him in person for being a good sport about my predicament and bringing you to the restaurant."

Kate shook her head. "Sorry, Harold's in Chicago.

He's preparing for a big lawsuit involving one of his corporate clients."

Did she imagine it?

Or did the expression in his eyes brighten slightly?

"Maybe your friend Alex could come with you," he said.

Kate almost laughed.

The last thing she needed was Alex tagging along.

Alex would probably rush to the grandmother's side, tell the old woman the truth, then beg the grandmother to marry the destined couple herself right there on the spot.

"Just give me the address," Kate said. "I don't need anyone to come with me."

"I'd be happy to pick you up myself," he offered. "Straight there. Straight back. Scout's honor."

Kate shook her head. "Definitely not a good idea."

He grinned. "You're probably right."

Meaning what?

No, dammit! Don't think about that.

Just get the address and get his cute ass out of here!

He finally handed over one of the restaurant's business cards. But when he pulled his billfold out of his pants pocket, Kate laughed out loud.

"Don't be ridiculous," she said.

He glanced up at her. "What? A deal is a deal. You've agreed to help me out. I'm going to buy your dress."

"But this *isn't* my dress," Kate explained. "I was only trying it on for my friends."

He seemed surprised. "You don't like it?"

Kate paused. "Actually, I love it. It's just not appropriate. I'm not having a big wedding. Harold and I are getting married by his mentor. A judge. In the judge's chamber."

He looked at her for a long time.

Too long.

So long, Kate felt the heat rise to her cheeks.

"What?" she finally asked.

"That's a damn shame."

"About the dress?"

"About the dress and the wedding. All women deserve a big wedding."

Who is this guy?

"What are you? A cop by day, and a bridal consultant by night?"

"Maybe," he teased back. "I have five younger sisters. I've attended enough big weddings that I could probably handle the job."

"Wow. Five sisters."

"And you?"

Kate shook her head. "Only child."

"Do your parents work in the gallery with you and your grandmother?"

Kate laughed. "Hardly."

"Why is that funny?"

"You think *you* have a crazy family? At least your parents aren't currently living in a nudist colony in northern California."

He shrugged, apparently not shocked at all. "Hey, it takes all kinds. It would be a pretty boring world if we were all alike. Right?"

Certainly not Harold's reaction.

Of course, Harold might have only acted so horrified because he was picturing himself and his gherkin walking around naked in a nudist colony.

Stop it!

He smiled slightly. "Would you mind if I ask you a personal question?"

Kate laughed. "Well, since I've just blurted out that my parents are nudists, and I doubt it can get much more personal than that. Sure. Why not?"

"Do you love this guy, Harold?"

Whoa!

She forgot she was talking to a cop.

She'd been rattling off her life story faster than if he'd jabbed her with a needle filled with sodium pentathol. Dammit, she'd seen *NYPD Blue* enough times to know a cop was trained to wrangle information out of people!

"Does the right to remain silent apply to that question, Officer Petrocelli?"

"Call me Tony," he said. "And I didn't mean to pry. I only asked because . . . well, you just don't seem like the typical happy bride, and . . ."

"And it's none of your business," Kate finished for him.

He said, "You're right. Whether or not you love Harold isn't any of my business."

Stop looking at me like that.

Like you really know me.

We're strangers, dammit. Strangers!

"So, *Tony,*" Kate said, hoping if she gave in and called him by his name, it would hurry things along. "I guess I'll see you tomorrow night, then. Around?"

"Seven o'clock," he said.

"Seven tomorrow night. Got it," she said.

He still hadn't taken his eyes from her face.

Kate couldn't help herself.

She stared right back.

"I really do appreciate this," he said.

"No problem," she said, "since you really were telling the truth. I am the only person who can help you get your mother out of her bedroom."

He kept staring.

She kept staring.

"And then I'll never bother you again."

"Just like you promised," Kate reminded him.

More staring.

He smiled. "And then you won't wear the dress. And you won't have a big wedding. But you will still marry Harold."

Kate nodded. "That's still the plan."

"And that's still a damn shame," he said. "Because you really do look beautiful in that dress."

Do something, you idiot!

Get him out of here.

Finally, Kate forced herself to look away.

Only when she broke eye contact did he turn and walk out of the dressing room, never looking back—the exact same way he hadn't looked back that day in Central Park.

Oh God. Oh God. Oh God.

What have I gotten myself into?

Kate didn't have time to ponder that question.

Alex and Eve rushed into the dressing room only seconds after he left.

"Didn't I warn you not to mess with destiny?" Alex squealed, all excited. "This guy is so into you, we could feel the vibes from outside the dressing room entrance."

"The two of you were eavesdropping on us?" Kate wailed.

Alex looked at Eve.

Eve blushed.

Kate sent both of them a mean look.

"I wouldn't call it eavesdropping," Alex said. "Eve and I were just making sure you were okay. Right, Eve?"

Eve nodded. "It never hurts to be too careful, Kate. You really don't know this guy. What if he'd . . . you know? Tried to get physical or something."

Yeah, what if?

She quickly pushed that thought aside.

Alex said, "I can't believe you didn't ask him what you were going to do if the grandmother declared you *were* the woman he's supposed to marry."

Kate paled. "Don't even talk like that."

Alex smiled her know-it-all smile. "Why? The grandmother predicted he would meet you in Central Park, didn't she? Maybe the old blind girl really does have the gift of seeing into the future."

"That's insane," Kate said.

Alex laughed. "Insane? Are you freaking kidding me? Insane doesn't even touch this whole situation. That's why it's so obvious. This man is your destiny, Kate. That's why fate keeps throwing the two of you together."

"I'm not even going to dignify that remark with a response," Kate said. She slammed the dressing room door.

"Well, you don't have to get all pissy about it," Alex called out as Kate slipped carefully out of the dress. "*I'm* not the one who made the stupid prediction."

Kate didn't answer.

She waited until she was sure Alex and Eve had left the dressing room area. Then she held the dress close to her breast one last time.

What had Tony said?

You really do look beautiful in that dress?

No!

Don't even go there.

And she couldn't believe she was actually thinking of him as "Tony." As long as he'd only been that "cop" or that "guy," she'd had no personal connection to him.

Tony.

God help me.

Kate placed the dress back on the hanger. She changed back into her street clothes. Then she jerked the dressing room door open, marched through the archway, and back out into the viewing area.

"But Kate," Eve said, sending Alex a nervous look. "Aren't you going to try on the bridal suits now?"

"No," Kate said. "I don't want to think about real weddings, predicted weddings, or any other kind of weddings right now. All I want is some kind of alcoholic beverage in an ice-cold glass."

Eve looked at Alex.

Alex looked at Eve.

"Does either of you have a problem with that?"

Alex closed her eyes and put her fingertips to her temples. "Hush," she said. "Madam Alexis is suddenly receiving a very important message. She predicts there are three delicious apple martinis in our immediate future."

"Screw you, Alex," Kate said.

She motioned for Eve to go in front of her, then started walking toward the front of the shop.

Bringing up the rear, Alex was still laughing even after they made it out the front door of the shop and onto the sidewalk.

A corporate attorney, Tony thought as he reached his car. He'd parked in front of the gallery on Broadway, around the corner from the bridal shop.

Yeah, he could just imagine what her fiancé had said when Kate told him about their meeting in Central Park. As if an uptown girl like Kate would be interested in some cop from Queens.

I bet Harold had a real good laugh over that one.

At least the guy was away on business. Having some big-shot attorney show up with Kate to look down his nose at him and his nutty family wouldn't have been a good thing for anyone concerned.

Or maybe I'm being too judgmental.

For all he knew, Harold could be a really nice guy.

Tony looked over his shoulder, then pulled the GTO out into the busy stream of traffic. Unfortunately, the thought of Kate's fiancé being a really great guy bothered him even more than assuming the guy was your typical pompous ass.

Damn, Tony thought. *I'm jealous.*

But how was that possible?

He'd only met Kate twice.

It's that damn prediction.

That was it.

Everyone had been talking about him meeting a blonde with green eyes for so long, when he finally did meet her, it was only natural he'd be a little disappointed to learn she was already engaged.

Hell, he was only human.

Plus, he wasn't seeing anyone at the moment.

The truth was, he really hadn't even been dating any-one for almost a year now. Not a conscious decision—

he'd just been busy. First, the new promotion with the mounted unit. Then the crazy work schedule that he'd volunteered his guinea pig services to try—an experimental schedule that changed his hours and his days off weekly. Second, the never-ending renovations on the apartment building he was trying to maintain, which was why the crazy schedule worked so well for him. Always, life in general.

Maybe after Kate came to the restaurant and ended his quarrel with his mother, he would make it a point to start looking around for a lady who would want to spend a little quality time with a mere cop from Queens.

Yeah, that's exactly what he'd do.

He'd take control of his own destiny.

But no more blondes.

Period.

After tomorrow night, the *blonde* chapter of his life would be closed forever.

He would sincerely thank Kate for her help in proving Nonna's prediction wasn't going to happen. Then he would sincerely wish her a long and happy life with her big corporate attorney husband, Harold.

Corporate attorney.

Tony shook his head.

Busy man. Busy schedule.

Had the guy's profession been responsible for Kate's lack of enthusiasm and the reason she refused to answer his question? Had she already taken a backseat to his clients more times than she cared to admit? Was she maybe even worried that his career would always come first—even in their marriage?

That's her business.

None of mine.

She'd told him so herself when he'd been brave enough to ask if she loved the guy.

Still, it was a cop's nature to analyze people and dig beneath the surface to uncover what really made them tick. And that made Tony wonder how Kate's away-on-important-business fiancé would react when she told him the cop had shown up in her life again.

Would Harold be jealous, too?

Maybe.

Maybe not.

All Tony knew for certain was that Kate deserved to have that special sparkle in her eyes on her wedding day.

I am certifiable.

Why should I care?

The woman is virtually a stranger.

He couldn't explain why Kate's happiness mattered to him, but it did. Maybe because he liked her. She was one of those people you just liked from the moment you met them. There wasn't any explanation for it. He could just tell she was really good people.

She'd been compassionate enough to help him out and agree to show up at the restaurant tomorrow night, hadn't she? What were the odds most women would be understanding about his ridiculous praying mother who had herself locked in her bedroom? Slim to none. Those were the odds.

A judge's chamber.

The groom's idea, no doubt.

In and out. Quick and easy. Harold probably wanted a short honeymoon, too. One he would spend with his cell phone to his ear most of the time.

67

Damn.

He was doing it again.

He didn't even know this guy.

He didn't really know Kate either, but could the guy really look at Kate and not know what a lucky man he was?

Get over it.

She was engaged. She would marry her corporate attorney. There was nothing he could do about it. It didn't even matter that they were attracted to each other.

Sure, he'd sensed that Kate was attracted to him.

He'd known it that first day in the park. And again a few minutes ago, when they kept staring at each other so intently back in the dressing room.

But I'd never act on it.

It just wasn't his style.

I'm one of New York's Finest, dammit.

Going behind some guy's back and making time with his fiancée was *not* going to happen.

Kate was off-limits.

Still, the thought of her marrying Harold bothered him.

Did her big important corporate attorney soon-to-be husband truly deserve her?

For Kate's sake, Tony hoped that he did.

CHAPTER 4

~~

"Good evening, Mr. Wellington."

Harold nodded curtly to the male desk clerk who promptly handed over his messages.

He'd always preferred male desk clerks to female clerks who felt the need for idle chatter that grated on his nerves almost as much as it bored him. He glanced through the messages, then headed across the exquisite lobby of The Peninsula to the elevators.

The admiring glances from several female guests as he walked past were wasted on him. Armani, Gucci, the Rolex, he had it all. He knew not one of the women had missed any of those luxuries only a man of his wealth and position could easily afford.

Mindless sheep, he thought briefly.

That had been his father's opinion of women in general.

To date, he'd never been able to make a strong case to contest his father's theory.

Most women were followers, not leaders.

Most women were always scrambling around to have

the latest trend in every facet of their meaningless lives. Clothing. Shoes. Jewelry. Even frantic to get the newest "new millennium" trend that had become so popular with women today—Botox or plastic surgery in all the right places.

"I feel sorry for the rest of you sons of bitches," his father had often boasted when he was alive. "I married the only genuine woman God ever put on this earth."

Harold hadn't been able to contest that statement of his father's, either.

Until the day he met Kate Anderson.

It was as if his father himself had yelled out from his grave, "That one!"

Kate was so much like his mother it sometimes scared him. She was beautiful, warm, and caring. Completely trusting. She'd make a devoted wife and a gracious hostess. She'd also make a wonderful mother. *If* he did decide later that he wanted any obnoxious offspring cluttering up his carefully planned-out life.

From their first date, he'd realized he would have to do everything in his power to sweep Kate off her feet. A long engagement had never been on his agenda. Nor would a big wedding be a possibility. Big weddings caused tensions to rise and gave friends like Kate's damnable best friend Alex chances to put doubts into people's minds.

He knew Alex didn't like him.

He wasn't going to take that chance.

He was going to keep doing exactly what he'd been doing from the moment he met Kate. He was going to overwhelm her with his charm and usher her to the altar as quickly as possible.

Sweet, beautiful Kate.

What man wouldn't want a trophy wife like her?

He wasn't an idiot.

He'd been on his best behavior from day one. He'd showered her with more attention than any woman deserved. He'd made it a point to make her believe he adored her completely. He'd even done a complete snow job on her grandmother and the unstable little twit who was currently living with her, Eve. Her friend Alex was the only thorn in his side.

He was sure Alex had been responsible for Kate's concern that as compatible as they were together, the physical attraction between them was lacking. When Kate brought the subject up, it had stunned him. No, it had infuriated him, actually. Thankfully, he'd always been a master at controlling his emotions. Had Kate not been so perfect in every other way, he would have dropped her at that first sign of insurrection.

Except Kate *was* perfect wife material.

More perfect than any woman he would ever find again.

He knew that.

"A successful man keeps his home life and his real life separate," his father had hammered into his brain. "Give the woman you marry everything a woman could ask for. Put her up on a pedestal where your *wife* belongs. But take your pleasure where money can buy you whatever you want in the bedroom. You do that, and you'll have a successful career, a successful marriage, and a sexually satisfying private life."

His father had proved that point on his eighteenth birthday. His birthday gift from dear old dad had been the type of woman you reserved for the bedroom. That coming-of-age experience had definitely been satisfying beyond his wildest dreams. It had also set the stage for his adult sexual preferences.

He often wondered what the couple's therapist he and Kate were seeing would say if she knew the real reason behind why he had no interest in Kate physically.

Harold smiled.

Dr. Elaine Markam had been so intent on bringing his "problem" to light, she'd quickly filled in all the blanks with her own absurd assumptions.

Clueless bitch.

However, when he thought about it, he decided he should actually double Dr. Markam's fee. After only two months into therapy, he'd proposed, and Kate had accepted.

Now Kate truly believed he was suffering from some imaginary penile inferiority complex. That meant she had stopped worrying about their lack of physical contact for the moment, getting her off his back. It also meant after they were married and he forced himself to take her to bed often enough to keep her happy, she would believe her patience and understanding had cured him—making her even more devoted to him.

But most importantly, she would never suspect the problem all along had been that nice girls like Kate had never been able to satisfy his sexual appetite.

Kate was going to be his wife.

He would put her on a pedestal where she belonged.

His pleasure he'd take elsewhere.

Harold smiled again as he waited for the elevator that would take him to the grand deluxe suite he always reserved when he stayed there—one of Chicago's finest hotels. There was no doubt in his mind that marrying Kate would be the best possible move he could make. Having

a beautiful wife and a gracious hostess would undoubt-
edly complete the image that went along with his already-
successful career. His finally getting married would
please his doting mother immensely. Also, having Kate to
take care of the elementary aspects of running his household would free him up for even more *private* life time
when he wanted it.

A sexually satisfying private life.

That was his ultimate goal.

"Good evening," an older gentleman said when Harold
stepped into the elevator. Harold ignored the man and
pushed the button for his tenth-floor suite. Arrogance was
another fond trait his father had passed down to him. Like
his father, he had no desire to waste time on empty conver-
sations with irrelevant people he had no interest in knowing.

But also like his father, he could turn on the charm
when it suited his purpose—as was the case where his
mother and his darling fiancée, Kate, were concerned.
When it came to the only two women who would ever be
relevant in his life, being so charming it often sickened
him would *always* suit his purpose.

He left the elevator, reached his suite, and slid the plastic key into the slot. Once inside, he tossed his briefcase
onto a chair, took off his suit jacket and loosened his tie,
then headed to the wet bar. A tumbler of Scotch in hand
a few minutes later, he walked to the living room area of
the suite, punched the remote, and slumped down on the
plush leather sofa as the large plasma screen came to life.

He had exactly fifteen minutes to relax before his
scheduled seven o'clock nightly call to Kate. If possible,
he would limit that call to less than five minutes. After
calling Kate, he would make an equally dutiful but brief

call to his mother. Then, he would finally be free to shower and head off to a less respectable room he already had reserved in a less than respectable part of Chicago.

He brought the tumbler to his lips for a long sip, thinking that the hefty tip he handed the desk clerk would be all that was required to arrange for the feature presentation he had in mind for the evening. The clerk had certainly never let him down in the past.

However, thinking about his last trip to Chicago made him glance at his Rolex again, wishing he already had those calls behind him so he could fully begin to anticipate the type of excitement only a certain type of woman had ever been able to give him. As usual, he would have only one requirement.

She had to be a redhead or a brunette.

No blondes.

His beloved mother and his bride-to-be were blondes.

***

"It's almost seven o'clock," Kate said as she pulled her cell phone from her purse. She looked across the table. The apple martinis Madam Alexis predicted would be in their immediate future had been found in a trendy new uptown restaurant. "I would appreciate no smart remarks when Harold calls. Okay?"

"Are you talking to me? Are *you* talking to me? *You*, are you talking to me?"

"No, Alex. I'm talking to Eve," Kate said. "And for the record, your De Niro impersonation sucks."

Alex stuck her tongue out at Kate.

But Eve's heart-shaped face screwed up in a puzzled

frown. "You're talking to *me*? But I've never made a smart remark about Harold in my life."

"Kate was joking, Eve," Alex said, rolling her eyes.

"And the only reason I let Alex get away with making smart remarks about Harold," Kate said, "is because Alex knows she's wasting her time."

"So far," Alex said. "One can always hope."

Eve looked over at Alex and blinked a few times. "I really don't understand you, Alex. Harold is crazy about Kate. Anyone who's around them for five seconds can see that."

"That's what worries me," Alex said. "Harold is too damn perfect around Kate."

"I've always thought Harold looks just like Pierce Brosnan," Eve said.

"Pierce Brosnan without a personality, maybe," Alex threw in. She took another sip from her glass, then smiled a catty smile when she said, "I assume you meant no smart remarks about your surprise visitor today, Kate?"

"I meant no smart remarks, period," Kate said. "Harold never talks more than a few minutes. I'm sure you can dilute your acid tongue with your martini until I finish my conversation."

Alex shrugged again. "If it doesn't bother you that the man you're going to marry schedules a specific time to call you every night, why should I care?"

"Harold's a little conservative, that's all," Kate said. "There's nothing wrong with that."

Alex laughed. "A *little* conservative? Harold's so conservative his private jet wouldn't even have a left freaking wing."

Eve looked at Kate. "When did Harold get a private jet?"

Alex said, "I wonder how conservative Harold's going to be when you tell him you have a hot date with the cop tomorrow night."

"You know it isn't a hot date," Kate said.

"But you are going to tell him about it. Right?"

Kate's cell phone rang promptly at seven before she could answer Alex's question.

She and Harold exchanged the usual hi-how-are-you pleasantries. But when he threatened to cut the call even shorter than usual, Kate broke in, and said, "Remember the cop I met a few weeks ago? The one who claimed his grandmother predicted he would meet the woman he was going to marry in Central Park? He came to see me again today."

"If he's harassing you, I can make one phone call and have his badge," Harold said in a self-aggrandizing voice.

"No," Kate said quickly. She turned around in her chair and turned her back on Alex and Eve. "He isn't harassing me, Harold. He just has a problem. He wants me to meet his grandmother. Just to prove to his family that I'm not the woman he's supposed to marry."

"You can't be serious."

"I know, it sounds bizarre." She left out the part about his mother being locked in her bedroom praying. That part was still hard for her to believe herself. "But his family is upset," Kate said. "And I did agree to meet the grandmother."

"You're too nice for your own good, Kate," he said, with a sigh. "People can sense that about you. The cop's problem with his family is *his* problem. Not yours."

"I know it's not my problem, Harold," Kate said, trying not to be miffed at the condescending tone in his voice. "But this is an unusual situation. I really am the only one who can help him."

He let out another disgusted sigh. "You agreed to meet the grandmother where?"

Kate squeezed her eyes shut, already anticipating Harold's reaction. Manhattan was the only New York City borough that existed for him. "I'm meeting the grandmother at his parents' restaurant in Queens."

"Queens," Harold said flatly. "Why doesn't that surprise me?"

Kate ignored him. "I'll take a taxi. Straight to Queens. Straight back. I just thought you should know. That's the only reason I mentioned it."

"Nonsense," Harold said. "I'll call my driver. If you're determined to go to Queens, he'll take you. When are you going?"

"Tomorrow night. I need to be there by seven o'clock."

"Morgan will pick you up at your apartment at six," Harold said. "But I want you to warn this guy that if he bothers you again, he'll be facing a restraining order."

A restraining order.

Nice touch, Harold.

"I really must get going," he said. "I'll call you tomorrow night at nine instead of seven. I'm having dinner with the CEO of the company I'm representing. I should be through by nine, and you should be back from Queens by then."

He hung up as Kate mumbled a quick good-bye.

"Well?" Alex said when Kate closed her cell phone and turned back around in her chair. "Is Harold upset that you agreed to go to Queens?"

"Not really. He's sending his driver to take me."

"Kate!" Alex said, shaking her head. "Please tell me you realize there's something wrong with Harold's reaction."

"Harold trusts me."

"Trusts you? Or is he just so arrogant he can't imagine you looking at anyone else? Especially some cop?"

Kate refused to answer.

"I'm just saying the first question John would have asked me if I told him I was going off to meet some guy who claimed we were destined to be together was whether or not I was attracted to the guy."

Eve sent Kate a sheepish look. "Sorry, Kate. But even the snake would have asked me the same thing."

Kate shrugged. "Okay. Maybe Harold is a bit overconfident. I don't see why that's a problem."

"It's a problem because you and Harold both treat your relationship like some business arrangement, Kate. So you like the same things. Big deal. So you're both at a point in your lives where you're ready to settle down. So what? Those are *not* reasons to get married."

When Kate still refused to comment, Alex said, "Tell us the truth. Why didn't you answer Tony when he asked you point-blank if you loved Harold? And don't give me that lame 'it's none of your business' line you gave him. I want to hear you say it with your own lips, Kate. Tell me you love Harold. If you do, I swear, I'll never make a smart remark about him again."

"I love a lot of things about Harold," Kate said. "I love the attention he gives me. I love the concern he has for his mother. I love that he's smart, that he's confident, that . . ."

Alex laughed. "See? You just can't say it, can you?"

Kate sighed. "Okay. Maybe Harold and I aren't madly in love with each other. But we both know what we want in life. And we're comfortable with each other. Being comfortable has to count for something."

"Bedroom slippers are comfortable, Kate," Alex said. "And speaking of the bedroom, that's another subject that should scare the living crap out of you."

"A great sex life doesn't guarantee a trouble-free marriage, Alex," Kate said right back. "Look at you and John."

"Oooh, that was a good one," Eve said, a little tipsily. She lifted her martini glass in a toast to Kate.

"Touché," Alex said. "But no woman in her right mind would marry a man she's never slept with."

Eve sputtered in her drink. "Excuse me?" She wiped clumsily at her mouth with only a tiny corner of her linen napkin. "Do I need to remind you that men and women have been entering into marriage without having premarital sex for thousands upon thousands of years?" Eve slurred slightly, but she got her point across.

Alex glared at her. "I think I like you better when you don't have an opinion."

Eve blinked innocently. "You're the one who's been telling me to be more assertive, Alex. I was just following *your* orders."

Alex looked back at Kate. "What do you think Harold would say if you called him back and told him the real reason you agreed to help Officer Petrocelli?"

Kate said, "And that would be?"

"Hot. Hunky. Wildly attractive?" Alex smiled. "Do you need any more descriptive adjectives?"

"Being attracted to someone and acting on that attraction are two different things, Alex."

Alex grinned. "I know. So let's go straight to the 'acting on that attraction' part."

"No!" Eve said with so much authority Kate and Alex both looked in her direction. "Leave Kate alone, Alex. I think we should drop this entire conversation."

Alex ignored her and looked back at Kate. "All I'm saying is, if you really are determined to go through with your being-comfortable marriage, you at least owe yourself one last wild, hot, sextabulous fling."

Kate shook her head. "You know I wouldn't do that."

"Not even if Harold gave you his permission?"

Eve giggled.

Kate rolled her eyes.

Alex said, "I'm serious. Call Harold back. Tell him that because of his inability to function at the moment, you were wondering if he had any problem with you having one last fling before you commit yourself to him for the rest of your life."

"I will not!"

"Why not? He's impotent, right? He's incapable of having any *hard* feelings against you."

"*Not* funny," Kate warned.

"Oh, come on, Kate," Alex said, grinning at her. "This could actually be a win-win situation for you. If Harold says yes, that he does have a problem with your having one last fling, at least we'll know he's human and he does care about you other than you just being a comfortable choice for a wife. And if he says no, he doesn't have a problem with you having one last fling, you can have hot sex with Tony tomorrow night with Harold's blessing."

Kate finally laughed. "You idiot. I am *not* calling Harold back."

"Silly me. I forgot," Alex said. "You've already had

your one scheduled nightly phone call from Mr. Totally Anal. Just curious, Kate. But are you ever allowed to call Harold?"

"I can call Harold anytime I want."

"What's wrong with now?"

"Alex, stop this," Eve said again.

But Kate grabbed her cell phone from the table and sent Alex a triumphant look. Her pleased look faded, however, as she scrolled down her phone list looking for Harold's cell phone number.

Alex pounded the table with both fists in glee. "Are you freaking kidding me? You're going to marry this man? And you don't even know his cell phone number?"

"Oh, shut up, Alex," Kate said.

So maybe she hadn't called Harold often enough to commit his cell phone number to memory. She didn't have to call Harold. He always called her. *Harold adores me, dammit!*

Maybe her third apple martini was kicking in a little strongly at the moment, too. Which was why she felt the need to prove to Alex once and for all that she and Harold were just as normal as any other engaged couple. That they could be just as spontaneous as anyone else. And that even though Harold hadn't whisked her off to the bedroom yet, he would still *not* want her to have one last fling before their wedding!

Besides, Harold was on the verge of a breakthrough.

Dr. Markam said so herself.

Plus, Harold adored her.

He adores me, dammit!

The call to his mother had lasted much longer than Harold anticipated. But if he hurried, he would still have time for a hot shower before he left for the evening.

He supposed some people might find it odd that he would never dream of taking a shower in anything less than a five-star hotel. Especially since he had no qualms about having sex with women who sold their bodies to strangers for a living.

The difference was, any scum off the street could stay in the types of hotels that turned a blind eye to the activity he frequently sought. But only men with his kind of money could afford the high-priced call girls he always selected for his in-the-bedroom company.

He had just reached the bathroom door when his cell phone rang. Harold cursed, but walked back over to the bed and picked up his phone. He expected the call to be from his office, a call he could ignore. The number that came up on his caller ID, however, shocked him.

Kate?

It wasn't like Kate to call him back.

He'd already told her he was busy.

He checked his watch and cursed again. The desk clerk with all the right connections would be off duty in less than an hour. If he missed the clerk, his entire night would be ruined.

He finally gave in and answered on the third ring.

"Kate? I told you I had a mountain of paperwork to do. What's the problem?"

He hadn't meant to snap.

But, dammit, he was running short on time.

"Sorry I bothered you!" she said, and hung up.

Perfect.

He kept forgetting Kate wasn't necessarily one of those mindless sheep. She had a feisty streak that could surface at a moment's notice. She'd only been irritated with him once or twice, and he'd easily handled the situation. But that had been when he wasn't rushed like he was tonight.

Reluctantly, Harold hit speed dial.

He willed himself to stay calm even as he watched the second hand tick, tick, tick around the face of his Rolex. When she answered, Harold said, "I didn't mean to sound so abrupt. But I'm busy. You obviously called for a reason. What is it?"

She remained silent for so long he said, "Kate? Are you still there?"

"Yes, Harold, I'm still here," she said, but the irritation in her voice was evident.

Harold willed himself to stay calm.

He couldn't pull it off.

"Well? Speak up, Kate. What did you want?"

"I wanted to ask you a question, Harold. And I don't appreciate your rude tone."

Son of a bitch!

He didn't have time for this.

There was nothing that irritated him more than whining women and their stupid questions.

"Then ask me, Kate. I'm waiting."

Her own tone sharpened when she said, "I was wondering why it never occurred to you that I might be attracted to the cop."

Unbelievable.

Alex had to be behind this. He knew she was with Kate. Kate had told him when he called at seven that she and the girls were out having drinks and were staying for dinner.

From the moment he met Kate, he and Alex had been playing their own mental chess game of sorts, with Kate as their pawn. The funny thing was, he normally enjoyed playing Alex's game.

Just not now. Now, he had a more pressing engagement on his mind.

He glanced at his watch again, seething. "I'm not sure where you're going with this conversation, Kate, but . . ."

"I'm asking you a simple question, Harold. Why did it never cross your mind that I might be attracted to the cop?"

Another look at his watch escalated his blood pressure. "It never crossed my mind, because I have no interest whatsoever in this cop! Now, if it's okay with you, I prefer to continue this conversation later."

"And I prefer to continue this conversation now."

What the hell is wrong with Kate? She's never been this irrational before. We've never even exchanged cross words in the entire eight months we've been together. He pictured Alex smiling over their first big squabble.

It infuriated him.

Before he could stop himself, Harold said, "If you're attracted to the cop, you do what you feel you have to do about it, Kate. But I think you're smart enough to realize that a five-minute quickie with some dim-witted cop could never compare to the life of luxury I can give you."

He heard her gasp.

He didn't care at the moment.

Just like he didn't care if Kate had sex with someone else before they got married. After they got married—that would be a different story. Kate would be his wife. Then he would put her up on a pedestal where she belonged and crush any man who came near her.

"Exactly what are you saying, Harold?" she demanded.

His grip on the cell phone tightened. Even if he left at that very moment, there was a good possibility he might still miss the desk clerk.

Fuck!

"Do I really need to spell it out for you, Kate?"

"Yes, Harold. Spell it out for stupid me. Plain and simple."

She wants plain and simple?

I'll give her plain and simple!

"I won't ask. You don't tell, Kate," Harold spat into the phone. "But when I get back home in two weeks, I want whatever you're doing with this cop to be over. Then we'll finalize our wedding plans. We'll get married on schedule. And neither of us will bring the subject up again!"

What?

Don't ask, don't tell?

Had Harold lost his mind?

A sick feeling in the pit of her stomach threatened to make her throw up. Worse yet, the wall of denial she'd been building around herself from the moment she'd met Harold came tumbling down around her all at once.

Kate shuddered.

Without a doubt, she'd just gotten her first glimpse of the *real* Harold Trent Wellington when things didn't go exactly according to schedule.

I'm such an idiot.

To think she'd been stupid enough to fall for his lies
and his long-winded declarations about how much he
adored her. That was really what had kept her holding on.
The idea that Harold adored her completely. She'd been
telling herself that Harold genuinely cared about her and
that a solid and comfortable marriage was all she really
needed.

Until now.

Now there was no turning back.

Harold didn't adore her at all.

A man who adored you *did not* offer to adopt a freaking don't-ask-don't-tell policy and give you permission to
sleep with another man.

"I want you to listen to me very carefully, Harold,"
Kate said, surprised at the calmness that had suddenly
settled over her. "There isn't going to be a wedding. Not
in six weeks. Not ever. Make sure and jot that down
somewhere on your precious schedule."

"Don't be ridiculous," he said. "We'll discuss this
when I get back from Chicago."

"We have nothing else to discuss," Kate assured him.
"It's over, Harold. Accept it."

Kate hung up before he could argue.

Harold snapped his cell phone shut.

Silly woman.

Let her stew the rest of the evening.

She'd never risk losing him and his money.

What sane woman would?

He headed across the room and locked his wallet, his Rolex, and his sacred 18 carat gold Harvard Law School ring that his father had custom made for him in the safe in the wall. His money clip he kept in his pocket, with more than sufficient cash to see him through the evening. Then he walked across the room and grabbed his suit jacket from the back of the chair on his way out.

Thanks to his suddenly irrational fiancée and her bitch of a best friend, he'd not only lost his temper, but there would be no possibility of a hot shower. There was also a good possibility there would be no brunette or redhead for his nightly entertainment, either.

That thought threw Harold into a full-blown rage.

He stomped down the hotel corridor to the elevator and pounded the elevator button with the ball of his fist. As he waited, he took his memo-mate from his inside jacket pocket. "Have Morgan pick up two dozen long-stemmed red roses to give to Kate when he arrives at her apartment to pick her up tomorrow night." He spoke into the microphone, then jammed the gadget back into his suit pocket.

Damage control had always been his expertise.

Tomorrow, I'll worry about pleasing Kate.

Tonight, dammit, I'm going to please myself.

Kate remained staring at her cell phone so long, Alex finally said, "Kate? Are you okay?"

Kate was too dumbstruck to answer.

"Kate, I'm really sorry," Alex said. "I never should have pushed you into calling Harold back. I'll call him back myself and tell him it was all my fault."

Kate never looked up.

She kept staring at her cell phone.

"I'm a total ass, and I admit it," Alex said. "I promise, I'll never say another mean thing about Harold again. I'll even come to the wedding. That's how sorry I am that I've caused trouble between you."

Kate finally looked up. "I owe you the apology, Alex. Harold's every bit the total ass you've always said he was. You knew it the first night he invited you and Eve to have dinner with us. You told me that night that anyone who is nice to you but treats the waitstaff like shit isn't a nice person. I just wouldn't let myself believe it until now."

Kate tried to laugh.

The laugh turned into a full-blown sob.

Alex was on her feet in a second.

"Kate, please don't cry. I'm so sorry about everything."

Kate sobbed even harder. "You're only saying that," she blubbered, "because you know I've never been able to cry quietly."

"True," Alex said, still patting Kate's back supportively. "Those donkey-braying sounds you're making are going to get us thrown out of here. Everyone in the restaurant is already looking at us."

Alex was only trying to lighten her mood.

But, dammit, she wasn't ready for her mood to be lightened yet.

"Let them look. I don't care," Kate said between her donkey-braying sobs. But she did take the linen napkin Eve handed over and wiped at her eyes.

"Better now?" Alex asked, handing Kate her water glass.

Kate nodded. "I just can't believe Harold talked to me

like that." She took a small sip from the glass. "I swear, he turned into this Dr. Jekyll/Mr. Hyde person without any warning. You should have heard the vicious tone in his voice. He said he was sure I was smart enough to re- alize a five-minute quickie with some dim-witted cop couldn't compare to the type of life he could give me."

"That bastard!" Alex swore.

"So much for you never saying another mean thing about Harold," Eve mumbled as she brought her martini glass to her lips.

Alex's eyes narrowed at Eve for a moment, but she sat down in the chair beside Kate. "It would serve Harold right if you do screw Tony's brains out tomorrow night."

"I'll drink to that," Eve said from the other side of the table. She drained her glass quickly and signaled for the waiter again.

"A five-minute quickie with a dim-witted cop," Alex repeated. "If he got a good look at your dim-witted cop, I doubt Harold would be so cocky."

"But, but," Eve stammered, obviously having a hard time following the conversation. "Why are you guys so upset? Harold gave Kate his permission. Right? A five- minute quickie counts as hot sex. Doesn't it?"

"Eve," Kate said patiently. "I am *not* going to have hot sex with Tony, or anyone else."

"Especially poor Harold," Eve said, covering her mouth when she hiccuped. "Because of his pitiful penis problem, I mean." She smiled happily when the waiter placed another round of drinks on the table.

"It's more than just the argument over Tony, anyway," Kate said. "I've known things weren't right between Harold and me from the beginning. I just believed we could work it out because he really cared about me. Now, I know he doesn't."

"Now, Kate," Alex began.

Kate shook her head. "I'm not kidding, Alex. You should have heard him when I called him back. He acted like I was some naughty little girl breaking the sacred don't-disturb-Harold rule. I just couldn't take his superior attitude tonight."

Eve pushed a fresh apple martini in Kate's direction. She did the same to Alex. "I say we drink to naughty *big* girls." She lifted her glass and took a long sip.

Alex looked at Kate. "We need to order food."

"And ruin my buzz?" Eve shook her auburn head, sending her springy curls in every direction. She wiped her mouth with the back of her hand. "No way. Eve Thornton will *not* drink to that suggestion."

Alex motioned for the waiter. She asked him to bring menus on the double. Then she turned back to Kate. "Listen, Kate, you know I don't like Harold, but for what it's worth, you guys just had your first real fight. People say things they don't necessarily mean when they're angry, and . . ."

Kate's mouth dropped open. "Don't you dare take up for him! Not when you've been begging me for months to wake up before I made the worst mistake of my life."

"I'm just saying Harold was obviously caught up in the heat of the moment, and . . ."

"No," Kate said, shaking her head. "My big charade with Harold is over, Alex. For good. There isn't going to be a wedding."

Alex let out a long breath. "So the leopard finally slipped up and showed you his true spots, huh?"

"And not a moment too soon," Kate said. She slipped off her engagement ring and dropped it into her purse. "I've always hated that ring, anyway. It's so over the top it looks fake. Just like Harold."

Eve looked as if she were about to cry. "Oh, Kate. Are you sure you know what you're doing?"

"Yes," Kate said, blinking back another round of tears. "I just can't believe I really have been such a big pushover. Even the night he proposed, Harold had the stage set so perfectly he knew I wouldn't have the heart to turn him down. Like the wimp I am, I didn't. And since that night I've been trying to convince myself I could be happy with Harold and a marginally comfortable marriage."

Alex hugged her. "Hey, stop beating yourself up. Only a heartless bitch would turn a guy down when he's a making a big production of proposing in front of *his* mother and *her* grandmother. And everyone knows if there's one thing you could never be, Kate, it's a heartless bitch."

"No, I'm just a stupid one," Kate said.

Alex hugged her again. "But look on the bright side. At least you don't have any big wedding to cancel."

"No, but I do hate disappointing Gram and Margaret."

"Better to disappoint them now than later, with a nasty divorce," Alex pointed out. "You have to know the marriage never would have worked long-term, Kate."

Kate sniffed again, but nodded in agreement.

"However," Alex said, "there could be another perfectly logical reason why you've suddenly had a change of heart about marrying someone you don't love."

Eve raised her hand like a schoolgirl. "I know the answer to that one." She grinned a goofy lopsided grin.

"Destiny," she said, and hiccuped again. "Destiny stepped in and changed Kate's mind."

"Destiny doesn't have anything to do with this," Kate grumbled.

Nor did Tony Petrocelli.

In fact, she had no intention of telling Tony when she saw him for the last time that her relationship with Harold was over. The last thing she needed was another man messing with her head right now.

What she needed was some time to herself.

She needed time to make sense out of why she'd almost settled for a comfortable marriage to a man she didn't love.

Harold obviously assumed his money could buy her.

Big mistake.

She was *not* for sale, thank you very much.

CHAPTER 5

━━◆━━

When Kate rounded the corner the next evening and saw the sleek black sedan sitting in front of her apartment building, she set her jaw determinedly and marched straight in its direction. She'd called Harold's driver first thing that morning to say she wouldn't be needing his services to take her to Queens. She would go to Queens on her own. She didn't need Harold *or* his money to get her there.

Morgan was out of his seat and waiting for her by the time she reached the car. "I know you called and said you didn't need my services tonight, Miss Anderson," he said quickly. "I'm here on other business for Mr. Wellington."

He opened the passenger-side door of the car, leaned in, and came out with a long flower box that he promptly handed out for Kate to take. "Mr. Wellington wanted you to have these roses," he said, "and I was also instructed to tell you that I'm at your disposal for the entire evening to take you and your friends anywhere you want to go. Is there anywhere else you'd like to go this evening, Miss Anderson?"

So, that was Harold's take on the situation, was it?

He truly didn't believe she had broken their engagement. He'd also automatically assumed that when she called Morgan to cancel she'd decided to be a good little girl and stay home.

Well, she had news for Harold.

Roses didn't change a thing.

It had been over for her the minute he suggested she could sleep with another man as long as she didn't tell him about it.

Kate looked down at the box, trying to keep the anger from burning its way up to her cheeks. She didn't want Morgan reporting back to Harold that she'd been anything other than indifferent about his pitiful excuse for a peace offering. "I have no intention of accepting the roses," she said, refusing to take them. "And I still won't be needing your services tonight, Morgan. I'm sorry you've made the trip for no reason."

Let Harold think what he wanted.

What she did or what she didn't do was no longer any of Harold's business. He'd sent his spy to gather information for him, but Morgan wasn't getting any information from her.

As if he sensed as much, Morgan tipped the brim of his hat and returned to the driver's side of the car. As he sped away, Kate was still mumbling unkind things about her now-ex-fiancé under her breath as she walked through the door that Mr. Womack was happy to hold open for her.

"Anything wrong, Katie?" the old man quizzed.

Kate knew he'd watched the entire scene with Morgan from the front door.

"No, nothing's wrong, Mr. Womack," Kate said as she headed toward the elevator.

What she didn't say was that she'd been a complete basket case all day. She kept telling herself one minute that seeing Tony again was the last thing she needed on the heels of breaking her engagement to Harold. Yet, the next minute she kept reminding herself she'd given Tony her word, and she should stick to her agreement to help him out with the problem he was having with his mother.

She'd also spent a good portion of her day coming close to hyperventilating every time she thought about how close she'd come to truly making the biggest mistake of her life. But she was angry mostly with herself, not Harold. Harold had been able to string her along, sure, but only because she'd been stupid enough to let him.

Roses, Kate thought.

So typically Harold.

Calling her at the gallery to apologize wouldn't have worked either, but it would have still been better than sending his driver over with flowers. Except calling her during the day had *never* been on Harold's fricking schedule.

To hell with Harold and his fricking schedules.

His schedules were none of her concern now.

Kate unlocked her apartment door and walked into the living room. Alex and Eve both jumped back from the window, guilty looks on their faces.

"Uh, we, uh," Alex began.

"Now the two of you are spying on me from the window?"

"Mr. Womack buzzed us to let us know Harold's driver was waiting for you," Alex admitted. "I still can't believe

Harold had the nerve to think flowers would change your mind."

Kate shook her head disgustedly.

She headed for her bedroom.

Alex and Eve followed right along behind her.

Eve said, "Is Harold really that clueless?"

"Believe me, Harold really is that clueless," Kate said. "He thinks all he has to do is send his driver over with a box of roses and everything will be back to normal again."

"Did he at least call you today to apologize?" Alex asked.

"Of course not," Kate said. "You know personal phone calls during the day aren't on Harold's *shed-ual.*" She mimicked Harold's exact pronunciation of the word.

"Right. I forgot."

"I'm sure he assumes because I called first thing to cancel his driver, that I'd changed my mind about going to Queens, too. Morgan didn't say that, but he let me know he was instructed to take me and my friends anywhere we wanted to go tonight. A bonus from Harold, I guess, for my shaping up and being a good girl. I sent Morgan on his way. Just as I had no interest in accepting the roses."

"I agree you shouldn't have accepted the roses," Alex said, "but you should have let Morgan take you to Queens. Harold at least owes you that much for putting up with him for more than eight months."

"Harold doesn't owe me anything," Kate said, "and that goes double for me."

She began pulling clothing from her closet in a frenzy. It was already after five. She still had to take a quick shower and get dressed by six. Then, thanks to her own

stubbornness, she'd have to hail a taxi for the trip to
Queens.

"So, Cinderella?" Alex said, as she and Eve peered
through Kate's open bedroom door. "What kind of gown
are you choosing for the ball tonight?"

"Kate's going to a ball?" Eve's eyes grew wide. "But I
thought Kate was going to meet Tony at his family's
restaurant tonight."

Kate stood looking down at the dresses she had strewn
across the bed. "I don't know why I'm so nervous about
what to wear. The grandmother is blind, for God's sake."

"Yeah, but Tony isn't," Alex said, with a grin.

"Don't start with that again, Alex," Kate warned. "I'm
doing the guy a favor. That's all."

Eve looked from one of them to the other. "The grandmother is going to be at the ball, too?"

"Eve," Alex said. "I was using a metaphor. Cinderella.
The Prince. The ball. Get it?"

Eve blinked. "Metaphors always confuse me."

Alex looked at Eve and sighed. "Are you sure you
aren't related to Jessica Simpson?"

Eve looked at Alex for a moment. "Oh. That's another
metaphor. Right?"

Alex rolled her eyes, walked across the room, and
stood beside Kate, who was still surveying the clothing
littering her bed. "Forget dresses," Alex said. "You aren't
going to some uptown affair, Kate. You're going to a
family-owned restaurant in Queens. You need to dress
casual. Jeans, a cute shirt, summer sandals. That's the
ticket. You can guarantee Tony is a jeans kind of guy
when he's out of uniform."

Kate chewed at her bottom lip. "I don't know about

jeans, Alex. I don't want to overdress, but I don't want to look like some waif off the street, either."

Alex walked over to her closet, selected a pair of jeans, an emerald green silk shirt that really was one of Kate's favorites, and hooked the hangers over the top of the closet door.

Kate still wasn't convinced. "You're sure about the jeans?"

"Positive," Alex assured her. "Add a cute pair of sandals, and you're good to go."

"I really don't know why I'm so nervous," Kate said again. And against her better judgment, she added, "I don't guess I could talk the two of you into coming to Queens with me?"

"Not me," Alex said. She walked back to Kate's closet and began surveying the hanging shoe rack on the back of her closet door. She extracted a pair of sandals from the plastic slots of the shoe rack and turned back around. "I was waiting until you got home to share the good news, but John finally called me today. He wants me to have dinner with him tonight."

"And?" Kate said, motioning for details.

Alex smiled a Cheshire smile and handed over the shoes. "He says he loves me. He misses me. And he wants me to come home."

"And?" Kate repeated.

"And he said he's ready to compromise. Which can only mean one thing. John has decided that I can take four more years to make senior executive before we begin our family."

"I'm so happy for you, Alex," Kate said, giving Alex a big hug. "I knew you guys would work things out."

"I was beginning to wonder," Alex said, and laughed. "I still can't believe John held out as long as he did." She reached out and put her arms around both Kate and Eve, pulling them close. "Thank you, guys, for putting up with me and letting me stay with you."

"We really are going to miss you," Eve said.

"Hey," Alex said looking at Eve. "Just because I can't go to Queens with Kate tonight, doesn't mean you can't go with her."

Eve started to protest, but Alex held up a finger.

"Oh, no you don't. No excuses. I know Kate's called off the wedding, but that doesn't mean we're going to let you fall back into hiding out in this apartment day in and day out. Those days are over. Right, Kate?"

Kate nodded.

Eve blushed. "I know those days are over. I promise. It's just that . . . well, don't freak out or anything, but I've actually met someone."

Alex and Kate exchanged shocked looks.

"You met someone where?" Alex wanted to know. "And when? You've been hiding out for over a year now, Eve."

"I met him online," Eve confessed.

"Are you nuts?" Alex exploded. "Don't you know how dangerous it can be hooking up with someone online?"

"I didn't meet him in one of those chat rooms or anything," Eve said quickly. "He's one of my new clients. I'm redesigning his Web site and we've been e-mailing back and forth. I finally broke down and gave him my phone number. He's going to call me tonight for the first time. That's why I need to stay home."

"Eve, you really do need to be careful," Kate said,

looking over at Alex for support. "What do you really know about this guy?"

"Everything," Eve said proudly. "His name is George Dumond. He's a musician. He plays the banjo, and he's actually quite famous in the folk music scheme of things. He lives in a small town in Connecticut. He's never been married. He likes the quiet and solitude of living out in the country. And . . ."

"And you're sure he's legitimate," Alex broke in.

Eve nodded. "I'm sure. And guess what? His screen name is Braveheart. Don't you love it? He's my very own Knight in Cyber Armor."

Neither Alex nor Kate cracked a smile.

Eve stamped her size four-and-a-half foot. "That was supposed to be funny, you guys. Knight in Cyber Armor? Get it? That's a metaphor. Right?"

Rather than tease Eve any longer, Kate and Alex both burst out laughing.

⟅⟆

"Anthony! Stop pacing back and forth in front of the door. You're wearing a hole in my floor."

His mother said this, then grabbed him by the arm and led him over to a booth by the window. When Tony plopped down on the seat, she motioned to his cousin, Tina, who was busy waiting tables.

"Bring my favorite son a glass of wine to calm him down," she said.

Tina turned and headed to the bar.

"I'm your only son," Tony reminded her.

"But my favorite son, still." She gave his left cheek a

not-so-gentle pat. "You drink your wine like a good boy. You calm yourself down. And we'll all be in the back at the family table when your intended arrives."

"She is *not* my intended," Tony said through clenched teeth. "What she is is a saint for agreeing to come here tonight."

"No need for blasphemy," his mother warned. "Not when the very Saints in Heaven above are responsible for you finally coming to your senses."

"I did *not* come to my senses," Tony mumbled under his breath. "Papa just couldn't take another damn night on the sofa."

If his mother heard his smart remark, for once, she let it slide. She headed to the back of the restaurant, where the rest of the family was gathered.

Tony turned halfway around in the booth and looked at the group sitting at the long table. They were already digging into Mama's fresh-baked bread, already stuffing their faces with salad, already anticipating Mama's famous baked ziti, which would be served as the entrée later. That meant the lively conversation around the table had died down for the moment while his sisters attended to their children and their husbands kept the bread baskets and the large bowls of salad circulating around the table.

His gaze rested on Nonna for a moment, sitting to his father's left at the head of the table. Her white hair was wound into a small bun on top of her regal head—her favorite heirloom brooch pinned at the throat of her freshly starched white blouse. Tony smiled when Nonna said something that made everyone at the table laugh.

At least he knew his family would play it cool when he introduced Kate to Nonna, and his grandmother didn't make the connection. As unreasonable as his family could be sometimes, he knew everyone sitting at that table would protect Nonna at any cost. He could count on them for that.

It didn't mean, however, that he wouldn't have to usher Kate out of the restaurant as quickly as possible. Better that than subject her to the thorough interrogation he was sure Mama and his sisters would put her through if he allowed them half a chance.

When he thought about it, his mother and his sisters were the ones who should have joined the police force. With their tenacious personalities, the women in his family could easily wear down even hardened criminals in record time and have them begging to make a confession, just to get some relief.

Thinking about women with unfaltering determination, sent his gaze right back to his mother.

If Mama kept her agreement and let him handle the situation tonight, there shouldn't be a problem. Except Mama often agreed, and just as often changed her mind about agreeing to anything.

So, he'd just have to stay on top of his game.

He'd have to usher Kate in.

Introduce her to Nonna.

And usher Kate right back out again.

Quick and easy.

Make her trip virtually painless, if possible.

Unfortunately, knowing his mother, Tony was actually contemplating whether or not a quick prayer to the Saints in Heaven above might not be a good idea.

"Here you go," Tina said, when she walked up and placed a glass of wine in front of him.

Tony thanked his cousin and turned back around in his seat. He waited until Tina went about her business before he picked up the wineglass and downed the red liquid in one easy gulp. Before the wine even reached his stomach, a warm tingle spread through his body, making him feel a little less on edge.

He was on the verge of yelling for Tina to bring him the whole bottle when a taxi pulled up in front of the restaurant and stopped.

Welcome to Nutsville, Tony thought.

He vaulted from the booth.

A quick prayer to the Saints on his lips just in case, he headed for the restaurant's front door.

Kate couldn't keep from smiling when the taxi stopped in front of Mama Gina's. It was exactly the type of Italian bistro no one would be able to resist. The restaurant had a crisp green-and-white awning over the door. A warm glow from inside radiated through the old-fashioned paned windows in front. Even from the street, the place looked inviting. She had no doubt people who ate here regularly were always encouraged to enjoy the food, join in on the laughter, and toast to the good cheer of everyone there.

Kate was still smiling when Tony walked out of the restaurant and headed for the taxi. Her smile faded, but only because her heart started pounding so badly it scared her.

What was it about this guy that rattled her every time she saw him?

Alex had been right about the casual dress.

But dear Lord!

No man had the right to look that good in faded jeans.

He grinned that little-boy grin of his when he walked up to the passenger side of the taxi. When he opened the door, he offered Kate his hand to help her out of the car. Kate took his hand and stepped out onto the sidewalk, but she wasted no time telling the taxi driver to wait for her. The last thing she needed was getting left in Queens without a way to make a quick exit.

Alone time with Tony Petrocelli was *not* an option.

Kate faced him.

He grinned again, and said, "Are you sure you want the taxi driver to wait? I'll be more than happy to drive you back to the city myself."

I'd be more than happy to let you, too.

That's the problem.

Kate shook her head. "No, I'll stick with the taxi."

He shrugged. "Okay. Second question. Are you sure you're really up for this?"

Kate said, "I don't have to help you break down your mother's bedroom door or anything, do I?"

He laughed. "No. All we have to do is walk to the back of the restaurant where my family is having dinner like we do every Friday night. I'll introduce you to my grandmother. And then I'll escort you right back outside to the taxi. Okay?"

"Okay," Kate said, hoping she sounded a lot braver than she felt. "Then I guess it's time to go meet . . ."

"Our destiny?" Tony teased.

"Your *grandmother*," Kate corrected.

If only he hadn't put his hand on her back as they started inside the restaurant. If only he hadn't touched her, Kate might have been able to ignore the rat-a-tat-tat inside her chest, and summon up the courage she needed to face the family she knew she was getting ready to thoroughly disappoint.

———✐———

Tony felt Kate tremble when he placed his hand at the small of her back. For a second he was tempted to turn her around and tell her to forget the whole thing.

She'd agreed to come of her own free will, sure, but he still felt guilty about involving her in the never-ending drama that always seemed to surround his family. The only thing that stopped him from putting her back in the taxi and sending her on her way, was knowing that after tonight Kate wouldn't have to deal with him or with his family again.

He took a deep breath, opened the door, and let Kate enter the restaurant ahead of him. When he stepped through the door himself, it was as if someone hit pause. The commotion going on inside stopped for a second.

"Do I really look that out of place here?" Kate whispered back over her shoulder.

"No way," Tony said, leaning forward close enough for her to hear him. "We're just not used to having someone so pretty show up in this place."

"Liar," she whispered back.

And she did look amazing.

Too amazing.

Even in jeans.

But it wasn't the time to let Kate or her sexy curves deter him from his mission. His goal was to get her back to the family table, prove she wasn't his intended bride, and rescue her before she was overwhelmed by the usual Petrocelli Friday night confusion.

He managed to usher her past the staring customers, toward the rear of the restaurant. But the second his mother looked up and saw them walking in her direction, she jumped up from her chair and hurried forward to greet them.

"Don't let my mother intimidate you," Tony warned.

His warning came too late.

His mother embraced Kate like the long-lost daughter-in-law she wasn't going to have.

Tony frowned. "We had an agreement, Mama. Remember?"

Her only response was to smile happily back at Tony over Kate's unsuspecting shoulder.

Kate wasn't prepared when the robust woman grabbed her in a bear hug. But it did cross her mind that she hadn't been hugged like that in a long, long time. For a second, Kate was reminded how much she missed hugs like that from her own mother.

"Well, don't just stand there, Anthony," she said, when she finally released Kate. "Introduce me to this lovely girl."

"This is Kate Anderson, Mama," Tony said. "Kate, my mother, Gina Petrocelli."

Kate was surprised.

Gina Petrocelli looked nothing like she'd expected.

She'd expected some frail, nervous little gray-haired woman, kneeling by her bedside praying. This woman was a beautiful, full-figured woman, not a wrinkle on her face, or a strand of gray in her hair. Her brown eyes danced with excitement as she sent Kate a big smile.

"Call me Mama Gina, Kate," she said. "First, we talk a bit. Then we take you to meet Nonna."

"Forget it, Mama," Tony said. "Kate's taxi is outside waiting for her. I promised her this would be quick. She needs to get back to the city."

"Tina," Mama Gina yelled over her shoulder.

Kate smiled at the lanky girl as she ambled in their direction. She looked to be somewhere in her early twenties. Her dark hair was spiked, her makeup was Gothic, and she was chewing her bubble gum ninety miles a minute.

"Take the taxi driver outside some pizza from the buffet and find out what he wants to drink," Mama Gina told her. "Keep him happy."

Tina nodded, and headed toward the buffet set up at the far end of the restaurant.

Mama Gina sent Tony a victorious smile.

Then she took Kate's hand and began leading her to a booth in the back, away from everyone else.

Kate had no choice but to follow. She looked back over her shoulder for Tony. He was following behind them, shaking his head disgustedly.

Mama Gina motioned Kate into the booth, then grabbed Tony by the arm and pushed him into the seat beside her. A little too close for comfort, Kate decided, when his leg touched hers for a second.

She scooted closer to the wall for safety.

After she seated herself across the table from them, Mama Gina sent them both another big smile.

Tony looked over at Kate, and said, "My mother promised she wouldn't do this, Kate. She obviously has selective memory tonight."

"What's wrong with me talking to Kate for a minute?"

Mama Gina frowned at Tony, then smiled warmly at Kate again. "Kate has been nice enough to come. I think she deserves to know why it is so important to your family that she meets your grandmother."

"I've already told Kate all about Nonna's predictions," Tony said.

"You've told her your way. I'll tell her mine."

"Show her your engagement ring, Kate," Tony said. "Maybe then my mother will accept the fact that you're already engaged and soon to be married."

Oops.

She'd forgotten about the ring.

Kate panicked for a second.

A plausible lie finally slipped through her lips. "I forgot to put my ring back on when I showered after work," she said, looking over at Tony.

He stared at her bare finger, then back at her.

He kept looking at her, as if he suspected the lie.

Double oops.

Kate looked away.

Mama Gina said, "Kate doesn't mind if we have a little talk first, do you, Kate?"

"I really don't mind," Kate said, looking back at Tony.

He was still staring at her bare finger.

Damn.

I really should have worn the ring.

Something was up.

Other than the fact that Kate was a lousy liar.

She was definitely lying about the reason for not wearing her engagement ring, and Tony knew it.

But why?

The mystery about the ring took a backseat, however, when his mother spoke up and said, "I wanted you to know a little bit about my Anthony, Kate."

Tony groaned. "Mama, please."

He could only imagine what was coming next.

And there was nothing he could do to stop it.

Kate glanced at him, an amused look on her face.

Shit.

"Anthony was raised right here with his five sisters." His mother pointed to the ceiling above them. "Right above this restaurant. Mario and I raised our children in the apartment upstairs, where we've lived since we first married and bought this building for our restaurant. A small space, yes. But our home has always been filled with a whole lot of love."

"And no privacy whatsoever," Tony mumbled. "Just like right now."

Kate giggled at his comment.

Tony looked at her, and said, "You really are enjoying this, aren't you?"

"Loving it," she said, and grinned at him.

They stared at each other for a second.

Tony broke eye contact first.

Off-limits. Off-limits. Off-limits. Off-limits.

"Even in kindergarten, Anthony was smart boy," Mama Gina said, and Tony groaned even louder. "Always at the top of his class. He graduated with honors from Princeton, too."

If I had my revolver, I'd shoot myself.

How embarrassing.

Especially since he didn't miss the surprised look on Kate's face when his mother mentioned Princeton.

"Surprised a cop would have a Princeton education?" He just had to ask.

"A little," she admitted.

"The police force wasn't Anthony's first choice in a career," Mama Gina spoke up. "He tried Wall Street first."

Tell it all, Mama. Dammit, tell it all.

Kate looked at him again. "Now, that does surprise me. I would never have figured you for the killer-instinct Wall Street type."

Is that a compliment?

Tony wasn't sure.

Mama Gina said, "Anthony decided there was more to life than making big money. He left Manhattan. He came back home to Queens. He went to the Police Academy. And he's made his father and mother very proud. He's made his community proud of him, too." She looked at Tony. "Tell her, Anthony. Tell Kate about the apartment building you bought and turned back into a safe place for people in your neighborhood to live."

Tony could feel himself blushing.

Enough is enough.

"I think you've bored Kate long enough, Mama," he said.

He slid out of the booth and stood up.

Mama Gina counteracted by reaching across the table and taking Kate's hand, holding her captive. "I've embarrassed my son, Kate. But I wanted you to know Anthony is a good man. I knew he'd never tell you himself." She lowered her voice, "Anthony's always been a little shy with the ladies."

"Mama!" *Jesus.*

"What?" Mama Gina asked defiantly. "Tell me once when you've brought a nice girl home for your mama to meet. Never. Until now."

"Kate's only here now, Mama, because she took pity on me when *you* locked yourself in your bedroom praying."

She ignored the reminder and turned back to Kate. "Still, I wanted you to know these things, just in case my mother-in-law realizes who you are tonight."

"Mrs. Petrocelli," Kate began.

"See," Tony spoke up. "Now you're embarrassing Kate."

Mama Gina patted her hand. "Don't worry. If Nonna doesn't make the connection, I won't say another word."

"You're my witness, Kate," Tony said, frowning at his mother. "When my grandmother doesn't have a clue who you are, my mother *isn't* going to say another word."

"But," Mama Gina added, because there was always an exception where his mother was concerned. "But if Nonna *does* make the connection, then I'm hoping Kate will consider that your nonna has never been wrong about one of her marriage predictions yet."

Tony looked at Kate. "What my mother isn't telling you, Kate, is that Nonna's previous predictions weren't all that hard to predict."

"Anthony!" Mama Gina scolded.

He looked back at Kate. "My grandmother predicted

my uncle Vinny would marry my aunt Annette. They'd only been boyfriend and girlfriend since the second grade. No big surprise there."

"And what about your uncle Ralphie?" Mama Gina asked.

Tony looked back at Kate. "Nonna predicted my uncle Ralph would meet his bride on the ferry. Not hard to predict, since he was already working on the ferry by the time he turned sixteen. He still drives the ferry from St. George's landing every day of the week."

Mama Gina said, "And I guess you think your father meeting me on the subway is a big coincidence, too. Just like your uncle Dominic becoming a priest is a coincidence, even though Nonna predicted he would do just that."

"Everyone knew Uncle Dom had the calling by the time he was twelve years old," Tony said. "Nonna's big prediction for Uncle Dom was that his love would always be the Church."

Mama Gina waved away his comment. "My son has an answer for everything," she said to Kate. She looked back at Tony. "So let's hear your explanation for why you found Kate in Central Park standing beside the Blessed Virgin, just like Nonna predicted."

The question caught Tony off guard.

Kate was even looking at him for an answer.

When he didn't have one, Mama Gina motioned for Kate to get up. "Come, Kate," she said, taking Kate by the hand again. "It's time to settle how well my mother-in-law can predict the future, once and for all."

Kate's mind was still reeling from the candid conversation she'd just witnessed between Tony and his mother. The Petrocellis were definitely open, honest, in-life's-face kind of people.

So different from her.

She had opinions, sure, but by the time she finished picking and choosing her don't-make-waves words carefully, the chance to state her opinions had usually passed. Which only reinforced her push-me-right-over personality. That's what had given Harold the upper hand—her inability to blurt out exactly what she was really thinking without weighing and balancing the risks.

Tony was like Alex. You always knew exactly where you stood with both of them. He'd been bold enough to ask if she really loved Harold, hadn't he? He'd just blurted the question right out there. Even said he could tell she wasn't your typical happy bride.

He knew I was lying about the ring, too.

Maybe she *would* tell him she had called off her wedding. After she finished her audition with the grandmother, of course. Admit that most of her life she'd been nothing more than a clueless guppy swimming around and around and around in the big bowl of life.

Not!

That would send him running in the opposite direction for sure. No straightforward guy like him would ever be interested in a ditzy chick who had accepted a marriage proposal from a guy because she didn't have the guts to make waves.

No.

She wasn't going to tell Tony anything.

Not tonight.

After she got her act together—maybe then.

When they reached the back of the restaurant, Kate found a table of smiling faces waiting to greet her. Mama Gina pointed down the table, spouting out names Kate knew she'd never be able to remember.

But the names didn't matter.

The energy in the room was warm and friendly.

Kate knew at a glance everyone was devoted to each other. It was the type of family anyone would want, and most people would never have.

"Kate, this is my husband, Mario," Mama Gina said, when they came to a stop at the head of the table.

Kate nodded politely, realizing she'd just caught a glimpse of what Tony himself would look like at his father's age. The resemblance was remarkable. Mario smiled, the same familiar laugh lines crinkling as he took her hand in his.

"Welcome to Mama Gina's," he said.

But the look in his eyes said more.

As if he knew some secret Kate didn't.

This really is creeping me out.

She couldn't help it. She was getting more nervous by the minute. She even felt a little light-headed when Mama Gina led her around the table to where the obvious matriarch was sitting.

The grandmother looked nothing like Kate had imagined, either. She'd imagined the grandmother rather Gypsy-like, shoulders stooped, dressed all in black, lace veil draped over her head and shoulders—your typical tea-leaf-reading icon. This woman was impeccably dressed, not a hair out of place on her snow-white head, and sitting as dignified as any queen holding court.

Had it not been for the slightly vacant look in her eyes, Kate never would have suspected she was blind. The old woman turned her head at the sound of their approach. That's when Kate realized whether she was blind or not, Tony's nonna didn't miss much.

By then, Tony was following so closely behind her, Kate could feel his warm breath on the back of her neck.

She shivered.

Oh, God, she kept thinking.

What if his grandmother did make some kind of connection? What if the old woman grabbed her in an embrace the way Mama Gina had done, and announced to the entire family that she really was the woman Tony was destined to marry?

Oh, God.

What will I do if that happens?

What will Tony do if that happens?

Kate glanced at the front door, fighting the urge to bolt. She was one second away from sprinting for the door when Mama Gina bent down to speak directly to the old woman.

"Nonna," Mama Gina said. "I have someone I want you to meet. This is Kate Anderson."

When the old woman held out her hand, Mama Gina said, "Kate, this is my mother-in-law, Rosa Petrocelli."

Kate sent a nervous look back over her shoulder at Tony when his mother took her hand and placed it into the outstretched hands of his grandmother.

"It's a pleasure to meet you," Kate said on cue.

She sent Tony a terrified what-do-I-do-now look when his grandmother kept holding on to her hand much longer than necessary.

The chatter at the table stopped completely.

Everyone held their breath.

The tension kept mounting.

Everyone kept waiting.

Waiting.

Waiting.

Waiting.

"Welcome," Nonna finally said. She released Kate's hand and promptly went back to eating her salad.

Welcome?

That was it?

Kate looked at Tony.

Tony looked at Kate.

And everyone started talking at once.

<hr />

Tony had no intention of losing control of the situation again. He bent down and kissed his grandmother on the cheek, told her he would be right back, then began pushing Kate forward, toward the front of the restaurant.

They were close to making their escape.

But his mother caught up with them just as they reached the restaurant's front door.

"Anthony! Where are you going?" she demanded. "No one leaves Mama Gina's with an empty stomach. I want Kate to stay for dinner."

God, it's tempting.

He'd like nothing better than for Kate to stay for dinner. The minute she walked out the door, he would lose her forever.

Staying for dinner isn't part of the deal.

Staying for dinner would mean that Kate would be subjected to Mama and more of her pranks.

It wasn't fair to Kate.

He had to let her go.

Tony shook his head. "No way, Mama. You'd be dropping hints to Nonna all night, and you know it. I think we've already put Kate through enough."

Mama Gina swatted Tony on the arm. "I wouldn't drop any hints to Nonna."

She looked at Kate for a second, then finally gave in and let out a defeated sigh. "I'm sorry, Kate. Tony's right. We've put you through enough drama tonight. But I am disappointed, and I admit it."

He glanced at Kate.

At least she was smiling.

"You have a wonderful family," Kate said. "I've enjoyed meeting all of you."

"You're always welcome here," his mother told her. "Bring your new husband with you next time. I'll treat you both to the best baked ziti in Queens."

Her new husband.

Tony winced in spite of himself.

Mama Gina stepped forward and gave Kate a final hug.

What?

Did he imagine it?

Or was it just wishful thinking?

Tony wasn't sure.

But just for a second, he thought Kate looked a little disappointed, too.

It had been awkward while Rosa Petrocelli held on to her hand with the whole family watching, but awkward didn't touch what Kate was feeling when she and Tony finally made it out of the restaurant and onto the sidewalk. The good news was, Tony seemed as eager to get rid of her as she was to get the hell out of there.

She'd almost blurted out for Mama Gina not to give up on her yet, that she had called off her wedding. But it wouldn't be fair to Tony. She needed to get things officially settled with Harold first. She'd already broken her engagement, yes, but she knew Harold well enough to know he wouldn't leave her alone until they had a face-to-face meeting when he returned from Chicago.

Which, in all fairness, Harold truly deserved.

Breaking their engagement on the telephone was not something she was proud of doing, she'd just been too angry to care after Harold's tacky don't ask, don't tell comment. Still, being angry was no excuse. She'd meet Harold face-to-face one last time and give him no reason to doubt it was over between them.

After the dust settled and her life settled back down, that was when she'd take a long walk through Central Park until she found Officer Petrocelli.

Waiting until I have my life together is the right thing to do.

Kate was sure of it.

He kept his hand at her back, practically pushing her toward the taxi. Before she could stop him, he dug into his pocket, bent down, and handed the taxi driver several folded bills through the open taxi window.

When he stood back up, he said, "I gave the driver

more than enough for your fare both ways, and a good tip. Don't let him tell you otherwise."

"That wasn't necessary," Kate told him.

He grinned. "Are you kidding? After what you've just done for me? I've been living with my grandmother's prediction for the last twenty years. Thanks to you, the curse is finally broken."

"And now you're a free man," Kate said.

"Yeah." He sighed. "I guess I am."

Was she mistaken?

Or did he seem a little disappointed?

Get in the taxi!

Now!

"I'd better get going," Kate said, reaching for the door handle.

He beat her to it and opened the car door.

"I can't thank you enough for coming," he said.

"Glad I could help," Kate told him.

Get. In. The. Damn. Taxi!

The last thing she needed was to end up in another one of those long soul-searching staring matches like the one back in the bridal shop dressing room.

I'd never survive it.

Too late.

He took her hand, pulling her closer.

Gulp.

They were standing only inches apart.

Oh, God!

His head came forward.

His hot mouth pressed against hers.

Zoom. Bam. Bop. Knock-you-right-out.

"I couldn't resist being the first one to kiss the bride,"

he said when their lips broke apart. "Have a happy life, Kate."

"You, too," was all Kate could manage.

Tell him! Tell him you aren't getting married!

She couldn't.

Kate slid onto the taxi's backseat, shaken.

Tony closed the door and stepped away from the car.

Kate said, "Go! Now," and the taxi driver placed his piece of pizza back in the to-go box on the seat beside him and sped away.

She willed herself not to look back, but she did.

Tony was standing on the sidewalk, staring after her.

CHAPTER 6

For once, Kate was relieved that Mr. Womack wasn't waiting to perform his doorman services. Pretending to be chipper, when chipper was the last thing she was feeling at the moment, wasn't at the top of her list of things to do.

She let herself in the building with a sigh, wondering how it was possible that her life had turned to crap in such a short time. She didn't want to be the wrong blonde, dammit! She'd realized that the second the grandmother didn't have a clue who she was.

The big letdown had stunned her.

Tony's blistering kiss hadn't helped matters, either.

Still, she'd done the right thing not telling Tony the truth. Kate assured herself of that fact as she put her key into the lock to her apartment. Tony was a really nice guy. It wouldn't be fair to send him mixed messages when she still had unfinished business with Harold.

The afteraffect of her calling off the wedding wasn't going to be pleasant by any stretch of the imagination. She was going to be the bad guy, regardless, and Kate knew it.

Worse yet, she also knew she deserved the title.

Sure, maybe it had taken Harold's stupid don't ask, don't tell comment to snap her back to reality. It didn't matter. She never should have accepted Harold's proposal in the first place.

She'd known it the second she'd said "yes." She just hadn't been brave enough to turn Harold down with her grandmother and his mother looking on, big smiles on their faces and huge tears of joy in their eyes.

Gram.

As much as she looked forward to her grandmother returning from Paris in the morning, the dread of having to tell Grace she was calling off the wedding washed over Kate like an ice-cold rain.

No doubt about it, she was going to be the bad guy.

Harold would possibly make an ugly scene when he returned because he wasn't getting his way. Her grandmother and Margaret Wellington were going to be devastated at the news they'd broken up. Any way you looked at the situation, she was going to be the villain.

She thought about Tony's kiss again.

And about the last thing he'd said to her.

Have a happy life, Kate.

Kate sighed.

Life for her was going to be anything *but* happy when she thought about how her grandmother was going to react to her calling off the wedding. Grace would not take her breakup with Harold lightly.

There was bound to be tension between them.

As much as she knew Grace loved her, she also knew her grandmother had always been waiting for the other shoe to drop, so to speak. Worried that eventually Kate was going to exhibit some of her mother's throw-caution-to-the-winds traits, that according to Grace had ruined her son's life, and sent poor Rob Anderson straight down the path to destruction.

So, maybe her mother was a little flighty when you compared her to someone as polished and adept as Grace. Maybe "Mystery" wasn't a name most women would choose for themselves, either. But her mother had decided to call herself "Mystery" because she said it was a mystery to her why her parents would name her "Gertrude" and not expect her to change such a horrible name.

Her parents marched to a different drummer, that's all.

Still, Kate loved them.

Burning incense and chanting all day—that was a different story.

But Kate did often wonder whether she might have been more assertive if she hadn't spent her formative years in a commune devoted to spreading peace and harmony throughout the world. The need to "please" and avoid any undue confrontation wasn't always the best trait to have.

Sometimes you had to go *against* the flow.

Like the confrontation she'd encountered with Grace after college, when Grace insisted she come back home to live with her, but Kate wanted her independence. Had it not been for Alex pushing her to develop a little backbone, she'd probably be thirty and still living at home with Grace now.

Chutzpah.

Did she have enough chutzpah to stand up to Grace and Harold over her calling off the wedding?

She thought about Tony's kiss again and decided that she did. She'd finally experienced that immediate knock-you-out connection she'd always assumed was just a myth. At last, that I-want-you-like-crazy feeling was real to her.

And, oh, how I do want Tony Petrocelli like crazy.

Just not right now.

Right now, my life is too complicated.

The first thing on her agenda had to be tying up loose ends with Harold. Then and only then would she be free to get on with her life.

And if Tony isn't available then?

Kate wouldn't let herself think about that.

That was one matter she *would* have to leave to destiny.

Feeling rather pleased with herself for analyzing the situation and, for once, coming to a mature conclusion about what she needed to do, Kate's mood unfortunately took another nosedive when she entered her apartment and found the place as silent as a tomb. No TV blaring as usual. No Alex ordering Eve around. No Eve scurrying around to do Alex's bidding.

Wait a minute.

No Eve?

Fearing something was wrong, Kate hurried down the hallway to Eve's bedroom. Her hand was poised, ready to knock on the closed door, until she heard Eve giggle. Shamelessly, Kate leaned forward and put her ear to the door.

Another giggle.

"Well, let's just say no one would pick me to be a runway model," she heard Eve say. "I'm what my friend Alex calls vertically challenged."

Giggle. Giggle. Giggle.

"Really, George? You're not just saying that? You really do prefer petite women?"

Kate smiled and tiptoed back down the hallway.

Good for Eve. Just because her own life was headed straight down the crapper didn't mean she wasn't thrilled to hear Eve sound so happy for a change. If anyone deserved a new start in life, it was Eve. The poor thing had more than paid her dues, and then some.

Kate headed for the kitchen, thinking that Alex evidently wasn't having any problem patching things up with John, either. She knew my-way-or-the-highway Alex all too well. Had John not given in and agreed to Alex's terms about postponing a family, Alex would have already beaten her back to the apartment.

Opening the refrigerator, Kate stood there for a moment, surveying her choices.

Frack.

If food kept serving as a replacement for her sex life, it wouldn't be long until she couldn't even get into her own pants.

She ignored the leftover Moo Goo, poured herself a glass of Pinot Grigio, and headed back to the living room to drown her sorrows alone. She'd no sooner settled herself on the sofa when the ring tone on her cell phone sounded loud and clear from her purse on the table by the door.

Kate glanced at her watch.

Nine o'clock sharp.

As usual, Harold was right on schedule, calling at the precise time he said he would call her on Friday night.

Kate took a leisurely sip from her wineglass.

She made no effort to answer her cell phone.

If she talked to Harold again, she'd do it in person.
She was so over Harold and *his* five-minute quickies.

Harold refused to leave a message on Kate's voice
mail. Let her save face by holding out and not talking to
him tonight. Fine with him. He wasn't completely over
his irritation with her, either.

That didn't mean he wouldn't turn the charm back on
when he called her again in a day or two. He'd give her
the rest of the weekend to calm down. Then he'd call.
When he did call, he had no doubt Kate would be so relieved finally to hear from him, she'd be more than happy
to put a stop to her Alex-induced behavior and beg him to
forgive her for suggesting something so stupid as calling
off their wedding.

She'd been smart enough to cancel the absurd trip to
Queens, hadn't she? He'd ignore her not accepting his
peace-offering roses. Roses were a bit too clichéd. But
Kate was a bright woman. There was no way she was
going to risk losing the perks and the prestige that went
along with becoming Mrs. Harold Trent Wellington.

He was offering Kate the world on a string.

Once they were married, she'd never want for anything
again as long as she lived. Just as his mother had never
wanted for anything since the day she married his father.

However, being a man who prided himself on always
having a backup plan, Harold decided it wouldn't be a bad
idea to touch base with Kate's grandmother. If anyone was
in his corner, it was Grace. He intended to keep it that way.

He glanced at his watch, calculating the time difference. If he stayed up until midnight, it would be morning Paris time. He would give Grace a quick call at her hotel before she left for the airport.

He'd pretend he was calling to wish her a safe flight home, then casually mention he was worried about Kate. They'd had a little spat, he'd say. Nothing serious. But with his being away in Chicago on business, he'd appreciate Grace doing what she could to help calm Kate's prewedding jitters.

A pep talk from Grace when Kate met her at the airport tomorrow would get his insolent fiancée back on track soon enough.

Harold was still smiling to himself over his own cleverness when a soft knock jerked his head toward the door of his hotel suite.

He frowned.

Dammit.

He'd given explicit instructions that he wouldn't tolerate being disturbed by housekeeping under any circumstances. Someone was falling down on the job. He'd make sure that person regretted it, deeply.

He walked to the door, ready to give the incompetent maid a lecture she wouldn't soon forget. Then he'd call the hotel manager and put the fear of God in him, too. A quick peek through the security hole in the door, however, shocked Harold to the core.

He jumped back from the door, astounded.

It just wasn't possible.

He'd always been so careful. He'd never carried any identification with him. Never once given anyone even the slightest clue about his identity.

The second knock was a little more forceful.

Harold ignored it.

Then the pounding started.

That's when he jerked the door open.

She walked into the room like she owned the hotel, and tonight she was dressed as if she had the money to buy the place. At least anyone passing her in the lobby would have assumed she was some top fashion super-model. She certainly looked the part. Classic little black strapless dress, the stiletto pumps, the clutch purse—all of it Garavani. He could pick out top fashion designers at a single glance.

It was one of Kate's flaws he intended to correct as soon as they were married. There would be no more "off the rack" for a woman carrying the Wellington name.

His surprise intruder turned around to face him.

She was breathtakingly beautiful. Classy. Chic. Nothing cheap-looking about her. Her services last night hadn't been cheap, either.

Harold slammed the door behind him.

Stupid twit.

She's picked the wrong man to antagonize.

"Why, Harry," she said, mischief dancing in her dark blue eyes. "You don't look happy to see me. And that certainly wasn't your reaction last night."

Harry?

Harold gulped.

Okay. She knew his name. She'd probably followed him back to the hotel. Probably slipped one of the desk clerks a few bills for his name, too. That's all. No need to panic yet.

"Of course, I doubt they call you Harry back at your prestigious law firm in New York City, do they? I'm sure

Harold is a more appropriate name for the sole heir to the impressive Wellington dynasty your rich daddy started."

Harold paled. "I don't know what you're trying to pull showing up here," he said through clenched teeth. "But you have two seconds to leave before I call the police."

Her smile was lethal.

She glanced at the phone sitting beside the king-size bed. Tossing her long, dark hair back over one shoulder, she said, "Go ahead and call, Harry. Tell the cops your story. Tell them how the prostitute you happily handed three G's last night, has shown back up to bother poor little you when you aren't feeling quite so frisky."

Harold took a menacing step in her direction.

She stepped forward herself, not one bit intimidated.

"Don't fuck with me," he warned.

She laughed. "That's *not* what you said last night."

She clicked opened the fancy clasp on her purse and pulled out a DVD disc. "Only one copy of many," she assured him. She even had the nerve to reach out and pat him sweetly on the cheek. "Poor Harry," she said with a sigh. "I really do hate to do this to you. But I've been trolling for a big fish like you for a long, long time."

"Oh, I bet you have, you . . ."

"Carla," she said, cutting him off before he could insult her. "My real name is Carla Matthews. So very happy to see you again."

She stuck her hand out.

Harold ignored it, glaring at her.

"We both know what's on this disc, Harry," she said, waving it under his nose. "You tell me. Do *you* think your uptown reputation could survive the world knowing you like to be spanked thoroughly for being a bad, bad boy?"

"Cut to the chase," Harold hissed. "How much do you want?"

She tossed the disc on the bed, walked over to the wet bar, and poured herself a glass of bourbon. She swirled the amber liquid around in the tumbler before she took a long sip. After licking her lips slowly and seductively, she smiled, and said, "It's not *how much* I want, Harry. It's *what* I want."

A muscle in his jaw twitched uncontrollably. "Keep talking."

"I want respectability."

Harold threw his head back and laughed. "As if money could buy a whore respectability."

She smiled. "Sure it can, Harry. Money can buy even a whore respectability. If she marries the right man."

His laugh was low and mean. "What self-respecting man would ever marry a whore?"

"Why you, Harry," she said, lifting her glass in a toast. "Unless you want the pictures on that disc to show up on the Internet."

❦

Tony had to hand it to his family. Not one of them had mentioned another word about Kate all evening. Nor had anyone dared to bring up the subject of the prediction. Not even after Uncle Vinny took Nonna home.

At last, Nonna's prediction was history.

Sadly, so was Kate.

He finished sweeping the main dining area, then glanced at his parents. They had their heads together at the cash register. Papa counting money, Mama going over the night's receipts.

He'd let Tina off the hook by offering to stay behind and help close up. After all, it was Friday night. His cousin had a hot date. As usual, he didn't.

Besides, he had another reason for hanging around until the restaurant closed. Since their little trip to the city morgue, Joey Caborelli had been working at the restaurant on the weekends. The best way to keep any surly teen out of trouble was to put him to work.

The kid hadn't let him down.

Joey had worked hard, and he did what he was told.

Tony knew the boy would never admit it, but he could tell by the pride he took in his work that Joey secretly liked having some responsibility. He'd taken more pride in his appearance, too. He'd dropped the rapper punk look in favor of jeans that fit and brand-name T-shirts like the Old Navy T-shirt he was wearing tonight. His dark hair was short now—and clean.

"What happened to your date?" Joey wanted to know when Tony walked back into the kitchen to put the broom and dust pan away.

"What date?"

"The blonde. She was hot."

"She went back to Manhattan where she belongs," Tony said, but he couldn't quite keep the disappointment out of his voice.

"Mama Gina said you were going to marry her."

"Yeah, well Mama Gina said you were doing a good job cleaning up back here, too," Tony grumbled, "but you missed a spot."

He picked up a wet dish towel and threw it at the kid.

Joey caught it easily but ran the towel carefully back over the kitchen counter one more time, just in case.

"If you get your lazy butt in gear and finish up in here, I'll give you a ride home," Tony said.

Joey frowned at him for a second. "Hey, you don't have to babysit me. I'm staying out of trouble."

Tony shrugged. "Suit yourself. If you don't want to drive the GTO, fine by me."

Joey's mouth dropped open. "Are you serious? You'd really let me drive the GTO?"

"Why wouldn't I?" Tony teased. "If you drive as slow as you work, there won't be any danger of your running into anything."

Joey mumbled something under his breath, but he kicked into high gear when he started loading the dishwasher.

Tony's thoughts, however, wandered right back to Kate.

He'd driven to the restaurant instead of walking, just in case Kate needed a way back to the city.

She nixed that option in a hurry.

Doing them both a favor, Tony decided, when he thought about it. Still, there was the question about the ring that had kept haunting him all evening.

Stop being such a masochist, dammit!

Tony grabbed a bag of trash and headed through the back door to the alley and the garbage cans.

Fully disgusted with himself, he couldn't believe he was still trying to find some evidence that Kate's engagement to Harold wasn't solid. That was exactly what he'd been doing since the first day he met her—refusing fully to accept she was engaged to someone else. He'd been hanging on her every word, studying her body language, even getting suspicious again tonight because she'd forgotten to put her ring back on after her shower.

Idiot.

He'd even been lying to himself, reasoning that it was only a cop's instinct always to question everything and everybody. But hell, who was he kidding? Being a cop had nothing to do with why he wanted to find some loophole in her relationship with her big, important corporate attorney.

He'd wanted Kate for himself from the second he laid eyes on her.

Too damn bad.

She's going to marry Harold, and that's final.

But talk about the irony?

For the last twenty years he'd been telling anyone who would listen that his grandmother's predictions were ridiculous. It was only fair, he supposed, that a whopper of a sucker punch had knocked him silly when his own prediction didn't come true.

"Hey!" Joey called out from the back doorway. "Who's dragging their feet now? I've been through in the kitchen for the last five minutes."

Tony jammed the lid down on the trash can and headed back inside. When he made it back into the main dining area of the restaurant, Joey was already waiting by the front door. His mother was waiting patiently by the door, too—ready to lock up for the night.

He stopped and kissed his mother on the cheek.

The look in her eyes said she wanted to say more, but Tony knew she wouldn't. Despite her ability to change her mind in an instant, his mother had said, "I give you my word," about never bringing the subject up again. That was sacred. A person's word was *not* something the Petrocelli family took lightly.

"You boys stay out of trouble," was all she said when they headed out the door.

Tony tossed his hand back over his head and closed the door behind them. But he stood by the door until he heard his mother turn the dead-bolt lock—signaling everything was locked up tight for the night. When he headed across the street to the GTO, Joey sprinted in front of him, then turned around, walking backward with his hands in his pockets.

Tony looked at him. "Is there something on your mind?"

"You're really not going to marry that blonde?"

"No. She's going to marry someone else."

"That blows."

Tell me about it.

"You're not even going to see her again?"

"No. I promised if she'd come to the restaurant tonight, I'd never bother her again."

"That was a dumb-ass thing to do."

"Hey," Tony said. "Be careful who you're calling a dumb-ass."

"Well, it was a dumb-ass thing to do," Joey said.

They reached the GTO and Tony walked around to the passenger side. Joey caught the keys when he tossed them over the top of the car.

Yeah, King of the Dumb Asses, that's me all right.

Joey had nailed it perfectly first try.

Tony opened the passenger-side door and slid onto the seat, in a worse mood than he'd been in before.

"Seat belt first. Always," Tony lectured.

Joey buckled his seat belt, then turned on the ignition. He looked up and down the street cautiously and pulled slowly away from the curb.

At least he was on vacation for the next week, Tony reminded himself. He'd leave town first thing in the morning, which wouldn't be a moment too soon. His being gone would allow plenty of time for everyone in the family to talk about the whole Mama-praying-and-Kate-not-being-his-future-bride episode without him being present. By the time he got back, the entire ordeal would have had time to blow over—becoming only a distant memory for the family.

For him, it would be a different story.

He could only hope Kate would become a distant memory for him someday.

Thank God for vacations.

He thought briefly about where Kate and Harold would do their vacationing once they were married. The answer he came up with was the equivalent of jabbing a hot poker deep into an open wound.

Manhattan corporate attorneys went to the Hamptons. Cops from Queens headed to the Catskills.

And this cop wouldn't have it any other way.

He'd bought the lakefront cabin a couple of years earlier. Stolen it actually, because it was in such bad need of repair. Hunter Mountain was a great place to hang out in the summer, and it was right in the middle of ski heaven in the winter. Plus, it was only about a two-hour drive from the metropolitan New York area.

He had gotten the cabin into great shape, but there was still plenty of work left to do around the place to keep him busy. Tackling the repairs on the dock, for instance. That chore had been on his to-do list much longer than he'd intended. Repairing the dock should be more than enough to keep his mind off Kate.

Hell, yeah!

Just thinking about heading up to the cabin put him in a better mood. A total change in scenery—that's what he needed. Fresh mountain air. Plenty of physical labor to wear his feeling-sorry-for-himself ass out before he became an official member of the Piss & Moan Club.

He'd be a brand-new man when he got back.

No doubt about it.

"I was thinking," Joey said, as he pulled to a stop at the red light. "Maybe you should call her. You know, just in case the blonde's changed her mind about marrying that other guy."

"Would you shut up about the blonde, already?"

"I can tell you really like her. You've been looking kinda sick ever since she left the restaurant tonight."

"You're going to look kinda sick if you don't drop the subject," Tony warned. He motioned Joey forward when the light turned green. "Now shut up and drive."

Joey looked both ways again, then eased forward slowly.

"What happened to that 'to achieve the impossible you have to attempt the ridiculous' crap you were telling me about when I told you what I really want to do is be a movie director? Was that just crap? Or do you really believe anything is possible if you put your mind to it?"

Tony looked over at him. "You're really starting to piss me off, Joey."

"You were already pissed off," Joey reminded him, "because the blonde's marrying someone else."

"I said drop it."

"I wouldn't drop it," Joey said. "If I liked some chick enough that she made me feel all sick inside, I'd do something about it."

Tony laughed. "Okay, Romeo. Let's hear it. What would you do about it?"

"You could always send her a present. Chicks really like presents."

"Great idea, Einstein. I'll send her a wedding present."

Tony jerked upright in his seat.

"What?" Joey said, sending him a nervous look. "I'm being careful, Tony. I'm not stupid."

Tony looked at him for a second, then grinned.

"Believe me kid, the *last* thing you are is stupid."

CHAPTER 7

The crowded terminal at JFK was impossible as usual, but anyone could have picked Grace Anderson out in the crowd without any problem. Even at seventy, Grace was the type of woman who demanded a second look. She was stunning, wearing her signature color, red—the smart-looking pantsuit a perfect complement to the silver hair she wore in a chic bob stopping just beneath her chin. Her stride was brisk, her statuesque frame held straight and erect, her figure trim.

Grace saw Kate and waved.

Kate waved back, took a deep breath, and hurried forward to meet her grandmother.

She'd decided she would go ahead and confess everything to Grace and get it over with. But seeing her grandmother's smiling face made her rethink that decision. Grace had been gone for an entire month, and Kate had missed her. Was there really any reason to ruin her grandmother's homecoming the second she stepped off the plane? Especially since Harold would be away in Chicago for the next two weeks?

I'll wait, Kate decided.

She grabbed her grandmother in a big hug.

The second Kate released Grace from their embrace, Grace said, "Now what's this nonsense about you and Harold having your first lover's spat?"

Kate was stunned.

"You've talked to Harold? When?"

Grace linked her arm through Kate's, leading her along as they headed through the narrow hallways of the terminal to the baggage claim area. "Don't be upset with Harold for telling me about it. He called me before I left Paris. He's worried about you, that's all."

The big liar, Kate thought, fuming.

Harold only worried about Harold.

"We think you should take a few days off," Grace said. "It will do you good, Kate. All brides get a little stressed the closer it gets to their big wedding day."

We think?

What a jerk!

And what wedding day?

How *dare* he use her grandmother to do his dirty work for him.

"I don't need any time off, Gram," Kate said, sounding every bit as pissed as she felt. "And I really don't appreciate Harold running to you with our problems. Besides, you just got home from your trip. You have to be worn-out."

"Now, Kate," Grace said again, squeezing Kate's arm. "Harold didn't run to me with your problems. He only called me to wish me a safe flight home. I'm the one who pressed the issue. When I asked if everything was okay he hesitated for a second. That's when I knew something was wrong."

"You don't know Harold like I do," Kate grumbled. "He was counting on you to press the issue, Gram, or he wouldn't have hesitated for a second."

"Oh, really, Kate," Grace insisted. "Harold adores you, and you know it."

Kate almost laughed at that statement.

Except it wasn't funny.

"And as far as my being worn-out from my trip," Grace went on to say, "that couldn't be further from the truth. I've spent the last month living the life of luxury in Paris, while you've been holding down the fort. It's your turn for a little R&R."

"I do *not* need any time off," Kate repeated.

Grace stopped walking and turned Kate around to face her. She took both of Kate's hands in her own and smiled. "My precious Kate," she said, "can't you take a hint? You need the time off. You have plenty to do. The type of last-minute things all brides do just before they go on their honeymoon."

Honeymoon?

Kate's eyes narrowed.

"Okay, Gram. You're obviously trying to tell me something, without telling me anything. What's going on that I don't know about?"

Grace let out a long sigh. "Harold is going to be so disappointed if I tell you."

"To hell with Harold," Kate vowed.

"Kate!" Grace scolded. "If you had any idea what that dear boy is planning for you."

"Tell me, Gram. I mean it."

Grace frowned. "You have to promise first that you'll never tell Harold I've betrayed his confidence."

"I promise," Kate said, trying to keep the anger out of her voice.

"Harold has a huge surprise for you, darling," Grace said, all excited. "When he comes home from Chicago."

"And what's Harold's big surprise?"

"He's already busy arranging everything himself," Grace gushed on. "And I promise you, it couldn't be more romantic. I'm supposed to get you to the Cocktail Terrace at the Waldorf Thursday after next, in the pretense that we're meeting Margaret there for afternoon tea. Harold will surprise you by showing up himself. And then he'll tell you he can't wait another minute to marry you. That's when he'll ask you to marry him right then, right there."

What?

Not then. Not there. Not ever!

"Thanks to me," Grace said with pride, "your bridal suit will already be waiting in a hotel suite upstairs. Once you're dressed, we'll head to the legendary Conrad Suite where Princess Grace and Prince Rainier had their engagement party." She squeezed Kate's arm again. "Don't you just love it? Judge Rowlings will be waiting there to marry you. And then, Harold is going to whisk you away to some fabulous villa he's rented in the south of France."

Kate was beyond furious.

The very nerve of him.

First, going behind her back and making her grandmother his unsuspecting coconspirator. And second, thinking the same don't-disappoint-Grace-and-Margaret trick he pulled when he proposed, would work with her again—even in the freaking legendary Conrad Suite—after she'd already told him there wasn't going to be a wedding!

A surprise wedding.

Harold was proof evolution *could* go in reverse.

It was on the tip of her tongue to confess everything. Instead, Kate held herself back. She couldn't risk Grace's panicking and calling Harold. Better to catch *him* off guard, this time.

"Aren't you excited?" Grace bubbled.

"Speechless," Kate said, and she meant every word of it.

"So," Grace said as they started back down the corridor. "Now that you know how busy you're going to be, which bridal suit did you finally choose, darling? The one you and I both liked best?"

Kate actually smiled.

"That's going to be *my* big surprise, Gram."

After what Harold was trying to pull, Kate didn't even feel guilty about the double meaning of her statement.

She'd show up at the Waldorf, all right.

And she wanted Grace and Margaret to be there.

She wanted them to be there when she told Harold she wasn't going to marry him—ever—to his arrogant don't-ask-don't-tell face!

Harold glanced at his watch—11:30 A.M. New York time. By now, Kate would have met Grace at the airport. If Grace didn't let him down, it would take her all of ten minutes to tell Kate about his plans to move up the wedding.

Women he knew.

There was no way Grace was going to let Kate be ambushed. Grace would want Kate to have the next two weeks to prepare herself—hair, manicure, pedicure, the works—even have her honeymoon wardrobe all picked out and ready to pack.

Women stuck together that way.

He was counting on it.

Kate would pretend, of course, that she never suspected a thing. And that was fine with him. Then they could go on their honeymoon and start their new life according to his *new* schedule.

He polished off the last bite of the brunch he'd had sent up from room service. But as he blotted his mouth with his napkin, he couldn't stop thinking about the other woman he could count on to do exactly what he expected.

Harold smiled again, pleased with himself.

Once he'd gotten over the shock of having Carla Matthews show up at his hotel suite, he'd taken control of the situation. He'd never been a fool. He'd had no intention of being played for one, either.

He'd turned the tables on his would-be blackmailer.

He'd shocked *her* speechless when he'd calmly written her a check for twenty-five thousand dollars. Good-faith money, he'd told her, proving he was willing to do whatever she wanted as long as she didn't use the photos on the disc against him.

Then he'd handed her another check—a reality check.

He'd reminded her politely that if respectability really was her price, making the man she was going to marry the laughingstock of New York City certainly wouldn't serve her purpose.

Such stupid creatures, women.

She'd seemed so surprised when he'd willingly given her his cell phone number, even given her his private office number in New York without her having to ask. Besides, what was the point? Since she knew who he was, he wouldn't have been able to hide from her anyway.

Miss Carla Matthews had actually turned quite agreeable once he'd duped her into believing she had the upper hand. Her whole demeanor had changed right before his eyes, just as he knew it would. Silly woman. She didn't have a clue that her own admission that marriage was the name of her game had ultimately been her downfall.

Call girl or not, Carla Matthews was still a woman—all about fairy-tale wishes and little-girl dreams.

Unfortunately for her, he was still a man.

A very smart man, even if he had to say so himself.

He'd dropped the tough-guy act the second he realized it wasn't working for him and fixed them both a drink. He'd led her to believe he had a softer side—one he knew she'd have a harder time resisting. His battle plan had worked perfectly. They'd talked for over two hours, as if her threat to blackmail him didn't even exist.

She'd even dropped her guard and told him a little bit about herself when he made it a point to ask. It was the kind of story he'd expected—rotten parents, hard life, her admitting her beauty had always been her only real asset.

Never once during those two hours had he come on to her, either, something else he knew would surprise her. He could tell his approach was working when she kept looking at him in a way she never would have looked at a paying customer. She evidently realized she was losing her edge, too, because she abruptly got up and declared she was ready to leave.

That's when he'd played his final trump card.

He'd told her he needed to finish his business in

Chicago over the next two weeks and go back to New York before he sent for her. He'd asked for one month to get his affairs in order, that was all. She'd agreed.

Harold smiled.

I'll be a married man by then.

Carla certainly couldn't marry a man who was already married, now could she?

But that didn't mean he wanted Carla out of his life completely. He'd realized what a perfect opportunity she was actually giving him as they'd sat there talking. The scare of her showing up at his hotel room had opened his eyes real quick to the fact that his days of cavorting with call girls needed to come to a quick end.

He would bring Carla to New York, just as he promised.

To offer her a consolation prize.

Being a mistress fell short of being a wife, yes, but it was still a big step up from her top-dollar career as a call girl. Especially if she was going to be mistress to a man who would buy her a luxury apartment, give her a staggering monthly allowance, and provide her with anything her heart desired.

He'd make her an offer she couldn't refuse.

A life of leisure in exchange for the photos.

She wouldn't turn him down.

Her accepting his offer would also be additional insurance that she'd never use the photos against him—even if she kept a copy of the disc on the sly.

Bite the hand that fed her?

Not likely.

One of the most important lessons he'd learned from his father was that loyalty always went to the highest bidder. With Carla, he'd make it a point always to be the highest bidder.

He was, after all, wildly attracted to her.

He even admired her spunk.

No one had ever dared to stand up to him before, much less threaten him. The challenge he would face in keeping a spirited woman like Carla under control turned him on immensely—almost as much as her willingness to participate in the games he liked to play in the bedroom.

Bedroom games.

Harold squirmed in his seat, the urge to see Carla again quickly overtaking him.

If he devoted his entire Saturday to the brief he was working on for his client, bedroom games wouldn't be out of the question for Sunday evening.

I'll call her tomorrow afternoon.

He had her private cell phone number. He'd surprise her and ask her to have dinner with him. Take her to dinner in one of the fanciest restaurants Chicago had to offer.

She'd boasted she'd caught her big fish.

Well, he could set the bait on his hook, too.

He'd give her a glimpse of the type of life she'd have with a man who had the power and money to give her anything she wanted. After dinner, he'd *invite* her back to his luxury hotel suite, reminding her that if she stuck with him, there'd be no more greedy pimps and seedy hotel rooms in her future.

With a little luck and a lot of charm, he'd reel Carla in *hooker*, line, and sinker.

Harold chuckled to himself over his little play on words, then pushed back from his chair. He headed for the writing desk across the room and the mountain of paperwork that needed his attention.

Yes, Carla had taught him one very valuable lesson.

His flirting-with-danger call-girl days were over.

Soon there'd be no need for dumpy motel rooms.

No need for random ladies of the night, either.

He'd have a proper wife at home where she belonged.

Even better, he'd have a sexy mistress waiting to satisfy each and every one of his bad-boy needs.

———

Eve looked up from her computer. "What are you doing back home? I thought you were going to the gallery after you met Grace at the airport."

Kate didn't say a word. She walked into Eve's bedroom and fell face-first on Eve's bed with a loud groan.

"Oh," Eve said. "I guess that means Grace took your calling off the wedding even worse than you expected."

Kate sat back up. "You mean the wedding Harold is moving *up?* The one he's convinced Gram we should have as soon as he gets back from Chicago in two weeks?"

"What?" Eve's hand slid off her mouse. She turned all the way around in her chair to face Kate.

"You heard me," Kate said, getting angry all over again. "Harold called Gram in Paris, telling her we'd had a quarrel and that he was worried the pressure was getting to me. He sucked poor Gram right in. He said he thought we should go ahead and get married as soon as he got back from Chicago. He even talked Gram into being his partner in crime, asking her to tell me we were meeting Margaret at the Waldorf for afternoon tea. He intends to walk in and surprise me and ask me to marry him right then and there."

"And you didn't tell Grace you've decided you aren't going to marry Harold at all?"

Kate let out a long sigh. "No. And I do feel awful about it. But you know Gram. She's my personal travel agent when it comes to guilt trips. She'd do everything in her power over the next two weeks to persuade me to change my mind and marry Harold."

"And you always have been a bit of a pushover," Eve mentioned.

Kate bounced off the bed. "Not this time, Eve." She stood in the middle of the room, hands defiantly on her hips. "But I am going to that afternoon tea, you can be sure of that. And when Harold waltzes in to surprise me, I'm going to yell 'surprise' at the top of my lungs, hand him his tacky megacarat ring, and march right out of his arrogant, insufferable, damn boring life."

Eve giggled behind her hand. "You wouldn't."

"You watch me!"

Eve blinked. "You mean *I'm* invited to the tea, too?"

"Tea? What about tea?"

Kate turned around to find Alex standing behind her.

"Well, look who finally came up for air," Kate said.

Alex grinned. "Guilty as charged. You know what they say about makeup sex."

"No," Eve said innocently. "What do they say?"

Alex ignored Eve and looked back at Kate. "Please tell me the tea you're talking about is in direct relationship to the tea *leaves* read by a certain Petrocelli grandmother."

"Not even close," Kate said. "The grandmother didn't have clue who I was."

"Oh, well, expecting her to know who you were was a bit of a stretch even for a psychic," Alex said. "What did Tony say when you told him you called off the wedding?"

Kate hesitated. "I didn't tell him."

"Kate! You said you were going to tell Tony you were finished with Harold."

"No, Alex," Kate said. "*You* said I was going to tell Tony I had called off the wedding. *I* didn't feel like arguing with you about it."

"Well, I hope you're proud of yourself," Alex huffed. "You missed the perfect opportunity to make a connection with a really great guy."

Oh, we definitely made a connection.

Kate decided to keep the kiss to herself.

"Forget about Tony," Kate said. "Harold's sudden interest in tea is my main concern right now."

Alex looked confused. "Harold's suddenly taken up tea-leaf reading?"

"No," Eve blurted out. "Harold's inviting Grace and Margaret to afternoon tea in two weeks for Kate's surprise wedding."

Alex's hands were on her hips now. "Kate Anderson, don't you dare tell me you let Harold talk you into . . ."

"Don't be ridiculous," Kate said.

When she finished repeating everything she'd already told Eve—including the part about what she intended to do when Harold arrived for his afternoon tea—Alex slumped down on Eve's bed, shaking her head in amazement.

"Clue Deficit Disorder," Alex said. "That has to be Harold's problem. How else could he possibly have believed you would go along with a surprise wedding?"

"Well," Eve mentioned again, "Kate always has been a bit of a pushover."

Kate frowned at her.

Eve mouthed, "Sorry."

Kate looked back at Alex. "Enough about me. I could use some good news today. Tell us about *you*. I take it things are A-okay with you and John?"

"I'm going back home," Alex said, not really answering the question. "That's why I'm here. I came to give you back your key and pick up my things."

Kate sent her a suspicious look. "But?"

"I'll just go get my things now," Alex said.

"Oh, no you don't," Kate said. She grabbed Alex by the arm as she started through the door, pulling her back into Eve's bedroom. "Something's wrong, or you'd be telling us every new position you and John tried last night, and you know it."

Alex walked back over and plopped down on Eve's bed.

"The only new position I'm interested in right now is CEO," she said. "But I don't want my marriage to fall apart, either. That's why I gave in and agreed to John's idea of the perfect compromise."

"Excuse me?" Kate said. "Did I really just hear the words 'gave in' and 'agreed' come out of *your* mouth?"

"I'm so excited!" Eve said, clapping her hands. "Alex is going to have a baby, and I'm going to be an aunt."

Kate kept looking at Alex. "Is that true, Alex?"

"Yes and no," Alex said. "Yes, John and I are going to have a child. No, *I'm* not having it."

"You're adopting?" Kate and Eve said in unison.

Alex got up from the bed and headed out of the room.

Kate and Eve followed right along behind her.

She walked over to the far end of the living room where she'd left her already-packed suitcase, picked up her purse sitting on top of it, and pulled out her keys.

When Alex started taking Kate's key off her key ring, Kate said, "Well? We're waiting, Alex. *Are* you and John adopting a baby?"

"No," Alex said flatly. "John is going to have his child with the help of a surrogate."

What!

"But, but," Kate stuttered. "That's so, so . . . wrong. You have to know that, Alex. Surrogates have babies for people who aren't capable of having children themselves."

"And that would be John," Alex said, the look in her eyes daring Kate to disagree. "Besides, why am I any different from male executives? Someone else has their children, and no one bats an eye. Just because I'm a *female* executive doesn't mean I shouldn't have the same option."

"Who are you trying to convince, Alex? Me? Or are you trying to convince yourself?" Kate shook her head, still in disbelief. "And I wouldn't count on finding a surrogate willing to have John's child just because his wife can't take time off from her career to start a family."

"Are you really that naïve?" Alex shoved the key in Kate's hand. "Money talks, Kate. Count on it."

"Maybe John is just trying to prove a point," Kate said. "Maybe he's counting on you being sane enough to realize how ludicrous him having a child with a surrogate really is."

Alex shook her head. "John wouldn't do that. He

really wants a child. Now. And I really don't understand why you think this is such a ludicrous idea. What if John had been married before? What if he already had children with someone else? Do you think I would love his children any less because *I* didn't bring them into the world myself? Of course I wouldn't. I'll love this child like my own because it *will* be John's."

Kate shook her head again. "You are so full of crap, Alex, and you damn well know it."

Alex's chin jutted forward. "Maybe I am. But I can't afford to take time off to have a child when I'm so close to making senior executive. And I'll lose John if we don't start a family as soon as possible. This way, John gets what he wants. I get what I want. And once the surrogate has the baby, the three of us will live happily ever after."

"Until you have to explain to little John or Alex Jr. that you were too busy to bring him or her into the world yourself," Kate said. "You'd better set aside some extra cash in addition to that college fund, Alex. The poor kid is going to need it for a lifetime of intensive therapy."

"Don't lecture me, Kate."

"Don't mess with Mother Nature, Alex."

The shrill sound of the doorbell ended the face-off.

CHAPTER 8

The young man standing in the hallway, when Kate opened her apartment door, had on a helmet and a bright orange vest that had CYCLE IT written across the front.

"Delivery for Kate Anderson," he said. "The old guy downstairs said it was okay to come up."

Kate reached for her purse on the table by the door. She gave him a five-dollar bill in exchange for the large box he handed over. She pushed the door shut with her elbow, dropped her purse back on the table, and stood staring at the familiar pink logo written in fancy script across the top of the box.

Alex was the first to follow her to the door. "What's that?"

"My punishment for not telling Gram the truth," Kate said. She looked at Alex and sighed. "This would actually be funny if it weren't happening to me."

"Life," Alex mused. "We're born naked, wet, and hungry, then things get worse."

"Save that speech for the baby you *aren't* willing to have yourself because you're too busy," Kate said.

She pushed past Alex and stomped back into the living room. After she slammed the box down on the coffee table, Kate flopped down on the sofa in a pout. "Gram knew which bridal suit I liked best," she said. "But I never dreamed she'd go ahead and buy the damn thing."

"Well, at least open it," Alex said, glancing at the box. "I'd like to see what you were going to wear if you *had* decided to marry outside your species. Wouldn't you, Eve?"

"But Harold isn't outside Kate's . . ."

It took only one warning look from Alex.

Eve shut up and nodded in agreement.

Kate stared at the box.

But she made no attempt to open it.

Alex walked around the coffee table. She bent over and sliced through the tape on all four sides of the box with her long, red fingernail. She shimmied the top off the box. She gently peeled back several layers of delicate tissue paper. She looked up at Kate . . .

And then Alex screamed like a surprised *Swan* contestant seeing herself for the first time at her long-awaited reveal.

Kate jumped up from the sofa.

She sat back down just as quickly.

She'd thought after Harold's surprise wedding and Alex's obvious surrogate insanity, nothing else could shock her today.

This Richter scale reading?

Off the freaking charts!

"There's a card, there's a card," Alex chanted.

She did a Snoopy dance around the room before she made one final workin'-it circular pivot with her hips, bowed politely, and thrust the card forward for Kate to take.

Kate only stared at the sealed card.

Instant-gratification-girl Alex tore the envelope open, jerked the card out, and forced Kate to take it.

Alex and Eve both leaned over Kate's shoulder.

They all three read aloud, "Be beautiful—Tony."

Tony let himself inside the cabin and dumped his duffel bag in the floor by the door. After a quick look around the A-frame, he headed through the great room to the back sliding door. A quick release of the security latch slid the door open. He stepped outside onto the large deck overlooking the lake, inhaled deeply, and filled his lungs with fresh mountain air.

That instantly-feel-better feeling didn't happen.

He might as well have been stuck in traffic on his Harley, sucking in exhaust fumes in the Queens Midtown Tunnel.

So much for a change in scenery.

He stood on the deck staring at the worn and weathered floating dock below the cabin. Had he not acted on his idea to make the trip to a certain bridal shop in SoHo, he would already have the rotted lumber stripped away from the dock.

But he had gone to SoHo.

He had bought the dress.

And, he regretted that decision.

He'd told Kate he would buy the dress that day in the bridal shop, sure, but that wasn't the reason he'd bought the dress. He'd bought the dress because he didn't want to spend the rest of his life wondering if their paths *had* crossed for a reason, and he'd just been too lame to do anything about it.

He'd sent the gift as a reminder.

Kate deserved a beautiful dress.

Kate deserved a big wedding.

And Kate deserved a man who would make her eyes light up at the thought of becoming his bride.

As for her being another man's fiancée, Tony had decided to hell with Harold, all's fair in love and war, and to hell with every other sane thought that kept reminding him he'd obviously gone flat-ass crazy. If Kate called him, nothing was going to stand in the way of his telling her exactly how he felt.

He wanted a fair chance.

He wanted time alone with her.

He wanted the opportunity for both of them to find out if the immediate attraction they felt for each other was purely physical or possibly the real thing.

But Kate hadn't called.

You cannot achieve the impossible without attempting the ridiculous.

Those had been inspiring words from his college days.

Words that sadly had him *perspiring* now over his spur-of-the-moment decision.

Tony glanced at his watch and his hopes plummeted even further. It was already four o'clock in the afternoon. He knew Kate had received the dress hours ago. He'd had the owner at the bridal shop call the gallery before he left the shop. Kate was scheduled to be at the gallery by noon. The woman had promised to walk around the corner and deliver the dress to Kate herself.

His home number was listed.

A quick call to information—she'd have his number.

But he'd checked his messages earlier.

Kate hadn't called.

Tony unclipped his cell phone from his belt and dialed his voice mail one last time.

"You have *no* new messages," the snotty voice informed him, confirming with each passing hour that the answer he feared most was becoming a reality.

Kate was obviously angry about the dress.

He'd taken a chance—it backfired.

It was just as simple as that.

Tony banged his fist against the deck railing, cursed himself for his poor judgment, then headed back through the A-frame and out to the car. As he unloaded his week's worth of groceries, he kept wondering if maybe he should try and call Kate at the gallery. Apologize. If he had upset her.

No.

Let her go.

He had to.

He'd made a big enough fool of himself already.

If he had any further contact with Kate Anderson, it would be because she called him. Or worse—because she filed a complaint against him.

And wouldn't that be just great?

Him, a respected cop until now, standing in front of the judge. Harold waving a restraining order under his nose. Him, trying to explain to the judge that he really wasn't a stalker at all—sending other men's fiancées wedding dresses just happened to be his latest hobby.

What the hell was I thinking?

King of the Dumb Asses.

That title didn't even touch his stupidity.

Tony put away the groceries, walked back out on the deck and down the back steps, heading for the dock. He needed to stop wishing for a phone call that wasn't going to happen, pull himself together, and stop acting like some lovesick teenager mooning over his first big crush.

I'm a grown man, dammit.

And a cop, for Christ's sake!

Get a freaking grip, already.

A rich Manhattan attorney?

Or a cop from Queens?

A no-brainer choice for any woman.

He stopped at the edge of the water, looking at the dock and mentally calculating which planks needed replacing and which planks didn't. The lumber and the tools he needed to get the job done were already in the basement of the cabin. If he got a move on, he could have the damaged planks stripped off before dark and begin rebuilding the dock first thing in the morning.

I need to get focused.

To hell with physical attraction.

Losing himself in some good old-fashioned hard physical *labor* was what he needed to do. Especially since the attraction he thought Kate felt for him had obviously only been a figment of his own warped imagination.

All foam, no beer.

He'd sure missed his mark on that one.

He walked out to the edge of the dock, testing the stability and making sure the rotten planks were all that needed attention. Everything was solid. The Styrofoam beneath the planks still had plenty of buoyancy. The repair wasn't going to be half as difficult as he'd expected. By the end of the weekend, he would have a brand-new dock with no problem at all.

And then what?

Spend his whole vacation hoping Kate would call?

Tony reached for his cell phone.

He stood there for a moment.

Shook his head.

Then threw the phone as far as he could send it, out into the middle of the lake.

"Diane? This is Kate Anderson."

"You got the dress?"

"Yes, but . . ."

"Thank goodness," Diane said with a relieved sigh. "Mr. Petrocelli was adamant that you received the dress today. I went to the gallery earlier to deliver it, but you weren't there. That's when I panicked and called the delivery service."

You went to the gallery!

"Was my grandmother at the gallery?"

"No, I didn't see Grace."

Thank God.

"I can't accept this dress, Diane. That's why I'm calling."

There was a long pause before Diane said, "I was afraid of that. That's why I made certain Mr. Petrocelli understood I have a strict no refund policy. He said it didn't matter. He insisted on buying the dress regardless."

"But, Diane," Kate said. "I haven't even taken the

dress out of the box." She looked back over her shoulder. The dress was not only out of the box, Alex was still waltzing around the room with it. She motioned impatiently for Alex to put the dress back.

"I'm sorry, Kate," Diane said. "Wedding dresses are like new cars. The minute they leave the showroom, they're used. It wouldn't be fair to my customers. I'm sure you can understand that."

No, Kate didn't understand that reasoning at all.

Any more than she understood why Tony would insist on buying the dress when he knew up front about the no return policy.

"Kate? Are you still there?"

"Thanks, Diane. It isn't your fault he bought the dress after you told him about your policy." But before she hung up, Kate did ask Diane not to mention the dress *or* Mr. Petrocelli to her grandmother.

She looked at Eve when she closed her cell phone.

"Diane won't take the dress back?"

Kate shook her head. "She has a strict no refund policy. That's what I don't understand. She told Tony up front about it. He bought the dress anyway."

"What are you going to do?"

"Pay Tony back, of course."

"Or not," Alex said as she placed the dress carefully back in the box. "I have a feeling if Tony has anything to say about it, this dress is going to come in handy a lot sooner than you think."

"Well, thank you, Ms. Rent-A-Womb," Kate said, "for spouting off even more babble you're trying to pass off as perfectly logical reasoning."

"Oh, please." Alex tossed a pooh-ha wave of her hand.

"Leave my psychodrama out of this. You have another important call to make, remember? A *booty* call?"

Kate rolled her eyes. "I'm not interested in falling madly in bed with Tony Petrocelli, Alex."

That was a lie, yes, but it was the kind of remark someone cleverly disguised as a responsible adult would probably make.

"But I will call Tony," Kate said. "Eventually. After I've had time to . . ."

"Analyze the situation?"

Kate sent Alex a go-to-hell look. "Yes, I want to analyze the situation, Alex. And I don't think even you can deny this is one situation that could use some serious analyzing. It just doesn't make any sense. As far as Tony knows, I'm still going to marry Harold. What could he possibly be thinking sending me the dress?"

Alex put her hands on her hips. "Did you forget to pay your brain bill, Kate?" She shook her head. "Read between the lines, dammit."

"Silly, there aren't any lines." Eve held up the card as proof.

"He sent the dress to put the ball back in *your* court," Alex said. "Tony has known from the beginning something wasn't right with you and Harold. He asked you himself if you really loved the guy. He's hoping you'll give him a chance to prove *he* could be your destiny." Alex shook her head again. "Poor guy, he could have saved himself the money and just sent you a box of condoms instead."

"But a box of condoms wouldn't have been nearly as romantic," Eve said.

Kate glanced at the dress and sighed.

Could Alex be right?

"I just don't know," Kate said. "He practically pushed me into my waiting taxi after his grandmother didn't know who I was. He actually seemed delighted to get rid of me."

"You had the taxi driver wait for you?" Alex wailed.

"Well, yes. Tony offered to bring me back to the city, but . . ."

"But you refused, of course," Alex said. "Just like you didn't tell him you had called off the wedding. My God, Kate, can you honestly stand there and say you don't realize how far this guy is going out on a limb for you?"

Kate didn't answer.

Alex held her hand out. "Give me your cell phone."

Kate didn't budge.

"I mean it," Alex vowed. "This is one time I'm not going to let you analyze the situation to death." She took a step forward and pried the phone out of Kate's hand. "Any guy who's willing to buy you a wedding dress just to let you know he's interested, deserves a phone call. You're going to call Tony, and you're going to call him *now*."

"Just get his number," Kate said, grabbing a pen from the coffee table. "Don't do that automatic dial thing, Alex, and I mean it. I need a few minutes to figure out what I'm going to say to him."

"Queens," Alex said. "Anthony Petrocelli." She ignored the pen Kate was holding out and punched a number instead. "Here," she said, holding out the phone.

"Dammit, Alex, I said *don't* do that automatic dial thing!" She grabbed the phone away from Alex anyway and put it to her ear.

"This is Tony."

The sound of his voice startled her.

"Tony?"

"I'm at my cabin on Hunter Mountain for a week," the message said. "I'll check my messages, so leave your number, and I'll call you back."

Kate closed her phone and tossed it on the sofa.

Alex frowned.

Kate frowned right back.

"You had me so rattled, I was talking to his damn voice mail," Kate said. "Tony isn't home. He's at his cabin on Hunter Mountain for a week."

She left out the "I'll check my messages" part.

"Tony has a cabin on Hunter Mountain?" Alex seemed impressed. "John and I go skiing there every winter. I've never been there in the summer."

"Well, Tony *is* there," Kate said. "For a week. I'll call him when he gets back. Satisfied?"

Alex got a sudden gleam in her eye. "You can't pass up an opportunity like this one, Kate. A mountain cabin? The two of you snuggled together in front of a roaring fire? What could be more perfect than that?"

Kate glanced at the window where her air conditioner was struggling to belch out a few puffs of cool air. "We already have a roaring fire, Alex, right outside in this ninety-plus-degree weather."

"That's here in the concrete jungle," Alex argued. "In the Catskills it gets chilly enough for a fire at night, even in the summer."

"You said you'd never been there in summer," Eve said.

Kate threw her hands up in the air. "Would someone

please tell me why we're even having this conversation? If I were stupid enough to go find Tony, which I'm *not*, a cabin in the Catskills isn't actually an address you could locate, now is it?"

Alex looked in her direction. "I'm sure Tony has a cell phone."

"And thank God there isn't an information number to call for cell phones," Kate said, "or you'd already have me packing my bags while you phoned Tony for directions to the cabin."

Alex smiled.

Kate didn't.

They both lunged for her cell phone at the same time. Alex was quicker. "And the name of his parents' restaurant in Queens would be?"

Kate's smile was a smirk. "Sorry. I'm afraid the name of that restaurant has totally slipped my mind."

"Wasn't it Mama Gina's?"

"Eve!"

"What?"

"Queens," Alex said into the phone with a smirk of her own. "Mama Gina's Italian Restaurant."

Kate drove out of the city Sunday morning, trying to decide what *wasn't* wrong with this picture. In addition to happily giving out Tony's cell phone number, Mama Gina had been more accurate than a global positioning system—after Alex had grabbed the phone away from her and boldly asked Tony's mother for directions to the cabin.

"Just in case," Alex had said, "that Tony's cell phone couldn't pick up a signal in the mountains."

Can you hear me now?

Evidently not.

She'd called his cell phone repeatedly. She'd also called his home number back and left a message to call her—regardless of the hour. She'd even slept with her freaking cell phone right there on her pillow.

Still, no word from Tony.

She knew it was irrational, but once she'd decided for herself that she wanted to talk to Tony—and couldn't—it had become an obsession with her. That calm, completely mature, totally rational adult she'd worked so diligently to become since her I'm-all-grown-up-now thirtieth birthday flew right out the window.

When Tony still hadn't called by nine o'clock that morning, Kate packed a bag—just in case he *did* pick up the signal she was going to give him when she arrived at the cabin. She gave Eve strict instructions not to tell anyone where she was. She called Alex and gave her the same lecture. Then she marched out of her apartment, out of the building, and hailed a cab to the nearest car rental agency.

A bright red SUV was what she rented.

It seemed like the type of vehicle to rent if you were headed to the mountains.

She was headed north on the New York State Thruway—Mama Gina's handy-dandy instructions within close reach—on a two-hour trip that Kate hoped had the potential to turn into a journey that would last the rest of her life.

Be beautiful.

How could any woman resist a guy like that?

Better yet, why would any woman want to?

Kate flipped her cell phone open and used her thumb to punch in the number she didn't have to scroll down her phone list to find—this number was already permanently stored in her memory. Unfortunately, the computerized voice told her the same thing it had been telling her for the last eighteen hours—the customer she was trying to reach was not available at that time.

She tossed the phone on the passenger's seat and picked up speed.

She'd been boldly going nowhere her entire life.

But not today.

Today, Kate had a date with destiny.

She intended to keep that date and see what destiny had to offer her.

If society only realized how therapeutic pounding the hell out of a board with a hammer could be—not to mention how cheap—there would be a lot of wealthy psychologists out of a job. Tony thought this as he hammered another nail—bam, bam, bam—deep into the wooden plank on the dock.

Man, but he did feel good this morning.

The second he'd chucked the phone into oblivion, it was as if the weight of the world had been lifted off his shoulders. His mind cleared. His stomach stopped churning. He immediately started feeling like his old self again.

He'd gone to work then and managed to strip every bit of the bad lumber off the dock by nightfall. After he finished stripping the dock, he'd tossed a mammoth steak on the grill, downed a few cold beers, and worked the Kate-induced knots of tension out of his shoulders with a long hot soak in the Jacuzzi on the deck.

When he finally hit the sack, he'd slept like a baby.

Something he hadn't been doing lately.

Truthfully, he hadn't been sleeping well since the day he came riding up the path in Central Park and saw . . .

Hell, no!

Jumping back on the train to Dumbassville wasn't even an option.

Been there.

Done that.

Learned a very valuable lesson.

What he was going to do was finish up the dock. He was going to take a nice dip in the lake to cool off. Then he was going to spend the rest of the day sitting on the deck with his feet propped up, the way every man *should* do when he was away on vacation.

Later, maybe he would clean up and run into town. Maybe call the restaurant and check on the family now that they had no way to contact him. Turning his cell phone into fish food wasn't the smartest thing he'd ever done, but it sure had been therapeutic.

No, skip going into town.

When he thought about it, going into town was not a great idea. Not if he wanted to go back home to Queens with his head on straight. The best thing he could do was isolate himself in blonde-detox for the rest of his vacation. Contact with a telephone might weaken his resolve and land him right back in the sad shape he'd been in when he first arrived at the cabin.

Besides, his family knew where he was.

If they really needed to get in touch with him badly enough, all it would take was a quick call to the local police. His good buddy Joe down at the station would run up and give him the message. His loving mother, bless her overprotective heart, knew that from experience.

That's how he'd gotten to be such good friends with Joe.

Tony picked up another plank, took a nail out of his mouth, and reached for his hammer.

Bam. Bam. Bam.

Bam. Bam. Bam.

Man, it was amazing how much better he felt since he'd finally accepted the fact that a certain green-eyed blonde was *not* going to be his destiny.

CHAPTER 9

Even though Kate made regular weekend trips out of the
city with Harold, she had never really relaxed in Bridgehampton. She realized that as she took the exit for Hunter
Mountain.

Weekends in the Hamptons really weren't any different from life in the city. Busy people. Busy lives. Always
the pressure to be seen at the most popular places, with
all the most popular people. Everyone making sure those
important connections that could be made only outside
the office were being made. Everyone making sure no
golden opportunities were ever missed over something as
silly as spending quality time with their spouses or their
families.

The only time she'd truly enjoyed herself was when
Harold was off doing whatever Harold was doing, and
she and Margaret were left alone. Then she'd find herself
relaxing a little, and enjoying the company of one fine
lady—even if Margaret did have a son who'd turned out
to be a first-class ass.

She'd always felt as if she and Margaret were kindred

spirits of sorts—smiling graciously on the outside yet struggling on the inside with exactly where they fit into a crazy mixed-up world. Margaret had even told her once that as much as she loved her son, she wanted Kate to be happy.

"My son is a lot like his father was," she'd said. "Harold has his own definition of what makes people happy, Kate. Make sure his vision is one you can live with."

Poor Margaret.

She should have asked Margaret point-blank what she really meant when she'd made that remark. She should have been a true friend to her. She should have given Margaret the opportunity to open up and say whatever she was trying to say—maybe even what she *needed* to say to someone she thought might understand.

But she hadn't done any of those things.

They'd both let the opportunity pass, both of them too cautious to step outside the boundaries of polite conversation.

Polite conversation.

She was definitely the Queen of Polite Conversation.

Except with Alex.

Maybe that's why she loved Alex so much.

She'd always been able to be herself and say whatever she was thinking with Alex. Alex, in fact, demanded that from her. Alex had always forced her to take those big bites out of life. And on those rare occasions when she had been brave enough to sink her teeth into a big messy slice of life, Alex had urged her just as strongly to spit out anything that didn't suit her taste.

But what is my taste?

Kate knew the answer before she asked the question.

*My taste is a guy who would tell me to be beautiful,
even if I were marrying another man.*

And to think she'd almost settled for a guy who preferred a don't-ask-don't-tell policy rather than interrupt
his precious schedule.

Scary.

No, terrifying *is a better word.*

Kate pushed any thoughts of Harold aside when she
saw the upcoming road sign. She slowed down to the required 25 mph speed limit, took a deep breath, and drove
into the town of Hunter just as the digital clock in front of
the First National Bank informed her it was 1:00 P.M.

She could certainly understand what had drawn Tony to
the place. The town was quaint and inviting. There were
old-fashioned storefronts on all the shops. Big potted bar-
rels sat on the sidewalks, overflowing with pretty pansies.

The town was filled with tourists, everyone enjoying a
beautiful summer Sunday afternoon. Happy families and
hand-holding lovers, all taking carefree Sunday window-
shopping strolls, just for the fun of it.

A little boy riding on his father's shoulders looked
over at Kate, gave her a big smile, and waved.

Kate waved back.

But she did have to wonder if the reason she was finally
seeing things so clearly, was because her tired-of-being-a-
wimp brain had simply gone on strike rather than continue
such a ho-hum existence. After all, her brain being on strike
was the only logical reason Kate had for why she was driving through Hunter now—Mama Gina's instructions
clutched tightly in her sweaty hand—watching for the
odometer to reach 3.5 miles from Main Street where she
would find the gravel road leading up to Tony's cabin.

And then what?

Kate took a deep, cleansing breath.

In 3.5 more miles, she guessed she'd find out.

Unless.

Ack!

She'd been so engrossed in her new obsession, she'd never stopped to realize there was a good possibility Tony wouldn't be at the cabin alone. Just because his mother said he'd never brought anyone home to meet the family didn't mean there weren't any women in his life.

She certainly hadn't phoned Grace to tell her she'd suddenly decided to follow her heart and head out of town in hot pursuit of a hunky cop who could very well be her destiny. What she'd done was wait until she was sure her grandmother had left for early-morning Mass. That's when she'd called and left a message on her grandmother's voice mail telling her not to worry. Telling Grace she was simply following her advice and taking a few days off to collect her thoughts.

Is Tony alone?

Not likely.

That would sure explain him not answering his cell phone. A terrific guy like Tony was bound to have all kinds of women willing to follow him to the ends of the earth just to get his attention.

Yikes!

Just like me.

Kate glanced at the odometer—3.5 miles exactly.

She could see the gravel road up ahead—the road that according to Mama Gina's instructions would take her up the mountain to Tony's cabin. That's when Her Royal Wimpness decided she would pull onto the gravel road only long enough to turn her rented SUV around and head right back to Manhattan where she belonged.

Until she reached the road and saw the sign.

The security gate blocking the private drive had been pulled to the side and left open. Kate pulled onto the road and stopped the car. She sat there for a moment, staring at the carved wooden sign attached to the gate.

Trail's End.

How appropriate.

She could continue on a road going nowhere.

Or find out what was waiting at the end of the trail.

She tried Tony's cell phone one last time.

When she still couldn't reach him, Kate stepped on the gas pedal. Before she lost her nerve, she zoomed through the open gate and up the gravel road, deciding once and for all, fate be damned.

When Kate finally reached the end of the gravel road and drove into a wide clearing, she decided Tony's cabin was nothing compared to the impressive Wellington estate that sat in the middle of ten manicured acres in Bridgehampton.

It was better.

She loved everything about this private spot on Hunter Mountain the second she saw it. The rustic cedar A-frame, a large deck running across the front. An absolutely breathtaking view from every direction. Even a flagstone chimney jutting upward past the peak of the A-frame, proving that Alex's enticing cuddle-in-front-of-a-roaring-fire prophecy was indeed a possibility.

Only one car was sitting in front of the cabin.

A shiny black sports car to be exact.

It gave Kate hope she would find Tony alone.

She got out of the SUV and started for the cabin.

If Tony did have someone with him, she would simply apologize for disturbing them, hand Tony the check she had already written out and tucked in the pocket of her shorts, and drive right back down the mountain and back to reality.

And if he's alone?

Suddenly, that thought scared her even more.

What if Alex had been wrong?

What if the only reason he'd sent the dress was because he'd told her he'd buy the dress that day in the bridal shop? What if she told him she'd called off the wedding, handed over the check, and he *didn't* ask her to stay?

Oh God. Oh God. Oh God.

She couldn't even think about that.

Not without throwing up.

Projectile vomiting.

Not exactly return invitation behavior.

Stop it! You can do this.

Kate squared her shoulders, walked up on the deck, and boldly knocked on the sliding glass door. Her heart was pounding so loudly she could hear every beat. She patiently counted to twenty, but no one appeared.

Kate knocked again.

Bam. Bam. Bam.

Bam. Bam. Bam.

One last plank, and the dock would be finished.

Tony grabbed his hammer.

Bam. Bam. Bam.

Bam. Bam. Bam.

"Tony."

The hammer stopped in midair at the sound of his name.

Tony jerked his head around.

From his crouched position the first thing he saw was two perfectly shaped legs. He shielded his eyes from the sun with his hand. His gaze kept moving upward, past a pair of white hip-hugging shorts, past a fabulous belly button, past a blue crop top, and right up to the one face he never thought he'd see again.

Heatstroke.

That was his first thought.

It wasn't until she pushed her sunglasses up on top of her head and looked out over the lake that he realized it was Kate—in the flesh—standing right there on the bank in front of him.

Tony was so stunned, he sat flat down on the dock.

"Nice dock," she said, smiling at him as if he had no reason to be shocked shitless that she was there. "Where's the boat that goes with it?"

Tony pulled himself up.

But he couldn't keep the goofy grin off his face.

The only thing he'd ever truly wished for had just come true.

"The boat comes later," he said. "You need a place to dock your boat first. Then you buy the boat."

She reached into her shorts pocket. "This should be a good down payment on one." She held out a check. "I can't let you pay for the dress, Tony."

So that's why she's here.
To pay me for the dress.

He glanced toward the cabin. Harold had probably brought her all the way to Hunter Mountain himself. Demanded that she put him in his place. Made sure Kate shoved his money right back in his face.

But hell, he couldn't really blame the guy.

He'd probably have done the same thing himself.

"Keep the money, Kate, whether you wear the dress or not," Tony told her. "I knew the dress couldn't be returned when I bought it. It's not your problem."

"But it is my problem, Tony," she said. "Just like your dock and your boat situation. There needs to be a wedding before you need a wedding dress."

His deep tan faded right before her eyes.

"God, Kate, I'm sorry," he said. "If Harold flipped out about the dress and called off the wedding, I'll . . ."

Kate cut him off. "No. I'm the one who owes you the apology. I should have told you at the restaurant I had called off the wedding. If I hadn't lied to you about why I wasn't wearing my engagement ring, you never would have bought the dress."

"Forget the dress," he said. He left the dock and walked right up until they were standing only inches apart. He took the check out of her hand and tucked it right back into the pocket of her shorts. "What's going on, Kate? Why did you call off the wedding?"

It was a simple enough question.

If he hadn't been so damn gorgeous—standing there

dressed in nothing but a pair of navy-and-white swim trunks, every muscle she'd ever imagined glistening in the bright afternoon sunlight—she might have been able to answer the question.

Tell him, dammit, tell him!

This is not the time for polite conversation.

And so she did.

Kate told him everything.

About their troubled relationship.

About their argument.

About Harold's don't ask, don't tell comment that had finally pushed her over the edge.

When she finished, Kate said, "So that's my story. And this is the part where you jump off the dock and swim for your life, rather than risk getting mixed up with someone so stupid she would accept a marriage proposal from someone she didn't love."

He looked at her for a moment.

"No," he said, "this is the part where I do this."

Kate was surprised when he cupped her face gently in his hands and kissed her so deliciously slow and soft she thought she might pass out.

"You really don't want to get involved with me," she said when their lips broke apart. "I'm one crazy . . ."

Another brain-rattling kiss silenced her.

A kiss that was harder, longer, and ten times better than the first. Kate couldn't help herself. Her arms slid around his neck, holding on, begging for more.

He didn't hold back.

It was the kind of kiss that was going to lead them straight to where her mind had been heading from the first day she saw him.

Unless I have the sense to push him away.

She didn't.

His hands slid to her hips, pulling her against him.

Kate gasped.

Mercy!

He could take her right there, and she'd let him.

In the grass.

On the dock.

In the water.

*Under*water if he wanted.

It just didn't matter.

He was the one to pull away.

But he didn't let her go.

They stood there, his arms clasped tightly around her waist, staring at each other.

"I think we need to slow down," he said.

Kate said, "I think you're right."

"And I know it doesn't make any sense, but I think we both felt an immediate connection that first day in the park."

"Yes," Kate said. "I think we did."

He smiled.

Kate smiled back.

Okay, her breathing was slowly returning to normal again. That kiss definitely had her motor running a little too fast, a little too soon. But Tony was right. They didn't need to jump into anything they'd both regret later.

Her pulse raced again when he pulled her closer to him.

"The important thing," he said, still searching her face, "is that you aren't going to marry Harold, and that gives us a chance to get to know each other better. Agreed?"

Kate nodded.

"Now," he said, "please say you'll stay with me tonight and not go back to the city."

Thank you, God!

"I'll stay," Kate said.

Let Tony think her staying was his idea for now.

She'd worry about explaining her overnight bag later.

"But," he added, "You have my word. No pressure. No expectations. You can trust me to be a perfect gentleman."

A perfect gentleman?

Kate sighed mentally.

Maybe she'd thanked God a little too soon.

Tony still couldn't believe Kate was with him.

Yet here they were, holding hands and walking down the main street in Hunter. Kate happily licking—quite seductively he might add—her two scoops of double fudge ice cream in a brown sugar cone.

Thanks to the kiss that almost had him doing backflips off the dock, he'd realized real quick that staying alone at the cabin with Kate wasn't exactly the best course of action. At least not until they did have time to get to know each other better.

He wasn't some horn dog with nothing but sex on the brain. They needed to take things slow, just like he'd told her earlier. He wanted them to ease into a comfort zone with each other before they took things to a different level.

His interest in Kate was a lot more than just a quick fling and a good time in bed. You didn't play around with something as serious as forever.

Forever deserved patience.

For Kate, he would wait as long as it took, for as long as she needed.

That's why he'd quickly showered and changed.

Then he'd taken Kate straight into town so there wouldn't be any further chance of his giving into temptation.

Only a real jerk would take advantage of a woman who had just broken up with her fiancé—eagerly rip her clothes off and ravish her body fifty ways from Tuesday. Except thinking about how much he wanted to ravish that gorgeous body of hers awakened more than just Tony's sense of fair play.

Tony glanced at her again.

That tongue of hers was definitely driving him crazy.

Down, boy. Down.

She looked over at him.

Tony squeezed her hand.

"What?" she said.

"I was just wondering," Tony said. "Are you purposely trying to torment me with every lick of that ice-cream cone?"

"You can have a bite," she said, and playfully shoved the cone under his nose.

Tony took a bite, but Kate knew exactly what he'd meant.

It certainly wasn't going to be easy being Mr. Take It Slow. Not if she kept teasing him the way she was teasing him now. The way she was dressed didn't help matters, either. Not that what she was wearing was inappropriate. She wasn't dressed any differently than any of the other tourists in town. It was the body beneath the shorts and the crop top he couldn't stop thinking about.

One more glance at her belly button, and I'm toast.

He looked away, wondering if maybe they'd get to know each other better if he ditched his plans to take her to dinner at a restaurant there in town. Maybe he should fix dinner for her himself. They'd certainly have more privacy than being jammed in a booth in a busy restaurant where they would have to shout to even hear each other.

Shouting at each other wasn't what he had in mind for their getting-to-know-each-other-better phase of things.

They could stop by the fresh market up the road a few miles. Pick up some fresh trout for the grill, some fresh greens for a killer salad, and a few bottles of good wine.

Then they could head back to the cabin. Enjoy the sunset from the privacy of his back deck. Soak in the Jacuzzi later, gazing overhead to see if their destiny really was written in the stars.

Like I could keep my hands to myself with Kate in a hot tub.

No, dinner at a restaurant was safer.

But instead of eating there in town, he would take her up the mountain to the resort village. There was always something going on in the village. After dinner, they could even hang out for a while at one of the pubs that had a live band.

That would be another safe thing to do.

Later, when they finally made it back to the cabin, he'd give Kate the only bed upstairs in the loft.

He'd bunk downstairs on the couch.

Sadly, but willingly.

No pressure, no expectations.

That's what he'd promised.

Maybe he could even talk her into staying for a couple of days. She didn't seem to have a problem missing Monday at the gallery. She was the manager, after all. Her grandmother owned the place.

Definitely.

I'll ask her to stay a few more days.

The more time they had away from the city, away from the daily grind, the better. He wanted Kate to know she could trust him. Completely. With her secrets, with her fears, and with anything else she wanted to share with him.

Kate was truly the first woman he'd ever wanted.

I am not *going to mess this up.*

Kate polished off the last bite of her ice-cream cone, thinking there had never been a nicer guy than the one holding her hand right now. Or a more gorgeous one. She hadn't missed the envious glances from women passing them on the sidewalk.

Tony was just one of those men who grabbed your attention the second you saw him. He was all male, muscle, and magnetism—a walking advertisement for every woman's dream come true.

They'd spent the last hour wandering around town, looking in all the shops. Her pretending she didn't notice that his biceps were so large that the short sleeves of his cotton polo shirt barely fit around them. Or that he looked terrific in a pair of shorts—the muscles in his legs making those guys on the *Nautilus* commercials look like underdeveloped weaklings.

Kate took a peek at those biceps again and sighed.

Would you excuse me while I scream now!

What the hell was up with Tony?

Nothing was up with Tony.

That was the problem.

Strolling through town certainly hadn't been a part of her fantasy. In her fantasy, the second she arrived at the cabin, Tony had her naked in two seconds flat, with her legs wrapped around his waist.

Penile dysfunction disorder again?

Not a chance.

So, what's Tony's problem?

Did he like her well enough, he just wasn't interested in her physically? Is that why he'd mentioned no pressure, no expectations, and given her that old line about being a perfect gentleman?

Or, did she just intimidate him?

Intimidation had been Alex's explanation for guys she'd dated in the past who'd expressed an interest in her, then backed off for no apparent reason. According to Alex, as much as men loved the idea of making love to a beautiful woman, they were a lot like a dog chasing a car—when they finally caught one, they had no idea what to do about it.

They stopped walking when they made it back to his car.

Tony let go of her hand and opened her car door.

He smiled, and said, "Would you like to ride up to the village at the ski resort? There's always something going on up there. The village has some really nice restaurants. We can grab dinner there in a few hours, then head over to one of the pubs that has a live band, and . . ."

Blah. Blah. Blah.—Blah. Blah. Blah.

Kate was sick of polite conversation.

She'd wanted Tony from the moment she saw him, dammit!

She was not interested in spending precious time on a freaking tourist expedition or tapping her toe to the music in some pub with a live band.

She was going to stop being her mealymouthed self.

She was going to take control of the situation.

For once, she was going to get straight to the *hard* of the matter!

Kate interrupted him. "Can I ask you a very blunt question?"

He looked surprised at her outburst.

He finally said, "You can ask me anything, Kate."

Ask him, dammit!

"I've already told you about my relationship with Harold," Kate said. "So tell me the truth, Tony. When you said no pressure, no expectations, what does that really mean? Are you just not physically attracted to me, either?"

Oh, no!

Now he looked shocked instead of surprised.

Kate bit down hard on her bottom lip, preparing herself for his answer.

He finally said, "God, yes. Yes, Kate. *Hell*, yes, I'm physically attracted to you! Making love to you is all I've thought about since the first minute I saw you. I just didn't want you to think . . ."

Kate leaned forward and kissed him senseless.

When she pulled back, Tony held up one finger.

"Give me two seconds," he said, then broke and ran.

Kate couldn't help herself.

She burst out laughing when Tony came charging back across the street from the pharmacy a few minutes later, dodging cars left and right, carrying a package tucked under his arm like a halfback heading for a winning touchdown.

CHAPTER 10

—⟡—

They were both completely naked.

But they'd never make it to the bed.

Not unless he carried her up the spiral staircase to the loft overhead.

Kate knew that whether Tony did or not.

For one thing, her knees were too weak to support her.

Another important factor—his searing kisses already had her head spinning until she was three shades past dizzy.

They almost hadn't made it back to the cabin alive, either. Thank God, it was only 3.5 miles from town. She probably shouldn't have kept kissing him and touching him like that while he was driving, but she just couldn't help herself.

"Mmmmmm," Kate murmured, as his hands slid down her bare back to her hips.

Her eyes flew open when Tony did pick her up.

Wow!

Countertops.

Who knew they were the perfect height?

He kissed her again, with more urgency this time.

When he reached for the box on the counter beside her, Kate looked away.

He tilted her chin up, forcing her to look at him.

Damn.

How did he always instinctively know if something wasn't exactly in sync with her?

Yes, dammit, she was nervous.

She'd made herself a promise she was not going to take anything that happened between the two of them seriously. It was just sex. She was only human. And he turned her on more than any man she'd ever met.

"If we're still moving too fast, Kate," he said, "all you have to do is tell me."

What?

I'm sitting on your kitchen counter, nude.

And you're saying you wouldn't mind if I suggested we turn on the Lifetime channel and forget the whole thing?

Oh, no you don't, Tony Petrocelli!

She hadn't driven two hours to watch the freaking movie of the week!

Kate leaned forward, slid her arms around his neck, and kissed him with everything she had. Tony kissed her back just as forcefully, fisting her hair as the kiss grew deeper.

Not serious. Not serious. Not serious.

His hot mouth slid to her neck.

Across her bare shoulder.

Onto her erect left nipple.

Kate got serious.

She closed her eyes, giving in to the delicious tingling sensation that set her entire body on fire. He found his way back to her mouth and kissed her again, gently this time. When Kate opened her eyes, he was staring at her.

His eyes never left her face as he ran his hand across her left foot, then slowly, tantalizingly up the inside of her entire left leg.

When his fingers got bolder, Kate gasped.

My God!

He pulled her head forward, kissing her deeply while his fingers worked their magic.

Yes. Yes. Oh. Mmmmmmmm. Oh. Ah. Yes!

Kate was so wet and ready, she grabbed Tony's hand.

They both moaned when he slid deeply inside her.

Even in her wildest dreams, she had never imagined anything could feel this wonderful.

She arched her back when his hot mouth covered her breast again. The tingle, God, that tingle instantly spreading through her body—pushing her closer, closer, closer to the edge.

His mouth slid up to her neck and Kate moaned again.

He grabbed her hips, holding her steady, moving faster and faster and faster, plunging deeper and deeper. His tongue toyed with her earlobe before he whispered low and husky, "Let it happen, baby. This is all about you."

Kate flashed hot all over.

Kismet? Fate? Destiny? Chance?

The words kept floating through her mind.

Oh God. Oh God. Oh God.

Kate slipped off the edge.

Right into paradise.

When she finally caught her breath, she fell against him, spent.

He reached up and pushed her hair back away from her face. "God, you are so incredibly beautiful."

She tried to mumble "you too"—she wasn't able.

He didn't seem to care.

He kissed her face, her eyes, even the tip of her nose. Then he slid his hands under her legs and picked her up from the kitchen counter so easily, it surprised her.

She got another big surprise.

Tony really was carrying her up the spiral staircase.

The king-size bed waiting for them took up almost every inch of the loft space. He placed her on the overstuffed comforter, lowered himself on the bed beside her, and leaned in for another long kiss. It wasn't until he reached out and caressed her cheek with the back of his hand—staring at her in that intense, soul-searching way he had about him—that Kate realized something very important.

As impossible.

As ridiculous.

As highly improbable as the entire situation had been from the first moment she met him.

She was madly in love with Tony Petrocelli.

This is still going to be all about you.

Tony thought this, knowing he could take his time and make love to Kate the way he wanted.

Slow.

Unhurried.

Every touch adding something special to the pleasure of the moment.

Sex was one thing.

Making love to the woman who had clearly stolen his heart was another.

He let his hand drift from her cheek, slowly down her neck. She closed her eyes and bit down on her bottom lip as his fingers gently traced the outline of each breast. The nipples he'd been taunting instantly sprang to life under his touch, begging for attention.

He didn't disappoint.

She cried out, her hands clasping the back of his head.

There was nothing he wouldn't do, nothing he wouldn't try, in order to take this woman to places she'd never dreamed possible.

Her breathing was becoming rapid.

He could feel her heart beating wildly.

Feel her body tensing, anticipating what was coming next.

Tony moved lower.

The feel of his mouth traveling down skin smooth as satin sent a moan to his own lips. His hands slid to her thighs, up the backs of her legs, gently pushing them apart for easy access to the place he was seeking.

She cried out his name.

The taste of her drove his own need higher.

But as great as his own need was, the desire to pleasure her again was greater.

She tensed when his own urgency to please increased the tempo. Her body arched, pressing against him. He slid his hands up her flat stomach, circled his fingers around both breasts, and kept his mouth buried exactly where it needed to stay.

She finally sighed, convulsing against him.

His own desire quickly took over.

He retraced his steps, his mouth moving upward, planting soft kisses up the full length of her body. He kissed her lips softly at first, then with the urgency he'd been trying to suppress.

He wasn't prepared when she reversed their positions.

Tony shivered when she took him deep inside her.

"God, Kate. You're driving me crazy."

His hands found her tiny waist, trying to slow her rhythm, trying to keep each movement slow and unhurried. He wanted to savor every moment, prolong the magic as long as possible. He kept drifting in and out, lost somewhere between this world and next, until her long silky hair brushed across his face as she bent down to kiss him.

It was more than he could take.

"Kate," he moaned again, begging for mercy.

She had none.

She grabbed his hands and held them down on the bed.

Slow and unhurried became fast and urgent.

"You," she whispered, moving even faster. "This one is all about you."

He exploded like a hand grenade.

The earth moved.

Time stopped.

Angels sang.

At least, Tony thought all of those things happened.

One thing, however, he knew without a doubt.

Forever would never be long enough to spend with Kate.

Tony pulled the corner of the comforter back over Kate's bare shoulder, deciding he would let her sleep.

When he turned to head back down the stairs, she called out his name.

He turned around.

She was propped up on one elbow, lazily pushing her hair back away from her face.

Is there anything more sexy than a sleepy tousled-looking woman lying in your bed?

Tony didn't think so.

He was tempted to undress and crawl right back into bed with her. Instead, he said, "I'm going to run to town for a second. I thought you might like more than peanut butter and crackers for dinner."

Her eyebrow arched. "You mean you aren't taking me to the village to one of those great restaurants, and later to a pub that has a live band?"

"Not a chance," Tony teased back. "From here on out, I'm placing you under strict house arrest."

"Can I roam freely about the cabin, Officer? Or am I confined to the bedroom?"

"Definitely confined to the bedroom," Tony said.

He walked back to the bed, leaned down, and kissed her.

"How does grilled trout, salad, and a nice bottle of Pinot sound?"

"Yummy."

He kissed her again and headed down the stairs.

Kate sat up in bed, pulling the comforter with her.

She called out, "Are you sure you don't want me to come with you?"

She heard him laugh.

"No way," he yelled back. "I can't trust you to keep your hands to yourself."

Is there anything sexier than a man with a great sense of humor?

Kate didn't think so.

She fell backward on the bed with a loud, wonderful, couldn't-be-happier sigh. It only took her about ten seconds before she sat back up again. She scooted to the edge of the bed, wrapped the comforter around her, and flew down the spiral staircase in search of her clothes.

Two seconds after she'd collected her clothing from the floor, the back of the sofa, and a nearby lamp shade, Kate wiggled into her lacy thong, into her shorts, jerked her top over her head, and dashed to the SUV for her cell phone.

Finding her bra?

She'd worry about that later.

She flipped open the phone and stared at the appropriate box informing her she had an unbelievable fourteen new messages waiting for her. Kate scrolled down the messages, shaking her head.

Ten of them (big surprise) were from Alex. Two (wince) were from Grace. And two (vomit) were from Harold.

Two from Harold?

When had Harold ever called her during the *day?*

Much less *twice* in one day?

Screw Harold.

But thank God she hadn't.

Tony had seemed ecstatic earlier when she'd admitted

she'd never slept with Harold, that their relationship had been platonic from the very beginning. She'd seen the look of relief wash across his face.

Thank God he was willing to overlook her stupid past mistakes and give her a chance to prove she really wasn't some desperate psycho chick he shouldn't get involved with.

Psycho chick.

Kate decided she'd better check her messages from her grandmother. Convincing Grace that her current behavior wasn't completely and categorically psychotic wasn't going to be that easy.

Message number one from her grandmother said, "Kate, call me when you get this message."

Message number two said, "Harold is concerned, Kate, and so am I. I understand you taking a few days off, but you could at least answer your cell phone."

Please.

Kate hit speed dial and called Alex instead.

"Jesus, Kate," Alex scolded. "I've been worried to death about you."

"Obviously," Kate said. "But was it really necessary to leave ten separate messages on my voice mail?"

Alex ignored her question. "Don't leave me guessing. Have you fallen madly into bed with Tony yet?"

"Madly," Kate admitted. She held the phone away from her ear when Alex screamed.

"Oh, God, I'm so excited. I feel like a proud mom sending her daughter off to the prom for the first time."

"Save that feeling for the daughter who's going to be too screwed up to go to her first prom," Kate said.

"Oh, please," Alex scoffed. "Do you really not know

me well enough to realize I never agree to anything unless I know I have the upper hand?"

"And you would have the upper hand letting a surrogate have your husband's child because?"

"I made John agree that the surrogate had to meet all of my qualifications. She has to be Caucasian. Brunette. IQ of at least 190. College graduate. And between twenty-five and thirty years old."

Kate laughed. "In other words, you, with maybe fudging a little bit on the IQ."

"Exactly. I convinced John that if a surrogate was going to have his child, it only made sense that she should be as much like me as possible."

"Knowing all along your qualifications could never be met."

"Are you implying I'm that devious?"

"I *know* you're that devious," Kate said, "that's one reason I'm calling. Gram has already left me two messages, Alex. I want you to call her for me. Tell her I'm okay. Make up a good lie about why I can't call her myself."

"Not a good idea," Alex said. "If I call Grace, that will only alert her to the fact that something really is going on. Other than your just taking time off to collect your thoughts."

Kate thought about it. "Yeah, maybe you're right."

"Use the low battery on your cell phone trick. Call her, but before she can quiz you or lecture you, tell her your battery is going dead and you'll have to call her later."

"You're a genius."

"So I've been told," Alex boasted. "But back to Tony. Where is he now? Have you left the poor guy in a sex-induced coma?"

"Tony's in town at the moment," Kate said. She added quite happily, "He just happens to be picking up things for the scrumptious dinner he's going to make for me later. And then I suspect he will carry me up the spiral staircase like he did earlier, to his loft bedroom in his A-frame cabin, which couldn't be any more romantic, where he'll again kiss every inch of my body and have me screaming and begging for more."

"Dear God," Alex said. "You really do have it bad. You should be careful here, Kate. Afterglow can be misleading. You should . . ."

Kate cut her off. "The quickest way to end this conversation, Alex, is to keep starting every sentence with 'you should.' I'm *over* everyone telling me what I should and shouldn't do."

"Don't get pissy with me, Kate. I only . . ."

"Alex? Alex?" Kate feigned. "I'll have to call you back later. My cell phone battery is going dead."

Tony had taken more time in town than he'd intended. He'd just wanted to make sure everything was perfect— the trout, the wine, even the fresh greens he'd picked for the salad. He'd also stopped by the drugstore again, this time for a few personal items for Kate—a comb, a brush, her own toothbrush.

A change of clothing wouldn't be necessary.

If Tony had his way about it, she'd never get a chance to wear them.

He grabbed the sacks from the passenger seat, whistling happily as he bounded up the steps to the deck

and into the cabin. When he walked into the great room
and dumped the sacks on the kitchen counter, he looked
up and saw her coming down the stairs.

His heart melted.

Breathtaking doesn't do her justice.

She'd obviously taken a shower. Her hair was still damp,
clinging to those magnificent high cheekbones and framing
her beautiful face. She'd changed clothes, too. Not a bad
idea since it did tend to get a little chilly in the evenings.

Whoa!

She's changed clothes?

Her soft-looking pink sweater was certainly alluring.
Seeing her in those tight jeans definitely made his mouth
water. Even her hot-pink-painted barefoot toes completely turned him on.

Still, Tony couldn't resist saying, "Nice jeans."

She blushed.

"I . . ." She looked at him for a second and put her
hands on her hips. "Okay. I admit it. It was presumptuous
of me to assume you were alone up here, much less come
prepared to stay. But if it makes any difference to you,
I've never wanted anything more than finding you here
alone and you asking me to stay."

Tony walked over and slid his arms around her waist.

"I was only teasing," he told her, and kissed the top of
her head. "I forgot to ask when I left for town if you
needed anything. But I bought you a comb and brush and
toothbrush just in case."

She looked up at him. "You did that for me?"

Tony nodded. "Does that sound like someone who's
ready for you to leave anytime soon?"

"I did try to call you first," she said after he bent down

and kissed her. "You didn't ask how I'd found you when I first got here, so I assumed you'd figured out your mother gave me directions to the cabin."

Tony laughed. "I'm surprised my mother didn't offer to bring you up here herself."

"She would have had to fight Alex for that privilege," she said. "Alex was ready to bring me Saturday night."

Tony bent down and kissed her again.

"Your mother gave me your cell phone number, too," she said. "And if you'd bothered to keep your cell phone on, I wouldn't be trying to explain myself now."

"I have a confession of my own to make," Tony told her.

She pushed back from him.

"Look," she said, "if your confession has anything to do with female guests you've invited to come up here later, that's really none of my business."

He pulled her back against him. "No female guests, Kate. Not ever. You're the only person besides my family who's ever been to Trail's End."

When she settled her head against his shoulder, he said, "I was referring to why you couldn't reach me on my cell phone."

Kate laughed when he finished his confession.

"You're serious? You really threw your phone in the lake?"

Tony nodded. "That's how disappointed I was when I'd given up all hope that you were going to call. And if it makes any difference to you, the first thing I thought when I turned around and saw you standing behind me, was that the only thing I'd ever wished for had just come true."

Could I possibly be any crazier about him than I am right now?

Knowing she could scared her.

But that didn't keep Kate from circling her arms around his neck and kissing Tony so thoroughly she felt his instant response as he pressed hard against her. She reached down, her touch saying everything he needed to know.

He led her to the sofa.

She sank back against the soft cushions.

Her breath caught as he unfastened the top button of her jeans. Her pulse raced, watching his own desire change the expression on his handsome face.

Afterglow?

Or ever after?

It didn't matter.

She would never get enough of this man.

Never tire of him touching her.

Never be able to spend another day without a desperate yearning for his kiss.

Madly.

Truly.

Deeply.

Whatever this was, it was simply beyond her control.

━━━━━◦

Kate snuggled closer when Tony leaned forward and kissed her ear. They were relaxing on the deck now, both sitting in the same lounge chair. His arms were around her, holding her close. She was settled between his legs, leaning back against his broad chest. Both of them listening to the night sounds—the lulling cadence of the crickets, an occasional splash from a fish jumping in the lake below, a screech from an owl somewhere in the distance.

He snuggled even closer to her.

She didn't resist.

The meal they'd just finished had been superb—once they'd left each other alone long enough to prepare dinner. The effort had been a joint one. He attended to the grill. She made the salad. She teased him mercilessly because all of his CDs were strictly eighties pop music. He teased her right back because she knew all of the words to each and every song.

"Are you cold, baby?"

"No, I'm fine," Kate said, but she couldn't keep from smiling happily to herself. How could she possibly be cold when a warm feeling spread through her every time he called her baby?

Such a simple endearment—baby.

Some people probably even found it silly.

But it wasn't silly to her, not when Tony said it.

Maybe because she'd never forget the first time he'd called her that—his voice husky with emotion, urging her to let it happen.

Let it happen, baby.

But exactly what in the hell *was* baby letting happen?

Besides the obvious, of course.

The obvious was that baby had lost her freaking head over Tony Petrocelli.

Maybe baby should call a proctologist and see if they can find it for me!

He nuzzled against her neck, flipping her emotions upside down again. Kate wanted more than anything to believe Tony felt the same way about her—that he couldn't stand the thought of losing her now that they'd finally found each other.

Yet, every time she felt herself slipping into that delirious state of happiness—exactly the way she'd been doing only a few minutes earlier—her better judgment tapped her on the shoulder, quickly reminding her that: (a) she was thirty years old; (b) she'd never truly been in love in her life; and (c) the probability that she was in love with a guy she'd seen a grand total of four times was as likely as poor John finding a surrogate to meet Alex's unmatchable qualifications.

However.

If Tony's only interest in her was just being a regular orgasm donor in her life, he was sure putting on one hell of a great act.

Excuse me?

Talk about great actors.

Does the name Harold Wellington ring a bell?

To hell with Harold.

Harold didn't deserve to share her same brain space with Tony.

She'd put an end to that embarrassingly sad chapter in her life. Or, technically, she *would* put end to Harold. Forever. Once she showed up for afternoon tea at the Waldorf.

She hadn't told Tony that part.

About Harold's big surprise wedding, and that she still had a face-to-face meeting with Harold looming in the distance.

But she would tell him.

Just not tonight.

The day had been too perfect.

The night had the promise of being even better.

She'd tell Tony about her upcoming meeting with Harold in the morning, before she went back to Manhattan.

Gulp.

And if he never wants to see me again?

He shifted their position and kissed her.

"Don't go back to the city tomorrow," he said, his strong arms circling around her even tighter. "Say you'll stay with me at least one more day."

"I'll stay," Kate said, slipping right back into delirious happydom. "I'll stay until Tuesday morning."

Pushover!

Kate was too happy to care.

Staying the rest of the week would be even better.

But Tony wasn't going to push her too fast.

She'd told him all about Harold, their argument, and why she'd called off the wedding. But that didn't mean seeds of doubt weren't still keeping him worried.

How could it not cross his mind that Kate's showing up at the cabin really was nothing more than one last fling before she settled down with Harold for the rest of her life?

Hadn't Harold challenged her to do just that?

Finish whatever was going on with the dim-witted cop before he returned from Chicago?

Tony winced inwardly at the thought.

Except, if that's what Kate's showing up at the cabin turned out to be, he knew he had no one to blame but himself. He, not Kate, had been the one who had opened the door far and wide for that disaster to happen.

Sending her the dress.

Sending her the message he was interested.

Breaking every rule he swore he wouldn't break.

Is this what love does to a guy?

Tony didn't have a clue.

He'd never been in love before, not even close.

It only made perfect sense he was confused right now, worried that Kate could never feel about him the way he already knew he felt about her.

Stop borrowing trouble!

True.

He needed to stop worrying about the future and enjoy what time he did have with Kate. Her showing up at the cabin was the closest thing he'd ever come to a miracle.

Unless I'm standing at the altar when Kate walks down the aisle in the wedding dress I bought her.

Jesus!

He really was on the verge of losing it.

So maybe his parents had gotten married within a month after *they* met each other. *As far as I know, love at first sight isn't hereditary, dammit!*

He needed to live for the moment.

He needed to enjoy spending time with Kate while he had her here in his arms. And most importantly, he needed to stop filling his stupid head with empty wishes that quite possibly would never come true.

"Look!"

Tony followed Kate's finger to the shooting star streaking across the ebony night sky.

"Hurry, make a wish," she said.

Baby, if you only knew the half of it.

She turned all the way around, pressing everything he wanted in this life fully against him.

"Did you make a wish?" she asked, nibbling at his bottom lip.

"I did," Tony told her.

"And will you tell me what you wished for?" she asked, teasing his earlobe with the tip of her tongue.

"Nope. Wishes told never come true."

Her lips moved back to his mouth for another teasing kiss before she said, "Well, if I remember right, Officer Petrocelli, the first time I saw you, you said you didn't have a superstitious bone in your body."

Tony tensed when her hand slid downward.

"Oops," she teased. "I think you were lying to me."

"You'd better be careful," he warned.

"Or what?" Her hand rubbed against him even harder. "How will you punish me? Place me back under house arrest unless I agree to strip off my clothes and get into the hot tub with you?"

"Uh-huh," was all Tony could manage.

She got up in slow motion, rubbing her body down the full length of his, then pulled her sweater over her head and let it drop just as slowly to the deck. The sight of her naked breasts bathed in the silvery glow of the moonlight took his breath away.

The jeans came off the same way, slowly and seductively.

When she shimmied out of her thong, Tony stood up.

He'd been wrong.

Occasionally, wishes did come true.

CHAPTER 11

On Sunday evening, Harold ushered his pretty dining companion to the best table available at *Une Fourchette*, the most expensive restaurant in Chicago when it came to French cuisine. He smiled inwardly as they walked across the room, knowing every eye in the place was focused in their direction.

The attention from his wealthy peers fed his ego.

That no one suspected his beautiful date's profession turned him on.

She was dressed to perfection again tonight, wearing a clinging royal blue Versace dress and carrying herself with more dignity than any *blue* blood he'd ever encountered. It struck him funny that, had she been from some notable family with a prestigious background, he wouldn't even be attracted to her.

Then, Carla Matthews would only be another pretty face.

Another boring female who had always played by the rules, never once daring to step outside the realm of what society perceived as acceptable behavior.

Carla's *unacceptable* behavior was what excited him.

Keeping her behavior unacceptable was his goal.

He remained standing while the waiter seated her, but a white-hot anger flashed through him when he noticed the leering expression in the young punk's eyes. It didn't matter how many men had enjoyed her body in the past, she was going to be his now. Only his. Any man who dared come near her again would rue the day he made that mistake.

"When I made reservations, I ordered the best merlot you serve here," Harold snapped, jerking the waiter's head in his direction. "I fully expected to have a bottle waiting when we arrived at our table. See that you don't disappoint me again."

The punk darted off, his face various shades of red.

Harold seated himself properly at the table and snapped his napkin open. When he looked across the table at her, Carla seemed anything but impressed.

"Are you always that rude, Harry?"

What?

"I beg your pardon?"

"No, you need to beg that young waiter's pardon," she said, staring him down. "He's the one you just talked to like he was dirt under your feet."

"Did I?" Harold feigned surprise.

"News flash, Harry," she said, tossing her long dark hair back away from her exquisite face. "When you talk to people like that, it doesn't make them look bad. It makes you look stupid."

Harold laughed.

But it was nervous laughter, not the ha-ha kind.

"How amusing," he said. "*You* giving *me* tips on social etiquette."

She replied, "How amusing *I* would have to give someone with *your* upbringing a lesson in common courtesy."

The sting of her words caught him off guard.

Who the hell did she think she was?

Did she not realize even being in a restaurant like this one with a man of his stature was a goddamn privilege for a woman like her?

The waiter hurried back to the table and quickly placed the wine in front of him. Harold glanced in her direction, then back at the waiter.

"My beautiful companion has just pointed out that I was extremely rude to you a minute ago," he said. "I hope you will accept my deepest apology for talking to you in such an unacceptable manner."

The young man nodded politely. "And please accept my apology, sir, for not having your merlot at your table when you arrived."

The waiter dispensed with pouring the wine, informed them he would give them a few minutes to peruse the menu, and hurriedly left the table. Harold pretended to study his menu for a few seconds, then glanced up at her nonchalantly.

"Well?" he said. "Happy now?"

She smiled slowly, drawing his attention to her full, glossy lips, and calling up heated memories that made him instantly grow hard for the want of her.

"You are one fine piece of work, aren't you, Harry?"

"Meaning?"

"Meaning heaven wouldn't have your ass, and hell would be too afraid you'd take over."

Harold laughed.

Ha-ha this time.

But a sudden thought scared him.

Everyone met his or her match sooner or later.

Harold feared *his* was sitting right across the table.

"Gram, it's me," Kate said on Monday morning.

She was standing at the upstairs loft window, watching Tony work as he put finishing touches on the dock. She winced at the sound of the long sigh on the other end of the line.

"Do you have your battery problem under control?" Grace asked. "Or is this going to be another dropped conversation?"

"I know you're upset with me, Gram," Kate said. She walked away from the window and sat down on the edge of the bed. "I'm just calling to let you know I'm okay. The last thing I would ever do is worry you on purpose."

Another long sigh.

"I take it this means you aren't coming home yet?"

Kate paused. "Is that a problem for you?"

"It could be a problem for *you*, Kate," Grace said, "and you know exactly what I mean."

Harold.

"I'll call Harold, Gram," Kate said, "as soon as I hang up with you, I'll call him. Okay?"

"Please do call him, Kate," she said, sounding rather desperate. "I feel bad enough that I've upset you by telling you about the surprise. I know that's what has you so upset right now. I almost confessed I'd told you when Harold called me yesterday."

"No, Gram," Kate said, "please don't tell Harold I know what he's planning. I promise, everything will work itself out when I get home."

"And when will that be?"

"Soon," was all Kate would volunteer.

"I just want you to know one thing," Grace said.

Kate steeled herself, waiting to hear the one thing her grandmother wanted her to know.

"Marriage is the biggest decision you'll ever make in this life, Kate. I might not agree with the decision you end up making, but I don't want to lose you the way I did your father. Whatever you decide, I'll accept it."

"I love you, Gram."

"Likewise," Grace said, and hung up.

Kate smiled, tapping the phone against her chin for a moment. She knew how hard it had been for her grandmother to tell her that. Grace and Harold were a lot alike in some ways—reserved, polite, never overly demonstrative. She suspected her grandmother's standoffishness stemmed from her losing her husband so young to a heart attack—then losing her son to a heart attack of a different nature.

She didn't have a clue what was truly behind Harold's fear of intimacy. Other than the fact that he liked to be in control. But the similarities in Grace's and Harold's personalities did contribute to the reason Harold had won her grandmother over so easily. They both preferred their lives neat and orderly and always on schedule.

She tried to imagine Grace sitting at the big family table at Mama Gina's amidst all the chaos and confusion, instead of being in her usual subdued and more formal surroundings. She couldn't. But she could imagine herself sitting at that big, boisterous Italian family table—loving every minute of it.

Kate walked back to the window.

Tony was in the water now, adding what looked like rubber stripping to the edge of the dock. As if he sensed she was there, he suddenly looked up at the window.

He waved.

Kate blew him a kiss and waved back.

Madly.

Truly.

Deeply.

When she stepped back from the window, Kate scrolled down her phone list, no longer dreading the call.

"This is Harold Wellington," the curt message on his cell phone said, "If you want a call back, leave your information in the following order: Your name. Your number. The time of your call."

Kate rolled her eyes.

Her first instinct was to tell Harold he could call her back at 1-800-SCREW-YOU! But that could possibly keep him harassing her grandmother. Better to keep her message civil, understated, and provide him with the least amount of information possible.

When the beep sounded, Kate said, "This is Kate, Harold. Gram said she told you I was taking a few days off. I have some things to figure out, so please give me the privacy to do that. I'll see you when you get back from Chicago."

Kate tossed the cell phone on the bed.

Skipped happily down the spiral staircase.

Hoping to spend eternity with her très hunky cop.

Harold had heard his cell phone ringing earlier, but he hadn't been in a position to take the call. The position he'd been in was another of the not-for-the-Internet variety.

As was the position Harold found himself in now.

It had never occurred to him that Carla would stay the entire night once they returned to the hotel after dinner on Sunday evening. Of course, it had never occurred to him how much fun they could have together once neither of them was watching the clock, either. Their bedroom games had lasted into the wee hours of the morning, until neither of them had any strength left.

He'd awakened with her head on his shoulder, shocked at how natural it felt to have her snuggled against him.

A cuddler, he wasn't.

Nor was he accustomed to sharing his bed.

Once he and Kate were married, he intended to work his way into separate bedrooms as quickly as possible. His late working habits would be his excuse. She'd soon tire of waiting up for him. Soon accept going to bed alone as part of the schedule. Even appreciate his not disturbing her when he did come home after hours.

But after last night, Harold decided staying overnight with his mistress would definitely become a new addition to his schedule. As would morning bedroom games like the one that had him in his present position.

He glanced across the room.

Carla was sitting on the floor, her legs contorted in a position he couldn't even describe. She claimed she was going through her morning yoga routine. It looked like sheer torture to him.

"I'm past the point of being amused, Carla," Harold said, trying again without success to loosen the ties around his wrists that had his arms pulled above his head and fastened to the elaborate headboard of the luxury suite's bed.

His three-hundred-dollar *silk* ties—to be exact.

She glanced up at him as she leaned forward and flattened her body against the floor. "Maybe *you* should combine exercise with kinky sex, Harry," she said, "then you would be *fit* to be tied."

"Great," Harold said, staring at the ceiling. "You're a comedienne, too."

"Yup, that's me," she said. "Your happy hooker at your service."

She pulled herself up from the floor and walked over to the bed. She was wearing one of his Brooks Brothers shirts with nothing underneath.

The nothing underneath made his pulse race.

She leaned over him, untying both hands.

Harold pulled himself up, resting his back against the headboard as he rubbed a little circulation back into his wrists. But the "happy hooker" connotation bothered him.

"I'd prefer you not demean yourself with the hooker reference from here on out," he told her.

She looked at him for a moment.

Then headed in the direction of the bathroom.

"Sorry, I forgot," she tossed back over her shoulder, "what self-respecting man would ever marry a whore?"

Harold flinched.

He hadn't been prepared to have his own harsh words thrown back in his face. Especially not when—for once—he hadn't been thinking of himself.

He'd been thinking about Carla and her own self-esteem. Life had been anything but nice to her. She might not be aware of it yet, but he intended to make sure Carla never again wanted for anything.

When he heard the shower running, Harold got out of bed and retrieved his boxers from the floor. It would soon be noon, and his exciting extracurricular morning activities had definitely left him famished. Thankfully, Monday's round of depositions for his client weren't scheduled to begin until around three o'clock. That meant he had plenty of time to order room service for both of them.

Over lunch he would inform Carla he wanted her to move into the hotel with him during the remainder of his stay in Chicago.

When room service answered, he said, "I would like luncheon enough for two, please. A variety of your best sandwiches would be perfect. And please include an array of fresh fruit and a chilled bottle of Dom Pérignon. Yes, that will be all. Thank you."

Harold returned the receiver to the phone, suddenly aware that he'd never said "please" or "thank you" in a nonbusiness-related conversation in his life.

How ironic.

Carla allowed him to be his bad-boy self in the bedroom, yet she brought out the best in his character.

He was still mulling over the whole paradoxical Carla situation when a beep from his cell phone reminded him he still had a message waiting. It surprised him when he walked over and picked up the phone and saw who the message was from.

He'd expected Kate to hold out a few more days before she called him back. He'd known Kate would be stunned when Grace told her about his surprise—even a little angry at first. He was positive Kate knew what he was planning. Grace had been too nervous when he'd phoned her yesterday.

Harold listened to the message, then erased it.

So, Kate had some things to figure out, did she?

Poor sweet Kate.

As if there was any doubt about what she'd decide.

Kate would marry him because that's what respectable women like Kate did—they married respectable doctors, executives, and lawyers like him.

Respecting her wishes and giving Kate *total* privacy until he returned to Manhattan, however, was something he'd be damn well happy to do. Harold decided that as his head turned toward the sound of the still-running shower.

He tossed his cell phone on the sofa and strolled happily in the direction of the bathroom, hoping to find his new playmate still wet and soapy.

CHAPTER 12

Kate tiptoed out onto the back deck wearing nothing but her panties and Tony's NYPD sweatshirt. She lowered herself onto the lawn chair, pulled her knees to her chest, and took her first sip of coffee as the sun took its first peek over the top of Hunter Mountain.

She'd slipped out of bed, leaving Tony asleep, so she could have some time alone to prepare herself for the inevitable. She couldn't put off telling Tony about Harold's surprise wedding any longer.

It still seemed unbelievable that leaving on Tuesday had been delayed to leaving on Wednesday, and leaving on Wednesday and Thursday had been delayed until now. Five whole days were what she and Tony had spent together—a lifetime as far as Kate was concerned.

Except her old life refused to be ignored.

Manhattan was screaming her name.

Literally.

Alex was in a tizzy, because the agency handling the surrogate search had supposedly found a willing womb lender who met each and every one of Alex's qualifications. Poor Eve was having panic attacks again, because her Braveheart was going to be in New York next week to play in a folk music festival and wanted Eve to join him and twenty or thirty thousand other delighted folk music lovers for the big event.

There was also the new exhibit at the gallery that began on Saturday, displaying all of the fabulous new pieces Grace had acquired on her buying trip to Paris. As gallery manager, Kate needed to be there. She didn't take her responsibility to the gallery or to her grandmother lightly.

The time to return to the real world had arrived.

The burning question was whether she and Tony would be able to survive as a couple in that world?

Elbows propped on her knees, and both hands clasped around her cup, Kate pushed that thought aside and took another sip of hot coffee. She'd rather think instead about how wonderful each and every day she'd spent with Tony had been—and not just their incredible lovemaking.

They'd hiked.

They'd swum in the lake.

They'd even taken a picnic to the top of the mountain one afternoon, and she was sure they had given the birds and the bees plenty of new material to pass down to the next generation.

It seemed funny that she and Tony had been barely more than strangers only five days earlier, yet now there wasn't much they didn't know about each other.

That's mainly what had her so worried.

She knew that, above all else, Tony valued honesty.

He'd told her how disillusioned he'd been with Wall Street and the occasional shady dealings that his own ethics couldn't ignore. How it had been such an eye opener to see what money was really capable of doing to people. She also knew how happy he'd been since he joined the police force and that never once had he regretted his decision.

She knew all about his sisters, his nieces and nephews, and how devoted he was to his parents. He'd told her about the apartment building he'd renovated. About the teenage boy he'd taken under his wing, hoping to keep the kid out of trouble.

In the course of conversation over the last five days, she'd learned a million other things about him, too—from his favorite sports teams to the favorite stops he and his horse, Skyscraper, made on their daily patrol.

Her basic life story, of course, had also come up.

She'd told him how quirky her parents were, but how much she loved them anyway. About her grandmother's heartbreak over her father's choice of lifestyle. About her decision to stay in New York with Grace rather than return to California with her parents.

She'd also admitted that controversy had always been a problem for her, and that most of her life she'd gone along with what others expected rather than stand her ground and make her own decisions.

She'd enjoyed telling him everything about Alex and Eve, and how close the three of them had always been since the first day they found themselves sharing a dorm suite at Wells College. She'd also told him a secret she'd never even shared with Alex—about her dream of one day having a small gallery of her own.

Not a prestigious gallery like her grandmother's. Something more eclectic, showcasing unknown local artists and making art available to customers who couldn't necessarily afford prestigious top-dollar gallery prices.

Tony had surprised her when he asked what was keeping her from making that dream happen. She'd told him she'd let him know the answer to that question when she figured it out for herself.

Kate smiled, thinking how hard he'd laughed when she admitted she'd been fantasizing about him naked the first time she saw him in the park. She didn't laugh when he told her that his first thought when he saw her was that she was his destiny—and that had been before he saw the painting sitting beside her.

There were so many things she loved about him. But one of the things she loved about him most was that Tony didn't push her. He didn't try to steamroll over her. He always asked what *she* thought. Never just assumed she would politely go along with whatever he had on his schedule.

He simply allowed her to be her own person.

But will he forgive me when he finds out I wasn't completely truthful about having unfinished business with Harold?

When Tony walked out onto the deck, Kate knew it was time to find out.

"You're up early," he said, grinning a sleepy grin.

He was barefoot, bare-chested, and wearing the bottom half of the sweats she had taken from the foot of the bed. A sharp pain pierced her heart, wondering if she would ever get to see him when he'd just tumbled out of bed again.

"I made coffee," Kate said, tightening the grip on her

cup to keep her hands from shaking. "Want me to get you a cup?"

He yawned and stretched. "No, you stay where you are." He bent down and kissed the top of her head. "I'll grab a cup of coffee and be right back."

Madly love him.

Truly hope he understands.

Deeply regret I wasn't honest from the start.

———

There was something serious on Kate's mind.

Tony had known it the second he'd walked onto the deck.

There wasn't much of a mystery, of course, about what that something was.

Kate was going back to Manhattan that morning. If she'd decided she was also going back to Harold, it was the time for her to tell him.

But am I ready to hear what she has to say?

Tony took a cup from the overhead cabinet and poured himself a hot cup of coffee. He remained standing at the kitchen counter for a second, trying to pull himself together.

If she told him it had been fun, but that now she was ready to go back to the real world and her corporate attorney, his only consolation would be that the last five days had been the happiest time in his life. He never would have believed he could have fallen in love so deeply and so completely in such a short time.

But that was exactly what had happened.

With every look.

With every touch.

With every moment they'd spent together, Tony knew he loved Kate.

It was just that simple.

If the Saints in Heaven above really had brought them together, and if Harold really was history, he had no doubt the rest of his life could turn out to be even happier than the last five days.

A high-stakes crapshoot.

That's what he was facing.

But whatever Kate told him, one thing would remain constant. He loved this woman. And unless she looked him in the eye and told him she didn't feel the same way, their fate was sealed.

At least as far as he was concerned.

Tony took a deep breath and walked outside.

She was staring out over the lake, a melancholy look on her face. "Thank you for having me here this week," she said, looking over at him. "I really do love this place."

"It isn't the Hamptons," Tony said, "but I like it."

She flinched.

And Tony instantly hated himself.

Damn.

Harold obviously did have a place in the Hamptons.

"I'm sorry, Kate," he said. "That comment was uncalled for."

She looked back in his direction. "No, your comment was pretty appropriate, actually. I have something I need to tell you."

He started walking in her direction.

She pointed to a deck chair several feet away from her instead.

"Please, Tony, sit down for a second and let me say what I need to say."

Not a good sign.

Tony reluctantly lowered himself onto the chair.

The last thing he wanted to hear was what he expected Kate to tell him.

She looked directly at him. "It's about Harold."

Shit! Here it comes.

"Even though I told him the wedding was off, Harold doesn't think I'm serious."

So? To hell with Harold!

But Tony forced himself to stay calm.

He'd seen more than his share of egotistical assholes like Harold on Wall Street. Climbing over everyone else to get what they wanted. Assuming the size of their bank accounts meant they could have whomever and whatever they wanted whenever they wanted it. Harold didn't know it yet, but there was one dim-witted cop who wouldn't think twice about kicking his rich arrogant ass!

Then Kate got to the surprise-wedding attack.

As soon as he heard that missing piece of the puzzle, any doubt Tony had whatsoever about personally getting up in Harold's snotty grill disappeared completely.

"I hope you understand that I have to go to the Waldorf next week and tell Harold face-to-face that it is officially over between us," she said. "And I'm sorry I wasn't completely honest with you from the start. It was selfish of me, and I know that. But I simply refused to let Harold consume even one second of our time together."

Tony was only half listening.

His mind was still stuck on that jackass Harold.

He finally said, "I understand why you have to go to

the Waldorf, Kate. I even understand why you postponed telling me about the jerk's surprise wedding. Just as I hope you understand that I'll definitely be going to the Waldorf with you next Thursday."

She paled.

Then she jumped up from the lawn chair.

"Absolutely not!"

Kate hadn't meant to act so horrified when Tony suggested going to the Waldorf. Nor had she meant to snap at him like that. It just never crossed her mind that he would want to attend her final meeting with Harold, much less assume it would be okay with her if he tagged along.

The angry look on his face said he didn't care for her over-the-top reaction, either.

"I'm sorry," Kate said, "What I meant to say is, no, your coming with me isn't necessary." She spoke while she frantically wiped at the coffee she'd just spilled down the front of his NYPD sweatshirt when she jumped up from the lawn chair.

He didn't look appeased.

She tried again. "I need to face Harold by myself, for myself, Tony. After everything I've told you this week, surely you can understand why I need to do this alone."

The way he was gripping the arms of the deck chair said that he didn't.

"What I understand, Kate, is that this guy has bullied you from the first day he met you. He won't get that chance when I go with you."

When?

What had happened to the Tony she loved?

The Tony who didn't try to steamroll over her?

The Tony who let her be her own person?

I do want to be my own person.

If she let Tony push over her now, Kate knew she never would be.

She repeated slowly, "You are not going with me, Tony. I'm sorry, but you're not."

A muscle in his jaw twitched.

"Harold already has the cards stacked against you, Kate. It's going to be three against one when you get to the Waldorf. Harold. His mother. And your grandmother. Let me even the odds a little."

Kate shook her head. "I said no."

He got up from the deck chair and turned his back on her, leaning on the deck railing as he looked out over the lake.

Kate walked up and stood beside him.

He turned his head to look at her.

"I guess I am nothing but a dim-witted cop," he said. "It took me a few seconds, but I think I'm finally beginning to see the big picture."

"And what's that supposed to mean?" Kate said, reaching out to touch his arm.

He moved out of her reach. "You tell me, Kate. Where does this leave us *after* next Thursday? Is this the part where you tell me we need to keep our relationship under wraps for a while? See each other on the sly now and then if you can sneak away? Wait six months, even a year maybe before you do get around to taking the dim-witted cop home and formally introduce him to your high-society grandmother?"

Kate blanched.

But she intended to set him straight about Grace.

"Since you brought it up, yes, my grandmother is one of the main reasons I don't want you to go with me next Thursday."

"You're contradicting yourself, Kate," he said. "You say you can stand up to Harold now. But you still can't stand up to your grandmother? What happened to the new Kate you were telling me about? The Kate who's decided it's time to start making her own decisions?"

Kate was astonished.

"Ex-cuse me?" she shouted. "That's exactly what I'm doing, Tony. I'm making my *own* decision. And no, I'm not interested in handing Harold his ring, then turning to my grandmother and asking her if she'd like to meet the man I've been sleeping with for the last five days while Harold was away in Chicago."

"And I'm not interested in being your dirty little secret," Tony shouted right back.

Kate flew mad.

"Well, thank you so much for clearing that up for me!"

She turned around and stomped inside the cabin.

"Dammit, Kate, come back here."

Tony stomped inside right behind her.

She went up the spiral staircase.

He came up the spiral staircase.

Kate turned around and glared at him.

"Do you mind? I'd like to get dressed so I can do you a huge favor and get out of your cabin and out of your life."

"I'd prefer that you stayed *in* my life," he said. "You're the one who almost passed out at the thought of having to introduce a reject like me to your grandmother."

Kate grabbed her overnight case from the floor and pushed him out of the way.

She marched back down the stairs.

He followed right behind her.

She stomped into the bathroom.

He stopped at the door.

"I. Did. Not. Almost. Pass. Out," she said, each word emphasizing the personal items she was slamming into her case. "If you'd turn off the damn testosterone clouding your brain at the moment, you'd realize I wanted my grandmother to like you for yourself, rather than forever think of you as the man who stole me away from *her* idea of the perfect husband! Of course, that was what I wanted five minutes ago when I thought we had a future together."

Tony exploded. "So that's your decision, Kate? You're saying we don't have a future together?"

"No, you said that," Kate said. "A *dirty* little future is how I think you put it."

A vein popped out on his forehead.

Kate didn't care.

She stormed back up to the loft.

He was smart enough not to follow.

She had her clothes on and her things packed in five minutes flat. When she came back downstairs, he was standing with his arm propped against the mantel of the fireplace. The same fireplace they never got to snuggle up in front of, and now probably never would.

His expression was stern when he said, "Don't do this, Kate. Don't walk out of here like the last five days haven't meant anything to you."

"You know how much these last five days have meant to me, Tony," Kate said.

He said, "I thought I did. Now, I'm not so sure."

Kate's heart sank.

"Remember what you told me? About your first thought when you saw me standing in the park that day?"

Tony said, "I thought—this woman is my destiny."

"What's it going to take for you to believe that, Tony? Me standing in the park beside the Blessed Virgin again? Do you even want me wearing the wedding dress you bought me, too?"

They looked at each other for a long time.

When he still didn't answer, Kate walked out the door.

Stop me. God, please stop me!

He didn't.

Kate was crying by the time she made it to the SUV.

She tossed her things in the back, slid behind the wheel, put the car in reverse, and turned the SUV around. She kept looking in the rearview mirror as she drove out of the clearing.

He never even came to the door.

By the time she made it to the end of the gravel road, she was making those obnoxious donkey-braying sounds Alex always hated. Kate glanced at the gate as she turned onto the main road.

The sign broke her heart.

Her trail with Tony had definitely come to an end.

Sadly, a final and bitter end.

Tony wasn't sure how long he remained standing at the fireplace. Ten minutes? Maybe even longer. He'd been too numb to move.

Maybe his testosterone *had* kicked into high gear, clouding his judgment about the situation. But how did Kate expect him to react? The thought of her facing Harold's potential wrath alone, not to mention the scorn of the two women who were in favor of the wedding, made Tony's blood boil.

His job was to protect and serve, dammit!

What kind of man would he be, if he didn't want to protect the woman he loved?

Love.

One hundred percent proof that misery loves company.

They'd spent five wonderful uninterrupted days together with no one else to consider and no decisions to make.

That was the problem.

He'd been caught up in the fantasy that an uptown girl like her would settle for a dim-witted cop from Queens.

Stupid. Stupid. Stupid.

Or was it?

Hope grabbed Tony by the seat of his pants and sent him hurrying to the door at the sound of tires crunching to a stop in the gravel driveway. Despair kicked him in the groin when he walked out on the front deck and saw who it was.

"You're in deep shit with your Mama for not calling her all week, buddy." Joe pushed his hat back off his forehead and leaned against his patrol car with a grin. "Mama Gina's exact words were 'don't make me come up there'."

Tony shook his head disgustedly.

"Sorry she bothered you, Joe. My mother thinks because I'm a cop, she has a hot line to every police station in the state of New York."

Joe laughed. "She thinks your future bride is up here with you, too," he said. "Mama Gina's exact words on that subject were 'don't screw it up.'"

Too late.

Tony walked back inside after Joe left, still shaking his head. He'd do better than head to town to call his mother. He'd show up at the Friday night family dinner.

After he gave Mama a stern lecture about using law enforcement as her personal messenger service, he'd set her straight that she wasn't going to be getting a daughter-in-law anytime soon.

Forgetaboutit already!

Besides, spending the rest of the weekend at the cabin now, wasn't even an option.

Hell, he'd probably sell the damn place as soon as possible. How could he not? He'd never be able to come to Trail's End again without the memory of the five days he'd spent with Kate being there to haunt him.

Tony headed for the stairs to go pack his things.

Another low blow hit him when he reached the loft.

Kate's check for the dress was lying on the bed.

It's final.

She's made her own decision.

He'd do them both a favor and leave it that way.

CHAPTER 13

Harold stroked Carla's hair as they lay in bed on Friday morning, her head resting comfortably against his shoulder. Having Carla with him the entire week had been spectacular.

They'd dined in all the best restaurants. He'd taken her shopping in all the best shops. He'd even taken her to a production of *Chicago*, an appropriate play to see under the circumstances, even if he had to say so himself.

Once he had Kate settled and brought Carla to New York, he'd show Miss Matthews the magic of Broadway.

Harold frowned.

Kate.

Damn.

He didn't want to think about Kate at the moment.

He didn't want to admit he was suddenly developing a goddamn conscience, either. His father's first rule of survival had been *never* develop a conscience.

He was a survivor, dammit!

He was Harold Trent Wellington.

There was no room for a conscience in his life.

Not if he wanted it all.

One of the things he definitely wanted snuggled closer against him, and Harold said, "I have a surprise for you this morning."

"Let me guess what it is." Carla lifted the sheet to peek under the covers.

"Dammit, I'm being serious, Carla." He shifted their positions and pulled himself up in bed.

She rolled over on her side, looking at him.

"You're always serious, Harry. It's boring."

"I can be spontaneous," he said, still pouting a little. "Like the surprise I have for you this morning. I've arranged for us to have a private couple's massage in the spa here in the hotel."

"Did you log it into your Palm Pilot?"

"Well, yes, dammit," Harold said. "But the idea was spontaneous when I had it yesterday."

He got out of bed and jerked on his boxers.

The fact that he was upset didn't seem to bother her.

She stretched languorously, instead.

"I've never had a professional massage," she said, "but I've given a few in my day."

"That *isn't* funny."

"Oh, stop being such a big baby," she said. "If I didn't know better, I'd think you were jealous of the men in my past."

Damn.

I am jealous.

He refused to admit it.

"You can stay here making up ridiculous accusations if you want," Harold told her curtly. "I'm going to shower; and then I'm going to the spa and enjoy my massage."

He paused at the bathroom door and chanced a look back over his shoulder. She'd rolled over in the bed so her back was to him, obviously going back to sleep without another thought that he might be upset.

Fine!

There was just no impressing this woman.

Even worse was the fact that he wanted to impress her.

It just didn't make any damn sense.

Harold kicked his boxers across the bathroom, turned on the shower, and adjusted the water. He grabbed the shampoo, stepped under the hot spray, and gave his head a good scrubbing—hoping it might stimulate some of the sense that seemed to be leaking out of his ears.

Maybe it was time to send Carla packing, he decided, her blackmail photos be damned. After all, he was *the* master—when it came to damage control. Plus, he had all the money he needed and all the power it required to put a spin on the story if she did follow through with her threat.

Photos of important people were doctored all the time, and everyone knew it. Who were people going to believe? Him, a respected Manhattan attorney? Or the woman he would expose for trying to blackmail him into marrying her?

Harold smiled.

He was definitely going to send Carla packing.

Let her throw away the chance of a lifetime.

Let her . . .

Harold jumped, startled when the shower door opened. Slender arms slid around his waist, then lower.

The idea of sending Carla packing went "poof."

Except packing for her trip to New York City.

Alex handed the tissue box to Eve who handed the tissue box to Kate. Kate grabbed a whole fistful of tissues. This was not a one-tissue sobfest. It was the first time she'd really let herself break down, except for those first few minutes after she left the cabin.

She'd made it back to the city around noon, turned in the rental car, and grabbed a taxi home, staying only long enough to shower and change. Eve had sensed she wasn't ready to talk about what had happened, and being the sweetie that Eve was, she hadn't pressed Kate for details.

When she'd reached the gallery, Grace had sensed the same thing. Kate and her grandmother had spent the remainder of the day getting ready for the exhibition, pretending everything was normal, and dancing around each other with polite conversation.

In other words, Kate had been reminded real quick how little her life had changed.

Except for her broken heart.

Now, it was Friday night all over again. Alex had stopped for their usual takeout from Mr. Woo's. Her two best friends were sitting beside her lending their support. And she was determined to cry Tony Petrocelli right out of her system.

Kate blew her nose.

Several times.

"And then what happened?" Alex asked.

"I reminded him that he thought I was his destiny the second he saw me in the park. And I asked him what it would take for him to believe it. I asked him if he needed to find me standing in the park beside the Blessed Virgin again, even wearing the wedding dress he bought me."

"And you do have the painting and the dress," Eve mentioned.

Kate and Alex both looked at her.

"Oh, another metaphor thingy," Eve said. "Got it."

Alex said, "And what did Tony say?"

"Not one word," Kate said. "That's when I left."

Alex sighed. "You don't want to hear this, Kate, but I can understand why Tony didn't want you to face Harold alone. You'd just finished telling him what an ass Harold is. How did you expect him to react?"

"My point exactly," Kate said. "And that's just what I *don't* need. Tony storming in, grabbing Harold by one of his three-hundred-dollar silk ties, and dragging him all the way to the freaking Conrad Suite to punch him out. No, Alex. I don't think so."

"Tony's an officer of the law," Alex said. "I'm sure he has more control over his actions than that."

"You didn't see the way he was gripping the arms of that deck chair," Kate said.

"Still . . ." Alex began.

"Don't confuse me, Alex," Kate said. "I gave Tony every opportunity before I walked out that door to tell me what he should have told me. He should have told me that he cared enough about me to respect my decision and let me settle things with Harold in my own way."

"*And* that he didn't mind being your dirty little secret for as long as you wanted?"

Kate blew her nose. "He never was my dirty little secret. He was the man I wanted to spend the rest of my life with. *Was* being the operative word."

"Yup, that's how love is," Alex said. "Fall in love in five days. Fall out of love in five minutes."

"Dammit, you know I still love him."

"*My* point exactly," Alex said. She leaned over and picked up the phone and handed it to Kate. "Do something about it."

Kate refused to take it. "I told you. Tony threw his cell phone in the lake."

"I'll bet you five hundred dollars Tony didn't stay at the cabin after you left," Alex said. She kept holding the phone out for Kate to take.

Kate shook her head. "No. I'm not calling him. Not until I settle things with Harold. If I call him now, we'll only end up in the same argument we had before I left."

Alex put the phone down. "You're probably right."

Kate and Eve both sent Alex surprised looks.

"Hey, it happens," Alex said. "I do agree with people on rare occasions." She paused for a second, then reached for the phone and picked it up again. "You said Grace told you she'd accept your decision, whether she agreed with it or not. So, settle things with Harold right now, Kate. Call the bastard. Put an end to his silly surprise wedding, and that'll solve everybody's problem. Then I'll run downstairs and hail you a taxi for your trip to Queens."

"No," Kate said. "I want to tell Harold face-to-face that I'm not going to marry him. And I want everyone to meet at the Waldorf just like Harold is planning. I want Gram and Margaret both to be there when I apologize."

Alex yelled, "Apologize!" and Eve jumped.

"Yes, apologize," Kate said. "I'm not a victim in this situation. I'm a cocontributor. I owe all three of them a huge apology for sitting there like some experiment in artificial intelligence and accepting Harold's proposal. I should have turned him down that night. Harold is a first-class ass, yes. But I was a first-class ass in accepting his proposal when I knew I didn't love him. I've hurt everyone involved. I need to take responsibility for it."

Kate blew her nose again.

Eve reached out and patted Kate's hand.

Alex only frowned.

"I really don't like you all grown-up, Kate."

"Stop frowning, Alex," Kate said. "I doubt wrinkled is what you want to be if you ever decide to grow up."

"Enough," Mario said, looking around the table. He motioned to Tony who was sitting three seats away and said, "Come with me."

"Gladly," Tony said as he got up from his chair.

But not loud enough for his mother to hear him.

His stern lecture for Mama had turned into a stern lecture *from* Mama. About why he'd messed up his golden opportunity to prove to Kate that their destiny was written in the stars—and that their destined marriage was in the immediate future.

When his sisters had jumped in to voice their opinions on what he should do about Kate, his father had taken mercy on him and offered him a way out of what was becoming an extremely uncomfortable conversation.

They left the family dinner table and the usual commotion behind. Tony followed his father up the back stairs into the apartment he'd grown up in. They passed through the kitchen, then up another flight of stairs that would take them to the roof of the building.

The roof had been where he and his sisters had played

when they were children. It was where his father often sneaked away now for a little peace and quiet.

His father pushed the door open and motioned Tony through. But when he closed the door, he grabbed a wooden handle from an old broom that was propped up beside the door. He dropped the handle into place—it across the door, both ends of the handle resting on two large hooks—and Tony laughed.

"So that's what you wanted with those old hooks I took down at my apartment building and was going to throw away."

Mario tapped his finger against his forehead. "A fool, your papa isn't," he said. "You want privacy in this family? You find a way to get privacy in this family."

Tony laughed again, then walked over and plopped down onto one of the aluminum folding chairs that were scattered around the roof. He shook his head when he saw why his father had suddenly taken such an interest in one of Mama's flower boxes.

Mario dragged a chair up beside him, dusting dirt from the large plastic baggy he'd hidden and buried in the soil. He pulled his pipe out first, then his can of tobacco.

"You think *I* just got an ass chewing?" Tony said. "You won't have an ass left if Mama catches you smoking again."

Mario tamped the pipe full, fumbled in the baggie, and pulled out a lighter. He waited until he took a few deep draws from his pipe before he said, "Mama knows about the smoking. She pretends she doesn't know, so I won't smoke in the house. I pretend I don't know she knows, so I can get away with it a little bit longer."

"I guess that's what thirty-seven years of marriage gets you, isn't it?" Tony said. "Compromise."

Mario glanced at him through the haze of blue smoke.

"Marriage gets you a lot more than just compromise," he said. "When you find the woman you love, you think your heart has no room for anyone else. But then she gives you the children the two of you can love together, and your heart swells to include them. Then your children give you the grandchildren who fill your heart with more love than you ever believed possible. Add all that up, and what you have is a lifetime of happiness."

Tony frowned. "I'm not in the mood to talk about a lifetime of happiness right now, Papa. I don't think that kind of happiness is ever going to be in my future."

"Maybe you should tell me about it," Mario said.

After Tony finished a rundown of the situation and his argument with Kate, he looked at his father and said, "So? What's your opinion about the whole situation?"

Mario said, "I think it's a blessing you're rid of this woman."

Huh? "What?"

"She's probably changed her mind about the attorney," Mario said. "He's a big important man, he has big money. He can offer her a big fancy life. We're simple people, Tony. She wouldn't fit in with our family."

"But that's just it, Papa," Tony argued, "Kate isn't like that at all. She's one of the most down-to-earth people you could ever meet. We might not have a future together, but she won't marry Harold. She won't change her mind about that."

"I don't know," Mario said. "Sounds like she was having second thoughts to me. If not, why didn't she let you go with her? Let you slay all those dragons in her path?

Show everyone concerned that you are the big man in her life now?"

Tony didn't answer—but he knew the answer.

Excess testosterone.

Too much testosterone obviously is hereditary.

"If you ask me," Mario said, "I think she was just stringing you along."

"That's ridiculous," Tony said, frowning at his father. "She didn't have to come to the cabin at all, Papa. She could have put the check in the mail. Or she could have done nothing at all. Not so much as even a thank-you note is what she could have done, Papa."

Mario shrugged, then took another draw on his pipe. "She still sounds like a user to me," he said. "In the future I'd watch out for women who just show up and move in with you for five days."

"She did not just show up and move in with me!" Tony was getting angrier by the minute. "Kate never would have stayed at all if I hadn't practically begged her to stay."

Mario frowned. "You practically begged her to stay? Why did you do a stupid thing like that?"

Tony launched himself out of the chair before he said something smart to his father that he'd regret later. He walked up to the concrete barrier around the roof, braced both hands on the concrete, and stood looking out over the street below.

With his back still to his father, he finally said, "I asked Kate to stay because I'm crazy about her, Papa. Hell, I'm past crazy about her. I love her."

When he turned back around his father was smiling.

Tony pointed a finger at him. "Why you old fox! You knew exactly what you were doing. Admit it."

Mario tapped out the ashes from his pipe onto the concrete floor, then got up from his chair and walked over to where Tony was standing. He slid the baggie back into its hiding place in the flower box next to Tony and put his arm around his only son. They both stood there for a few minutes, surveying the neighborhood they both loved from their lofty position on the roof.

Mario said, "If you love something, son, set it free. If it comes back to you, it's yours. But if it doesn't come back to you . . ."

"It never was," Tony said, and sighed.

"No," Mario said, "if Kate doesn't come back, you go to Manhattan and get her. *After* you give her the freedom to do what she needs to do."

Harold looked around the hotel suite, satisfied that everything was perfect. He'd decided they would dine in tonight, skip the hassle of dressing formally and making an appearance in some fancy restaurant in town.

They'd started the morning off with a relaxing massage. He thought Carla might enjoy ending the evening on a relaxing note with no specific schedule.

No specific schedule.

A first for him.

But didn't everything have a first time?

Room service had already delivered a feast fit for a king and his queen—lobster and filet mignon, the perfect combination. All of the other bases were also covered.

Champagne, chilled and waiting. Lights, dim and romantic. Billie Holliday singing softly in the background.

The only thing missing was his guest of honor.

She'd told him she'd be back at the hotel by seven, that
she had errands to run she couldn't put off. Harold
glanced at his watch, becoming a little concerned that it
was already half past seven and Carla still hadn't arrived.

Friday night traffic, most likely, he decided, but he
glanced at the bedside phone just in case. No blinking
light, indicating a message. He even checked his cell
phone. No message there, either.

For lack of anything else to do, he walked back over to
the room service cart and adjusted the crisp linen napkin,
making sure the long blue velvet box was hidden completely. The late Audrey Hepburn had nothing on Carla
when it came to a neck made to wear pearls.

Carla having nothing on *but* pearls?

That wasn't a bad idea, either.

Harold breathed a sigh of relief when he finally heard
the click of the electronic lock. He walked toward the
door and smiled when she walked into the room.

She didn't smile back.

"Is something wrong?"

She looked at him for a long time.

Then she fished into her purse and tossed a DVD disc
on the bed. "You're off the hook, Harry," she said. "I can't
blackmail you."

What?

Was she nuts?

Of course, she was going to blackmail him.

It was part of his fucking master plan!

"Don't be ridiculous," Harold said. He walked over to

the bed, picked up the disc, and stuffed it back into her purse. "You're going to blackmail me, and that's final."

"You're not listening, Harry," she said. "All that crap I told you about wanting respectability? Well, that's exactly what it was, just a bunch of crap. I was after your money, that's all, and I wasn't going to risk the chance of being arrested for extortion. I was going to marry you. And then in a few months I was going to divorce you and take you for every penny I could get. I just never expected that I would . . . I would . . . I would like you, dammit."

"You like me?" Harold was surprised.

He wasn't sure if anyone actually *liked* him.

"Believe me," she said, "liking you is a big shocker for me, too. You're not that easy to like."

"My mother adores me," Harold informed her.

"I wouldn't be too smug about that," she said. "I'm sure even your mother has her moments."

She turned and headed for the door.

"Carla, wait," Harold said. "We can still work this out."

She whirled back around. "Are you deaf, Harry? This whole game we've been playing is over. I don't want to marry a man I have to blackmail into marrying me. Especially if I like him too much to swindle him out of his money."

"But that's the beauty of this whole situation," Harold said, grinning from ear to ear. "I lied to you, too. I wasn't going to marry you at all. I'm actually getting married next Thursday. To my fiancée back in Manhattan."

The color drained from her face.

It came rushing back—red and angry.

"And what were you going to do with me?" Carla demanded, hands on her hips now. "The plane ticket to New York? The key you've already given me to the apartment I'm supposed to move into in a few weeks? Were those arrangements nothing but lies, too?"

Harold walked over and took both of Carla's hands.

"You're going to be so happy when I tell you this," he said in a cheerful singsong voice. "The ticket, the apartment, everything I've told you about your allowance, your charge cards, everything. All of that is absolutely one hundred percent true. I've planned for you to come to New York from the very beginning. Just not as my wife. As my . . ."

"Mistress?" Carla finished for him.

"Yes!" Harold said, delighted that she'd finally caught on. "See? Everything is going to work out fine. You can be my full-time mistress. And I'll give you anything you want whenever you want it."

Carla jerked her hands from his.

The look in her dark blue eyes turned icy.

Harold shivered for a second.

"You'll give me anything I want?" she asked.

"Anything," Harold assured her.

"Then lose my number, Harry. I'm done here."

She turned around and headed for the door.

She stopped long enough to take the disc from her purse and toss it back on the bed again. When she opened the door, she looked back at him one last time.

"Don't worry, that disc is the only other copy," she said. "I only made one copy for me and one copy for you. Keep your copy for those nights when you're bored with your respectable life and your respectable wife, Harry. Give my copy to the bride as a wedding present from the woman who is *not* interested in becoming your mistress. I'm sure she'll be thrilled to add the pictures to your wedding album."

Carla slammed the door.

Harold slumped down on the edge of the bed, stunned. "What the hell just happened?" he yelled out.

None of his yes-men were there to give him an answer.

CHAPTER 14

—◦—

Alex held her hand out.

Eve placed her hand on top of Alex's.

Kate placed her hand on top of Eve's.

"We can do this!" they said in unison.

It was a ritual they'd started back in college. Except back in college they'd only been facing final exams. The grown-up stakes were higher. They were going their separate ways later today—facing much more serious problems than final exams.

Alex had even taken the day off—completely unheard of for her. Her usual nerves of steel had begun to crumble over John's insistence that he go ahead and sign papers with the agency, now that a proper surrogate had been found.

Eve was a nervous wreck. But she was also fully determined not to let her crowd phobia keep her from meeting her Knight in Cyber Armor at the River-to-River Folk Music Festival at South Street Seaport.

As for Kate?

It was also the day of Harold's big surprise afternoon

tea at the Waldorf. As eager as Kate was to get the dreaded experience behind her, facing Margaret and knowing she was going to disappoint Harold's mother was not something she was looking forward to doing.

At least Grace already expected what was coming.

Her grandmother had only asked Kate about the bridal suit once more. When Kate told her she'd take care of the bridal suit herself, Grace had dropped the subject.

The day of reckoning had arrived.

For her, for Alex, and for Eve.

It had been Alex's idea to hold an emergency breakfast meeting so they could all gather strength from each other. She'd arrived at the apartment bearing what she called "brain food"—sinful chocolate éclairs and rich Starbucks coffee. The three of them were sitting around Kate's kitchen table now, stimulating their systems with total caffeine overload.

Kate licked the chocolate from her fingers, looked at Alex, and said, "You really are going to let a surrogate have John's child?"

"Yes," Alex said without hesitation. "Unless time stands still and the entire city of New York grinds to a screeching halt, I'm going to stand by silently when John signs the papers with the surrogate agency this afternoon. I love John too much to lose him. And I want my promotion too much to take time off to have a baby just because he can't wait a few more years."

"Then I'll support you any way I can," Kate said. "As long as it goes on record that I do *not* agree with your decision, and never have."

"Me, too," Eve spoke up.

"Thank you both," Alex said, looking from one to the

other. "For your support. And for realizing this is my decision to make, whether the two of you agree with it or not."

"Which brings us to my decision," Kate said, "which I also hope you, Alex, will respect as much as I respect your decision. I've decided *not* to pursue a relationship with Tony."

"Now, dammit, Kate," Alex began, but Kate held her hand up.

"He's had five whole days to call me since I left the cabin. Not once has he dialed my number. Just like he had the opportunity to say something before I walked out, and he had the opportunity to stop me from leaving before I drove away. He didn't do any of those things. Only a fool wouldn't be able to see that he's just not interested."

"Or, that he's just giving you the space you asked for," Alex said, "so you can finalize things with Harold."

"You don't have to agree with my decision, Alex," Kate said, "just like I don't have to agree with yours. But as far as I'm concerned the Tony subject is closed. Forever."

Kate dismissed Alex and looked over at Eve. "How about you, sweetie? Are you sure you're going to be okay today?"

Eve nodded.

"You'll be fine," Alex assured her. "Just remember the trick I taught you."

"It's impossible to think about two things at once," Eve recited on cue.

Alex nodded. "Take a taxi to South Street Seaport. Hop out of the taxi when you arrive at the restaurant where you're going to meet him. Grab George by the hand and don't let go. Then, focus on him, just him, and nothing but him. Got it?"

Eve nodded.

But she took a deep breath, and said, "Only I've decided not to take a taxi. I'm going to be brave and ride the subway instead."

Alex looked at Kate.

Kate looked at Alex.

"You might want to rethink that, Eve," Alex began, but Eve shook her head, sending her springy auburn curls flying.

"No," Eve said. "If I take a taxi I have a greater chance of starting to panic the second I get there. If I take the subway, I'll be forced to pull myself together before I get to the restaurant."

"Well, listen to you, Eve," Alex said, smiling. "I have to say I'm extremely impressed that you've thought this out all by yourself."

Eve smiled back, obviously pleased with Alex's praise.

"Still," Alex said, as only Alex would, "it might not hurt to be honest with the guy when you do get there. Tell George the truth. Tell him you've had some social anxiety problems lately, and . . ."

"No," Eve said again, and with just as much authority. "I think George really could be the one, Alex. I'm not going to lay a ton of baggage at his feet before he even has the opportunity to get to know me."

"I agree with you, Eve," Kate said, before Alex had a chance to keep chipping away at Eve's confidence.

She sent Alex a stern look.

Alex took the hint.

She got up from the kitchen table to leave.

But she looked at Kate in a funny way for a second.

"What?" Kate asked.

"Have you seen my Kate Spade bag?" Alex wanted to know. "The zebra one? I know it's silly, but I've always thought of it as my good luck charm. I can't find it, and I want to carry it today."

"Try the hall closet," Kate said. "Wasn't that where you were keeping most of your things?"

"Good idea," Alex said.

She hugged them both and hurried off.

When she left the kitchen, Eve leaned over to Kate and whispered, "But isn't it bad luck to be superstitious?"

"Eve," Kate said patiently, "think that question over very slowly."

"Oh," Eve said after a few seconds.

"Found it," Alex yelled from the hallway.

When the door slammed, Kate let out a deep sigh.

August 14.

She wasn't sure why, but something told Kate it would be a day none of them would soon forget.

Tony had actually been relieved when he received his work schedule when he returned from vacation on Monday, and saw he would be working second shift on Thursday. Being confined to Central Park on duty meant he couldn't pull any last-minute dumb-ass stunts and show up at the Waldorf to kick Harold's ass.

At least verbally.

Whether Kate approved or not.

He'd almost called her more times than he could count

over the last five days, but he'd kept himself from making that mistake. Besides, calling before her big breakup date with Harold would only lead them into another argument about the same damn thing.

He still believed she should have let him go with her.

Not to embarrass Kate.

Not to make her grandmother hate him.

Not because he was afraid Kate would change her mind.

She should have let him go with her because, to him, denying him that privilege was the same thing as saying *I'm not exactly sure where you fit into my life yet.*

That's why he'd decided not to follow his father's advice. He wasn't going to call Kate later tonight. He wasn't going to call Kate at all. If he ever talked to Kate Anderson again, it would be because she *had* figured out where he *did* fit into her life and had come looking for *him*.

Verdict in.

Case closed.

Tony tossed his trash bag into the can at the side of his apartment building and slammed the lid soundly to make sure it was in place. When he turned back around, he found Joey standing behind him.

Joey shoved the basketball at him.

Tony caught it with ease.

"Wanna play a little one-on-one?"

Hell, why not?

It was still early.

He didn't report for duty until three that afternoon.

Which happens to be the exact time Kate will be sitting down to tea at the Waldorf with asshole Harold.

Tony pushed that thorn-in-his-side thought aside.

"Sure, I'm up for some one-on-one," Tony said. "If

you're up for getting your scrawny little butt kicked this early in the morning."

Joey grinned. "You're not going to kick my scrawny little butt today, old man. I've been practicing."

"Bring it," Tony said.

They headed for the new basketball court he'd had put in at the back of the building—the one that had been used practically nonstop by every kid in the neighborhood almost before the concrete had time to set up.

"Ready?" Joey asked when they reached the court.

Tony nodded. "I'll even let you go first."

Joey did a few fancy dribbles, keeping his distance.

He charged forward for the layup.

They both jumped at the same time.

Tony missed the block.

Joey made the basket.

"I'm bad. Oh, yeah. I'm bad," Joey chanted, strutting around the court, flapping his arms and doing a poor imitation of a chicken.

"Lucky shot," Tony told him.

Joey passed him the ball.

Tony dribbled back to midcourt.

Just before the ball left his hands, Joey said, "I heard you screwed things up with the blonde."

Tony missed the shot.

"Thanks," he said, glaring in Joey's direction. "And you heard wrong. I didn't screw things up. *She* did."

Joey shrugged, then went to retrieve the ball.

He did more of his fancy dribbling, first around one leg, then around the other. "So? The blonde made a mistake. So what? Mistakes are only lessons in life. Right?"

"Are we going to play ball?" Tony barked. "Or are you more interested in quoting Dr. Phil this morning?"

"I wasn't quoting Dr. Phil," Joey said with a grin. "I was quoting you."

Joey broke for the goal before Tony could block him.

He grinned at Tony when the ball went through the net.

"See? I told you I've been practicing."

If Tony hadn't been in such a foul mood, the proud look on the kid's face would have made him smile. Tony did smile—but only when Joey wasn't looking.

"You've been practicing, all right," Tony said. "Practicing on how to keep your opponent's mind off the game so you can cheat and win."

"Back to the blonde," Joey said, spinning the ball around on one finger—proving he'd been practicing more than just his dribbling and his layups. "I was hoping I could get some tips from you about chicks. But man, maybe you should be getting some tips from me. I can't believe you had her up at that cabin all alone and still screwed it up."

He tossed Tony the ball.

Tony missed the shot.

"Man, your game is way off today," Joey said, grinning at him.

More than my game's off, you little shit.

His whole life was off.

It had been since the day he met Kate.

But who am I kidding?

Hell yes, I'll call her tonight.

No.

He *would* take his father's advice.

He'd show up at her Manhattan apartment.

Just as soon as he got off duty.

He'd throw Kate over his shoulder—if he had to.

Then he'd take Kate home to Queens.

With him.

Where, dammit, she belongs.

—————

"Thank you," Harold said, and handed his beverage glass to the pretty flight attendant.

"Why, you're very welcome, Mr. Wellington," she said with a great deal of surprise. "Thank *you.*"

Harold looked at her a little more closely.

He grimaced when he finally recognized her.

He'd given the young woman a hard time on his flight going to Chicago a few weeks ago, over something so insignificant he couldn't even remember what it was. She'd walked to the front of the first-class cabin area, but she kept looking back at him while she whispered something behind her hand to another pretty flight attendant.

Jesus.

What had he been thinking?

She was barely more than a kid, twenty-five tops. Blond and cute in that girl-next-door sort of way. Why hadn't he noticed she was just a kid before? Just a young kid trying to do her job with as little hassle as possible.

Harold motioned for her.

Her expression said she was already mentally preparing herself for the worst as she walked in his direction. He used to enjoy seeing that tentative look on people's faces. It made him feel important.

At the moment, all he felt was ashamed.

She bent down when she stopped beside his seat.

"We should be landing at JFK in about fifteen minutes, Mr. Wellington. Is there anything else I can do for you?"

"Yes," Harold said, looking up at her. "I hope you can accept my apology for being so rude to you a few weeks ago. My behavior was totally unacceptable. I deeply apologize."

She smiled, dimples flashing. "Oh, don't you worry about it, Mr. Wellington." She patted him on the arm. "Everyone has an off day now and then."

A bell sounded.

She hurried off to assist someone behind him.

An off day?

How about an off life?

That's what his entire life had been—way off.

It was a sobering experience to wake up screaming and realize you weren't asleep—realize that you'd always been one of those people who brightened up a room only if you *left* it.

He'd certainly been a chip off the old block, all right. He'd been exactly the type of son his dear old dad had always wanted. Except lately, thoughts of his father made him incredibly sad.

Poor self-centered Dad.

What a bitter, wasted life.

Funny, that it had taken Carla walking out on him before he finally started seeing himself through everyone else's eyes. Not that it had done him any good where Carla was concerned.

He'd tried to call her cell phone repeatedly, but to no avail. When he'd finally realized she never intended to answer his call or call him back, he'd also realized he didn't know a thing about her.

He'd never even asked.

Not where she lived.

Not if she had family in Chicago.

Not who her friends were.

Nothing.

It simply hadn't mattered to him.

He'd logged Carla's life right into his Palm Pilot like he did everything else, assuming because of his money and his power she would follow right along with his schedule like everyone else around him had always done.

Biggest mistake of my life.

He'd also thought of contacting the desk clerk, seeing what information he could get out of the clerk, but he'd eventually decided against it. Besides, what was the point? Carla had made it perfectly clear she had no interest whatsoever in becoming his mistress.

Plus, he already had a fiancée.

The fiancée who was going to become his wife that afternoon.

Kate.

Harold leaned his head back against the seat, thinking that at least maybe he would be a better husband to Kate now that he'd had a complete attitude adjustment. He didn't love Kate, but he would be good to her.

He knew she didn't love him, either, but they'd talked about the whole "love" dilemma before he ever proposed to her. They were both big skeptics when it came to love. Which was why they'd both agreed they were a compatible life match.

Compatible life match.

Something Carla definitely wasn't.

Men like him married well-bred women like Kate.

Plus, I could never disappoint Mother.

His mother adored Kate.

So, he and Kate would be married that afternoon.

He'd put Kate on a pedestal where a wife belonged.

He'd give Kate everything she ever wanted.

As for him?

Sadly, he'd spend the rest of his life aching and long-ing for Carla.

Kate had dressed as if she were going to a wedding—just not her own. Afternoon tea at the Cocktail Terrace called for dressy attire—casual dressy or better.

She'd chosen a pale yellow dress, simple but elegant. She was also wearing the only pair of Manolos she owned. The open-toed d'Orsay pumps with a three-and-a-half-inch heel were the same color as the dress. The shoes had been a birthday present from Alex, who claimed by the time you reached thirty, every woman should have at least one pair of five-hundred-dollar shoes in her closet.

Transportation to the Waldorf for Margaret and her grandmother had been provided by Harold's driver, but Kate had declined that invitation. She'd taken a taxi instead.

This was not a day for polite conversation.

Her goal was to say what she had to say.

Then she intended to leave as quickly as possible.

With that thought in mind, Kate took Harold's en-gagement ring out of her purse. She slipped it on her fin-ger for easy access, then walked up to the hostess with a forced smile on her face.

"The Wellington table, please."

She followed the hostess into the dining area and looked across the room when the hostess pointed in that direction. Margaret and Grace were already seated at the table, looking exactly like what they were—two extremely attractive well-dressed women enjoying each other's company and the formality of sitting down for afternoon tea.

If she aged as well as either of them, Kate would be happy.

Margaret's beauty in particular had always left Kate in awe—her natural blond coloring, her gentle ways. She'd asked Margaret once why she'd never remarried after Harold's father died. She'd known the reason couldn't have been for lack of interest. They were rarely out together that Kate didn't notice men Margaret's age and even younger openly admiring her.

Margaret's reply had been "one husband was enough for me." At the time Kate had taken the remark as a tribute to her late husband. In retrospect, she wondered if Margaret had meant it that way.

Kate continued making her way across the room, but winced when she noticed two large elegantly wrapped presents sitting on the floor beside Margaret's chair. Parting gifts for the happy couple, no doubt. Margaret was thoughtful that way.

"Here is our girl now," Margaret said, when Kate walked up to the table. She turned her smooth cheek up for Kate to kiss.

Kate kissed Margaret fondly, then repeated the same gesture for her grandmother.

Her worry about polite conversation, however, was unfounded. She'd no sooner seated herself at the table when she saw Harold heading across the room in their direction.

Only something was wrong.

Harold usually commanded a room.

Today he looked subdued—almost humble.

Harold humble?

That was a laugh.

Unless.

Unless her grandmother had felt so guilty, she'd finally called Harold to warn him there wasn't going to be a wedding. Or, he'd simply figured it out for himself. After all, they hadn't spoken directly to each other since their don't-ask-don't-tell fight on the phone.

The thought that Harold knew she'd been serious about calling off the wedding was a relief in one way, yet it scared her in another. If Harold already knew she wasn't going to marry him, that meant he'd had plenty of time to come up with a dozen reasons why she should change her mind.

Pushover?

Not this time.

Harold seated himself at the table without saying a word to anyone.

He looked at Kate.

Kate looked at him.

"I can't marry you," they said at the same time.

"What?" they both echoed again.

Grace looked at Harold.

Margaret looked at Kate.

"I'm sorry, Kate, I've fallen in love with someone else."

"But that's fabulous, Harold, so have I."

"What?" Margaret and Grace both shrieked.

Kate leaned across the table and handed him the ring.

"The cop?" Harold asked, slipping it into his pocket.

"Yes," Kate said, "and he's wonderful."

"Carla is wonderful, too," Harold said with a big grin.

Grace looked at Kate. "What cop?"

Margaret turned to Harold. "Who's Carla?"

Afternoon tea at the Waldorf turned into a downright hootenanny after that. Harold was out of his chair, giving her—of all things—a big genuine I'm-so-happy-for-you hug. Kate was hugging him back, wishing him nothing but happiness with the new woman in his life.

Harold pulled her aside for a moment, leaving Grace and Margaret sitting at the table, stunned looks on their faces.

"Kate, I owe you a huge apology," Harold said, "and if I've hurt you in any way, I'm terribly sorry for that. I knew I was pushing you into something you didn't want to do. There's no excuse for my behavior."

"I owe you an apology, too," Kate said. "I never should have accepted your proposal. I want you to know I truly do hope you're happy."

He smiled. "Who knew two skeptics like us would actually fall in love?"

"Who knew?" Kate agreed, smiling. "But aren't you glad that we did?"

They walked back to the table.

Harold pulled her chair out for her.

Kate sat back down.

He remained standing.

He looked at his mother, then at Grace, and shrugged.

"Well, I did say I wanted this to be a big surprise."

Kate laughed.

Margaret and Grace didn't.

Harold making a funny?

She couldn't believe it.

This Carla had to be some woman.

Love had definitely made Harold a better man.

"Well," he said brightly. "You ladies continue enjoying your afternoon tea. Morgan will be at your disposal for as long as you need him. But I'm off to hail a taxi. With any luck, I'll be back on a plane to Chicago within the hour."

He bent down and kissed his mother on the cheek, waved good-bye to Kate and Grace, and hurried out of the dining area.

"I'm not sure what just happened here, are you, Grace?"

"The only thing I'm sure of, Margaret, is that there isn't going to be a wedding today."

Kate reached out and took Grace and Margaret both by the hand. "I'm so sorry we've disappointed you," Kate told them. "But Harold seems happy, and so am I. I hope you'll both forgive us."

They each mumbled responses that were more than acceptable under the circumstances.

Kate looked down, then back up at Margaret. "And I'm so sorry you went to the trouble to bring presents, Margaret. Save those presents for the woman Harold *is* going to marry."

"I didn't bring those," Margaret said, looking down at the packages herself. "One of the waiters brought them over shortly after we arrived and said they were for you. We assumed they were presents from Harold."

"Isn't there a card?" Grace said. "I thought I saw a card attached to the top package."

Kate scooted her chair back and looked down at the prettily wrapped packages. She bent down, picked up the card, and opened it.

She recognized the handwriting immediately.

All the card said was—Go for it!

Alex had found what she was looking for in the closet.

It *wasn't* her lucky Kate Spade bag.

Kate sat there for a moment.

She looked up at Grace.

She looked over at Margaret.

"I'm going to need your help," Kate said, and stood up from the table.

CHAPTER 15

Really, Kate," Grace fussed. "What is the point in all this nonsense?"

Kate didn't answer.

She turned around so Grace could zip up the back of her dress.

"Do you really have to torture me and poor Margaret further by showing us the dress you would have worn. *If* you and Harold hadn't suddenly lost your minds?"

"But it is a beautiful dress, Grace," Margaret said, smiling at Kate. "And Kate looks absolutely beautiful in it."

Kate turned around and looked at herself in the full-length bathroom mirror.

A tad wrinkled?

Yes.

Did she think Tony would notice?

Not a chance.

"I'm not showing you the dress, Gram," Kate finally said, "I'm going to wear it."

Grace's mouth dropped open. "Wear it? Where?"

"To Central Park," Kate said, as if that made perfect sense.

"Central Park?" Margaret and Grace both echoed.

"Sorry, I don't have time to explain right now."

"Well, you'd better take time to explain right now," Grace told her. "You're acting as crazy as . . ."

"My parents?" Kate finished for her.

Grace refused to answer.

They stared at each other in the bathroom mirror.

"I guess I am as crazy as my parents after all, Gram. I'm crazy in love. Just like they've always been. But I'm not going to leave you. I'm not going anywhere except to tell the man I love that I can't imagine my life without him in it. Before I lose him forever, I'm going to tell him that, Gram. Please say you understand."

Grace stood there, looking at her for a moment.

"Oh, go on," Grace said with a sigh. "If you love him enough to go wandering through Central Park in a wedding dress, go tell him."

Kate tore open the second package.

She pulled out the framed sixteen-by-twenty painting.

She fumbled in her purse for a twenty-dollar bill.

She kissed Grace and Margaret.

Then she bolted for the door.

"I love you both," she called over her shoulder, "and thanks for taking care of my things."

"I'm not sure what just happened here, Grace, are you?" she heard Margaret say on her way out.

She heard her grandmother reply, "All I know, Margaret, is that I'm definitely going to need something stronger to drink than afternoon tea."

"Central Park. The entrance near the Met. As fast as you can get me there," Kate told the taxi driver.

He was a young guy, cute. She didn't miss his slightly raised eyebrow at her wedding attire, but he didn't ask. That's what she loved most about New York City—everyone just accepted the fact that trying to figure each other out was too damn exhausting to even put forth the effort.

When the driver pulled away from the curb, Kate propped the painting up beside her and fell back against the seat with a relieved sigh. Until she realized she didn't even know if Tony was on duty. He'd told her about his crazy work schedule, how he rarely worked the same shift two days in a row.

A glance at her watch only increased her angst.

It was already 4:15 P.M.

If Tony had worked days, she would miss him.

She held to the hope that destiny wouldn't let her down. *Please let him be on second shift.*

"Work with me here, destiny," Kate said aloud.

"Did you say something?"

"No, forget it," Kate said, but she was getting more anxious by the minute. Especially since the taxi was inching along at a snail's pace. She looked behind her. They were still practically right in front of the Waldorf.

Kate leaned forward. "Can't you go any faster?"

"Sure," the guy said, holding her gaze in his rearview mirror. "I'll just have Scotty beam us up and over this nasty old gridlock."

Smart-ass.

Kate leaned back against the seat again.

They were completely stopped.

Sheesh.

Did every day have to be the dawn of a new freaking *error* for her?

She tried not to count the minutes.

She couldn't stop herself.

Two minutes.

Five minutes.

Ten damn minutes.

What is going on?

Kate jerked upright in the seat.

People were pouring out of the buildings on both sides of the street. Fear's cold hand grabbed her with an icy fist. The same fear no New Yorker would ever be free of again.

Her eyes met the driver's in the mirror.

She knew he was thinking the same thing.

"Hey, what's going on," he yelled out the window.

A guy with his cell phone to his ear was cutting in front of the taxi. The guy hurried back to the driver's side of the cab and bent down to look in the window.

"Blackout," the guy said, holding up his phone. "Can't even get a cell phone signal. None of the buildings have power, either. Everything in the city must be shut down."

"Holy shit," the driver said.

Kate sat there for a moment.

She tossed the twenty over the seat.

Grabbed the painting.

Opened the door.

Hopped out of the taxi.

"Hey," the driver yelled after her. "You don't owe me anything. We hardly even moved."

Kate kept walking and never looked back.

———————

"Don't worry, babe, I'm sure this is only a minor glitch. We'll be out of here in no time."

Alex reached for John's hand and finally found it in the pitch-black elevator. They were stuck somewhere between the ninth and tenth floors of the Madison Avenue office building where the agency was located.

She knew that's where they were stuck, because the agency was on the tenth floor. She'd been watching the digital numbers as they changed, praying John would change his mind before the elevator came to a stop.

The elevator had come to a stop.

An abrupt stop.

Knocking out the lights just as quickly.

At least they were alone, Alex kept reminding herself.

There were no other people in the elevator with them to increase her growing hysteria. Her hope that John would change his mind was the reason she had kept him from piling into an elevator with a crowd of other people when they first arrived in the lobby. She'd held him back, wanting him to be on the elevator alone with her.

She'd wanted to give him that one last-minute opportunity to turn to her and say they should forget the whole surrogate nightmare. She knew her husband well. Even if he'd felt that way, John never would have discussed their private business in front of anyone else.

But how long had they been trapped?

Fifteen minutes, maybe?

Twenty?

Longer?

She wasn't sure.

But it had been long enough for both of them to feel their way along the side of the elevator car and sit down in the floor. Fearing the worst, she knew—yet sparing each other the agony of saying out loud what both of them were already thinking.

This wasn't just an isolated elevator glitch.

They'd checked; neither of their cell phones worked.

Whatever had happened, it couldn't be good.

John's strong arm slid around her shoulder, pulling her close. Alex couldn't keep from thinking how tragic it would be if this really was it. If life really was going to cheat her out of growing old with John.

She'd always teased John that the thing she liked best about marriage was finding that one special person you wanted to annoy for the rest of your life.

Suddenly, that joke wasn't funny.

John had to love her to have put up with her all these years. If anyone had ever annoyed the hell out of someone, she'd sure annoyed the hell out of him.

Alex reached up and touched his face. She couldn't see him, but she didn't have to. She knew exactly the look that would be there in his kind gray eyes. A look that told her he loved her whether she was a giant pain in the ass or not.

She reached up farther and pushed his sandy blond hair away from his forehead, knowing instinctively that his stubborn front cowlick had caused his hair to fall forward despite his attempt to keep it slicked back with gel.

What if this really is it? Alex kept asking herself.

What if I've wasted my life worrying about all the wrong things?

What if life isn't going to give me a chance to have my own children with John one day?

What if this is my punishment for not realizing that my husband and the children I do want matter more to me than any CEO position ever could?

Alex wiped at the unexpected tear as it rolled down her cheek. She just wasn't one of those sentimental people who slobber all over everybody, dammit!

But Alex was sentimental enough to snuggle against her husband and say, "Whatever happens, John, I want you to know that I love you with all my heart even if I don't show it most of the time."

"What's that?"

"I said I . . ."

"No," John said. "That!"

Alex heard the banging.

They both managed to pull themselves to their feet.

"Hello," John yelled out. "I'm John Graham. My wife and I are trapped here in the elevator."

A man's voice yelled back, "Just stay calm. We'll have you out as soon as possible."

"What's going on out there?" John yelled back.

"We've had a blackout," the guy yelled. "The whole city has ground to a halt."

Unless the entire city of New York grinds to a screeching halt.

Her own words came rushing back so fast, Alex gasped.

John grabbed for her. "Don't panic now, babe. You

heard the guy. They'll have us out of here as soon as possible."

Don't panic?

Panic didn't touch what she was feeling.

Life had just slapped her in the face with a huge wake-up call.

Alex yelled out herself, "How long do you think we'll be in here?"

It took a second, but the guy yelled back, "An hour, maybe a little more. Just remain calm. We'll get you out as soon as we can."

One hour, maybe a little more.

Destiny had granted a reprieve from her selfish ways.

Alex didn't intend to waste a perfect opportunity to prove she was sincerely grateful for her second chance.

"Now, dammit, Alex," John said when her wandering hand found exactly what she was seeking. "Stop that! Unless you happen to have your diaphragm, the condoms, and that spermicidal spray stuff in your purse, don't play games with me."

"Poor John," Alex said, lowering his zipper. "I guess I have been a bit obsessive when it comes to birth control, haven't I?"

"Obsessive?" John laughed and pushed her hand away. "I'd say hysterical is a better word. So, stop it, Alex. I'm not kidding."

"I'm not kidding, either," Alex told him.

"Alex?"

"John?" Alex said.

She pulled her devoted husband back down onto the floor with her. The devoted husband that she hoped would get her pregnant on the first try.

"Oh. God. You *are* serious. Oh. Man. Alex!"

"Just promise me one thing," Alex whispered as she helped guide John right where she knew beyond a shadow of a doubt that she wanted him. "Promise me we'll never tell our child he or she was conceived in an elevator. That could screw the poor kid up for life."

The pole. Just the pole. Nothing but the pole.

That's what Eve was thinking as she held tightly to the pole beside her seat in the subway car. At the moment it was so dark she couldn't see a blessed thing.

Which was actually a relief.

She didn't have anyone staring at her.

Nor was she imagining that everyone was staring at her.

The backup lights in the car had been coming on, then going off again for the last thirty minutes or so. The first time the lights went off, several people screamed.

Everyone had settled back down for the moment.

But Eve knew everyone was still nervous.

Too bad she still had to listen to the faceless voices who kept coming up with the type of worst-case scenarios she never would have thought of on her own.

"At least we're not stuck in the tunnel," some woman said. "We're sitting right here in the station. We'll be the first ones to be rescued."

True, Eve decided.

They had just pulled into the station when the lights went out, and the power shut down, trapping them inside the subway car. She'd been sitting right by the door, only one second away from walking out of the subway car, right up to the street, and several blocks over to where George was waiting for her at the restaurant.

But was George safe?

That was her biggest fear.

She'd tried to call, but the cell phones were out.

Like everyone else, she could only assume something terrible had happened.

Please let George be safe.

The thought of losing him before she even met him would have made her shiver, had it not been so hot inside the car.

Eve let go of the pole long enough to swipe at a trickle of sweat running down the back of her neck. The air conditioner was off, and the heat was becoming unbearable.

At least everything was quiet again.

Until a male voice said, "Whoever just said we're better off sitting here in the station is a nutcase. We'd be better off if we were in the tunnel. We could just as easily be sitting ducks if . . ."

"Shut up!" several people yelled.

"Hey, I got your shut up right here, you bozos," he yelled back.

The pole. The pole. The pole.

"Does anyone smell that? I swear I smell something. Oh, God. You don't think it could be nerve gas, do you? Isn't that what caused all those people to get sick in that Tokyo subway? Wasn't it nerve gas?"

"Hey, I smell it, too."

"So do I."

"Would everybody just calm down," some guy said. "It's me, okay. I can't help it. I've got this irritable bowel thing that flares up whenever I'm nervous."

"Hey, what's your name, dude?" some guy yelled.

"Norm, why?"

"It's not nerve gas, people, it's Norm's gas."

Several people laughed.

"Jesus," somebody else said. "Too many freaks. Not enough circuses."

"Look! Over there. I see flashlights."

"See, I told you we'd be the first ones to be rescued."

The policeman walked up to the car, holding his flashlight under his chin so everyone could see his face. "We've had a citywide blackout," he told them. "Nothing serious to worry about. Keep calm. We'll start letting you exit the car as soon as possible."

It took thirty more minutes before they were finally set free. Eve bolted out of the subway car like she'd been shot out of a cannon. She didn't even care that more bodies than she wanted to think about were pressing against her as everyone made a mad dash for the street.

She climbed the stairs and drank in a deep breath of fresh air the second she reached the street.

And then Eve almost passed out.

A too-familiar, too-handsome face was shining like a beacon amidst the sea of swarming people.

The snake!

Her worst fear was actually walking up the street, heading straight for her, his arm draped possessively around a tall, lanky blonde.

Eve stumbled back away from the subway entrance, flattening herself against the building. She kept praying the steady stream of people still coming up the stairs would keep the snake from seeing her.

Oh God. Oh God. Oh God.

She couldn't breathe.

The sidewalk was starting to move beneath her feet.

Eve leaned her head back.

That's when she saw it.

A beautiful white gull, flying overhead.

The gull. Just the gull. Nothing but the gull.

Flying lower.

Lower.

Lower.

Ewwwwwwwwwwwwwwwwwww.

Eve reached up and slowly wiped the poop from her face at the exact same time the snake and his latest fiancée stopped right in front of her.

At that moment, Eve decided something very important.

She'd been crapped on for the last damn time.

The snake hadn't changed much. He still had the look-at-me blond highlights in his spiked brown hair. Still had the same God's-gift smirk on his face. He looked her up and down before he smiled the kind of smile that used to make her swoon.

"Eve? Is that really you?"

"No," Eve said. "It's Jessica Simpson."

He sent the blonde a snide whatever look.

"What on earth are you doing down here by yourself on the riverfront?" He hugged the blonde even closer. "We have tickets for the folk music concert. Folk music has become our latest passion. Hasn't it, pumpkin?"

Pumpkin nodded rather snootily.

"Then you might have heard of my boyfriend," Eve said proudly. "He's one of the musicians *playing* in the concert. George Dumond? World-class banjo player?

There's a big write-up on him in the front of the festival program. Check it out when you get a chance."

His snotty smirk instantly faded.

Eve, however, couldn't stop smiling.

He was *so* five minutes ago—as Alex would say.

No doubt about it.

She was over the snake for good.

"Enjoy the concert," Eve told the happy couple and walked off.

She never looked back.

It was a different Eve Thornton who pushed and prodded her way through the crowd of people as she kept making her way toward the riverfront restaurant. She ignored the occasional looks from passersby. She didn't even care if she still had traces of bird poop on her cheek, or that her hair was frizzled and her blouse was sticking to her back from the sweltering heat inside the subway car.

George was waiting for her.

All she cared about was George.

Just George.

Nothing but George.

She saw him before she crossed the street.

He was pacing back and forth in front of the restaurant, a worried look on his face. She knew it was him the second she saw him—he looked exactly like the picture he'd sent her for his Web site.

Not a pretty boy like the snake.

He was a big teddy-bear-looking man.

One you knew would also have a big teddy-bear heart.

"George," Eve yelled, waving madly.

He waved back, a big grin spreading across his face.

Her Braveheart.

Her brave heart.
Today, Eve had found them both.

"That's absurd!" Harold shouted, and the pretty ticket agent jumped. "I understand there's a blackout. I understand no planes are landing and no planes are leaving. I even understand there's a problem with no power to operate the security systems. What I *don't* understand is why you can't put me on a list or something so you can issue me a ticket the minute things *do* return to normal!"

"Are you always that rude, Harry?"

Harold whirled around.

His heart whirled around fifty times faster.

Carla?

Thank God!

"How did you ever find me?" was all he could think to say.

"Oh, get over yourself," she said. "I wasn't looking for you. I heard you yelling all the way across the terminal."

She turned and walked off.

Harold hurried after her.

He grabbed her arm, stopping her.

She jerked her arm away from him.

"You're in New York," he said. "I still can't believe it. You're here in New York."

She shrugged. "I didn't see the point in letting a plane ticket go to waste. I switched the ticket date, but I sure picked the wrong day to arrive in the Big Apple. My plane landed over an hour ago. Who knows when I'll get my luggage."

She's here. She's here. She's here.

Harold couldn't keep the silly grin off his face.

"Would you drop the grin?" she said. "It's starting to scare me."

"I can't help it," Harold said. "You're here."

Her eyebrow arched. "On *business*," she emphasized, "that has absolutely *nothing* to do with you."

Harold frowned. "What kind of business?"

"Bigger fish than you business," she said, and walked off down the corridor again.

Harold ran ahead and stopped in front of her, blocking her path.

"Don't you have a wedding ceremony to attend somewhere today, Harry?"

"God, I hope so," Harold said, grinning at her again. "Say you'll marry me, Carla. Say you love me and you'll marry me."

"Are. You. Nuts?" she hissed.

"I'm nuts about you," Harold said.

He grabbed her and kissed Carla like crazy.

She finally pushed him away.

"Would you stop it!" She looked around them, flustered. "Everyone is staring at us, you idiot."

"I'm serious, Carla," Harold said. "I called off the other wedding. I couldn't go through with it. You're the one I love. You're the one I want to marry. I was trying to get a plane ticket so I could go back to Chicago and find you."

She looked at him for a moment, then shook her head.

"You said it yourself, Harry. What self-respecting man would ever . . ."

Harold refused to let her say it.

"I don't care about your past, Carla. All I care about is your future. The future I hope you say you're willing to spend with me."

Her blue eyes narrowed. "What do you think I am, stupid? We both know I'm *not* the type of girl you take home to good old Mom. I doubt you'd want to introduce me to any of your big-shot associates, either."

"Is that what you think?" Harold said. "You think I'll be ashamed of you?"

"Thanks for saying it for me," she said. "It makes it easier to walk away."

"What will it take, Carla?" Harold demanded. "You want proof I'm not ashamed of you?"

"Go away," she said, and tried to push past him.

Harold threw his head back and shouted as loud as he could, "I love this woman. Do you hear me, New York? I love this woman, and I'm begging her to be my wife."

Several people stopped walking to watch.

Harold dropped down on his knees, his hands clasped together in a plea. "See? I'm begging, Carla. In front of all these people, I'm begging you. Please, say you'll marry me."

"Get up!" Carla said, cheeks blazing.

"Only if you'll say you'll marry me."

A larger crowd had gathered now.

Everyone was watching.

Everyone kept waiting.

Harold kept waiting.

Waiting.

Waiting.

"Okay, okay," Carla said, rolling her eyes. "Get up and I'll think about it."

"Did you hear that, New York?" Harold shouted. "At least she's going to think about it!"

The crowd started cheering.

Everyone started clapping.

Even the agent at the ticket counter was clapping.

Harold jumped up and pulled Carla into his arms.

Carla relented and slid her arms around his neck.

Her sweet lips close to his ear, she whispered, "You deserve a good spanking for embarrassing me like that, Harry."

Harold stiffened.

In more ways than one.

He grabbed her hand and bolted for the front entrance.

Blackout, or no blackout, he *would* find them a taxi.

No matter what the cost.

CHAPTER 16

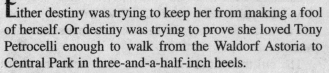

Either destiny was trying to keep her from making a fool of herself. Or destiny was trying to prove she loved Tony Petrocelli enough to walk from the Waldorf Astoria to Central Park in three-and-a-half-inch heels.

Kate did love Tony that much.

But her feet kept screaming they didn't.

She'd given up trying to hurry, it was pointless. She'd never seen so many people on the streets at one time in her life. Except maybe in Times Square on New Year's Eve.

She'd finally stopped wincing at the strange looks she kept getting as she hobbled along in a wedding dress with a painting under her arm. Just as she'd learned to ignore the smart remarks from less-than-desirable guys who kept trying to get her attention.

"Hey, sweetheart, I'll marry you. Come over here and let me prove I'm your type."

Like that guy.

Definitely one Froot Loop short of a full bowl.

Please.

Kate sighed and stopped with a million other people, waiting to cross the street. The two teenage girls standing beside her looked over at her and immediately started snickering.

Kate glanced at the girl standing closest to her.

She had a pretty face, but she was wearing way too much makeup for a girl her age.

She looked down at the girl's feet. "Size seven?"

Both girls giggled.

"Yeah, so?" The girl punched her friend and they both giggled again.

Kate stuck her foot out. "Manolo Blahniks," she said. "Five hundred dollars' worth. Trade with me and you can sell them to buy yourself several new pairs of tennis shoes."

The girl thought about it. "You don't have any weird foot fungus or anything, do you?"

"No. Do you?"

When she shook her head, Kate said, "Follow me."

They made it across the street and stopped in front of an outside café long enough to make the trade. Her feet breathed a welcome sigh of relief when she slipped on the tennis shoes.

"Those totally look crunk on you, Lisa," the girl's friend said, admiring the pumps when the girl put them on.

Lisa smiled at Kate and grabbed her friend's hand.

They quickly disappeared into the crowd.

Afraid, most likely, she was going to change her mind.

Not a chance.

Even though now she was three and a half inches shorter.

A wedding dress and tennis shoes.

Not what Vera Wang had in mind, she was sure.

Kate put the Blessed Virgin and her child down long enough to pick up the hem of her dress and drape it over her arm to keep the hem from dragging. She hoped to wear the dress for real one day.

The fact that she was begging for more smart remarks now that she'd hiked Vera's lovely creation up to only a hair longer than a miniskirt, didn't even faze her. She picked the painting up again, squared her shoulders, and headed off in her new tennis shoes determined to reach her final destination.

But Kate had decided one thing.

After everything she was willing to go through, if she did find Tony and if Tony *didn't* say he loved her the second he saw her.

She was going to pistol-whip him with his own damn revolver!

Once the blackout hit, Tony had been too busy to worry about afternoon tea at the Waldorf. He had, however, said more than one silent prayer that Kate was safe.

With the city in turmoil, he was positive his shift wouldn't be ending at its regular time, either. That nixed his idea of heading to Kate's apartment as soon as he was off duty. But at least maybe by nightfall communication would be restored, the streets would clear out, and Kate would have made it home safely.

Then he would call her.

He'd beg her to forgive him for being so stupid.

And hopefully have her in his arms as soon as possible.

It did make him wonder though, if the blackout had been destiny's way of telling him to leave her alone.

Or?

Was destiny just reminding him that life really could change in a New York minute?

A cop like him, always living on the edge to a certain degree, needed to be reminded of that now and then. Reminded that life was short, and the best way to have no regrets was to hold on to love if you were one of those people lucky enough to find it.

He loved Kate with all his being.

He'd tell her that this time.

The second she answered her phone.

With that settled in his mind, Tony turned his attention back to the current situation. People had poured into Central Park from every direction, seeking a likely place of refuge away from the mass confusion on the crowded New York streets.

The good news was, everyone seemed to be in a good mood, even taking the inconvenience in stride—once word spread through the city that a major power failure along the entire Eastern seaboard was the cause of the problem.

However, there's always one more imbecile than you counted on.

The only time Tony had heard anyone mention what had been on everyone's mind, was one wise-ass in a suit and tie who had joked, "Who needs terrorists? We've got ConEd."

Angry looks had told him real quick no one was amused.

Tony surveyed the area one last time. When he was

sure nothing was amiss, he pulled on the reins, signaling to Skyscraper it was time to head to the next section of the park. They'd barely made it fifty feet when he heard someone yelling.

"Officer! Hurry. We need your help."

Great.

That would teach him to relax even for a nanosecond.

Tony tugged the reins to the right, turning Skyscraper back around and directing the horse toward a man who was now motioning frantically in his direction. A group of people had already gathered around the man, everyone looking concerned.

It wasn't until Tony dismounted, secured Skyscraper's bridle to a nearby bush and made it to where the group was standing, that he saw the problem.

Someone had failed to tell Mother Nature about the blackout.

The woman sitting on the park bench had both hands flattened against her enormous stomach, her eyes were squinted shut, and she was panting like crazy to fight off the pain.

"Officer, hurry. We need an ambulance. My wife's . . . uh . . . well, her . . ."

"My water broke, Tom!" his wife yelled. "Just say it. This is no time to be embarrassed."

The mother's outburst caused the toddler standing beside her to pucker up and burst into tears. The husband had no sooner picked the little girl up to comfort her, than a loud wail erupted from the baby carriage that was pulled up next to the other end of the park bench.

The poor guy looked ready to cry himself.

"I'll take care of the baby," said an older woman standing in the crowd. The baby stopped crying when she took the infant out of the carriage.

The husband looked ready to kiss her.

Tony quickly radioed for help.

No need to panic, he kept reminding himself.

It could take hours after a woman's water broke before she delivered. Even under the current circumstances, there should still be plenty of time for an emergency medical crew to arrive and take over.

His job was to keep everyone calm.

To keep the crowd back and out of the way.

To keep his own head clear and focused.

That was his game plan until the husband walked up, still jostling his daughter in his arms, and whispered, "How soon do you think it will take the ambulance to get here? I'm worried. We barely made it to the hospital with our son. Once she goes into labor, my wife delivers real quick."

Perfect.

"Help will arrive in plenty of time," Tony assured him. "Just remain as calm as you can. Your wife needs your support right now."

The man nodded and walked back to stand beside his wife.

Jesus.

Now Tony was worried the ambulance wasn't going to make it before a brand-new little citizen to protect and serve showed up.

Another woman had thankfully come forward from the crowd to help. She was currently blotting the wife's forehead with a tissue. Tony motioned the crowd back to give the poor woman some privacy. He walked over and mumbled more words of encouragement to the husband.

He even finally got a smile out of the little girl by tickling her tummy.

It didn't change a thing.

Mother Nature crooked her finger.

The wife threw her head back and screamed.

"The baby's coming. Oh, God. Somebody please do something!"

Tony launched into action.

He motioned for the husband still holding his daughter and the woman holding the baby to move away from the bench.

"You stay," he said, pointing to the woman blotting the wife's forehead. "I'm going to need your help."

"Okay," he said, "everybody else form a circle with your backs to this woman. We need to make a barricade and give her some privacy."

People started falling into line without him having to ask again, linking their arms, and placing their backs to the soon-to-be new mother. He turned back around and the woman who had stayed to help was now holding the wife's hand, helping her lie down on the bench.

Tony grabbed the blankets and the soft mattress out of the baby carriage. Then he grabbed the diaper bag sitting at the end of the bench. He'd changed his own nieces and nephews enough to know there wasn't much a woman didn't keep in her diaper bag. At least he should have enough to make do until official help arrived.

He kneeled down beside her. "What's your name?"

"Judy," she groaned, grabbing her stomach again.

"Judy, I'm Tony," he said. "You've done this before, and so have I. Everything's going to be fine. Okay?"

She looked at him. "You've delivered a baby before?"

Tony nodded.

"Okay, Tony," she said, and grabbed on to his hand.

Him delivering a baby before?

A blatant lie—Tony was scared shitless.

The relieved look that washed across her worried face? Well worth going to confession later.

By the time Kate walked the twenty-plus blocks from the Waldorf Astoria to Central Park, she figured she could land the role as an understudy for the freaking *Bride of Frankenstein*.

Be beautiful?

Ha!

Being beautiful was not something she'd been able to pull off under the circumstances.

She walked through the entrance of the park and headed for the area where she'd been standing the day her entire life changed. And she wasn't being dramatic. Without a doubt, nothing about her life had been the same since she first saw Tony galloping up the path in her direction.

Please God. Let me find him.

She'd already decided she'd have a better chance running into Tony if she stayed in one place. Her walking randomly in one direction, and him possibly riding off in the other direction, could result in them missing each other altogether.

Plus, she was exhausted.

If Tony (Please God) did happen to be on duty, he'd keep patrolling the area. She'd let him find her standing right where she'd been standing the first time he saw her—happily waiting to finally become his destiny.

Make that sitting *where he first saw me,* Kate decided when she noticed a vacant spot on a park bench in the same general area.

She walked over and gently propped the painting against the end of the bench. She spent the next few minutes removing every bit of dust—and any other suspicious-looking particles—from the back and the seat of the bench with her bare hand.

The older woman sitting on the opposite end of the bench had been watching her with great interest the entire time she cleared a safe place to sit. But the woman had never said one word.

That won't last long, Kate thought, and finally sat down.

The woman was just one of those people you knew at a glance would ask you a million questions and never think a thing of it.

She was around sixty, rather large, and had a bad perm and a worse dye job. Her flowered muumuu had a torn pocket. Her pair of run-down sneakers looked as if they possibly could be home to some type of weird foot fungus.

"What happened to you?" she asked, just as Kate knew she would. "Did the groom run off when the lights went out? And you decided to steal the Madonna's picture from the church to get even?" She smiled at Kate, fanning herself with the paperback novel she held in her hand.

Kate glanced at the title.

A mystery.

Great. Granny's a supersleuth.

"No, the lights finally came on up here," Kate said, tapping her forehead. "And if I'm lucky, my future husband is going to come riding through here any minute now."

"Your Fairy Godmother told you that, did she?"

Kate laughed in spite of herself.

"I'm Lorraine," the woman said, sticking out her hand. Kate shook it.

"Kate."

"So, Kate," she said. "The streets are still swarming with people. I'm not going anywhere until the crowds thin out. You're sitting here waiting for your prince to ride by. Why don't we pass the time by you telling me what really happened to the groom?"

Oh, what the hell?

Why not tell the woman her story?

She probably wouldn't believe it anyway.

Kate almost didn't believe it herself.

By the time she finished giving Lorraine the highlights of her tea-leaves, Blessed Virgin, wedding-dress saga, Kate had even started to wonder if she really had just made the whole story up.

"And after everything you've been through, you're just going to sit here hoping destiny will send Tony riding up the path again?" Lorraine looked doubtful.

Kate was doubtful.

About finding Tony.

Also about what the outcome would be if she did find him.

Kate sighed. "I don't know what else to do," she told her new friend. "I'm afraid if I start wandering around the park looking for him, I'll miss Tony completely."

Lorraine thought it over for a second.

"I have an idea," she said.

Tony had remained calm through the delivery.

He really hadn't had much to do.

With the other woman's help, he had managed to slide the mattress beneath Judy only seconds before he saw the baby's head crowning. All he'd done next was basically catch New York's newest little citizen in the baby blanket.

When the woman bent forward and wiped the baby's face and mouth with a baby wipe, the little guy had let them know real quick what he thought about the whole situation.

"He's definitely a New Yorker," Tony's smiling assistant had said. "He's screaming his head off before he even knows what's going on."

Tony barely remembered shouting out to the crowd that the baby was a boy. He had just finished placing the newborn carefully on his mother's stomach when the emergency medical crew arrived to take over.

The happy family was gone now.

The crowd had dissipated, going about their business.

He and Skyscraper were back on their watch.

But Tony couldn't keep his hands from shaking.

Aftershock.

There wasn't a cop alive who hadn't experienced the same thing after the fact. After the adrenaline stopped pumping and the danger was over, aftershock was the reminder that your subconscious was still going over a long list of the things that could have gone wrong.

But what an incredible experience.

He couldn't imagine anything more amazing than witnessing the miracle of the birth of a child. Except one day being lucky enough to witness his own child being born.

Kate.

He had so much to tell her.

He just hoped she gave him that chance.

Tony glanced around him, searching the crowd, looking for anything else that might be out of order. The park was still overloaded with people, even though it was almost seven o'clock.

Some people were still waiting for the crowds to thin out. Some people were just now showing up and preferring being outside to stuck inside in their hot apartments.

From the reports he'd been getting, it could be midnight or later before power was restored. He'd already resigned himself to the fact that this was going to be a long, watchful night.

"Officer. Wait!"

Tony pulled Skyscraper to a halt and turned halfway around in the saddle, looking behind him.

A nice-looking young couple holding hands both waved.

They were about a hundred yards or more behind him. They started running to catch up. Both were dressed in jogging attire, their water bottles hanging from the straps around their necks.

Tony tensed for a second, praying nothing as serious as what he'd just faced was the reason for them running in his direction. They were slightly out of breath when they reached him.

"Is your name Tony?" the guy asked.

"Yes, I'm Tony."

"Lorraine asked us to stop you if we saw you. She said

she needed to see you, and you knew who she was. We'll show you where she is."

Lorraine?

Who the hell is Lorraine?

Tony racked his brain trying to place the name, but the search came up empty.

"Describe her for me," Tony said.

The guy immediately looked over at the girl.

"She's an older woman. Heavyset. Curly sort of orange-looking hair."

The guy nodded in agreement.

"She said you knew her," the girl reminded him again.

One of Mama Gina's customers maybe?

He couldn't even count the number of times he'd heard his mother tell her customers to look him up if they ever needed anything in Central Park.

"You need something? You find my boy Tony. He'll take care of it for you."

The woman was probably stranded in the park. No way back to Queens anytime soon. Thanks to his mother, the poor woman probably fully believed all she had to do was summon Gina's boy Tony, and he would send for the S.W.A.T. team to escort her safely home.

Jesus, Mary, and Joseph!

"Show me where she is," Tony said with a sigh.

He pulled on the reins and turned Skyscraper around. They'd barely gone a couple of feet when two teenage girls on in-line skates zoomed up beside him.

"Tony?" the girl wearing a pink helmet said.

"Yeah."

"Lorraine asked us to stop you if we saw you."

Are you f'ing kidding me?

"Already got the message," Tony said, pointing to the joggers who were now walking up the path ahead. "They're going to show me where she is."

The girls waved and both skated away.

He hadn't expected the no-nonsense-looking business-man carrying his briefcase to stop him with the same message from Lorraine.

Or the burly biker with the tattoos.

Or the street performer with his guitar case.

But when the Hasidic Jew in his black clothing, hat, and earlocks stopped beside him, Tony saved the poor guy the trouble. "Lorraine wants to see me, right?"

He nodded, his curls bouncing above his long beard.

Tony thanked him and nudged Skyscraper forward.

But he had decided one thing.

His mother was way overdue for that lecture.

If he had to tie Mama to a chair.

Put duct tape over her mouth to keep her quiet.

Even make Papa promise not to untie her until he left.

Mama was definitely going to get a stern lecture.

"Here come some of our carrier pigeons back now," Lorraine said, looking over at Kate with a big smile.

Kate looked up.

The girls on the roller blades were trying to outrace each other back to where she and Lorraine were sitting. The girl in the green helmet skidded sideways to a stop in front of them, beating her friend who was wearing the pink helmet.

"We found the cop," the girl said proudly. "He's just a little ways behind us."

Kate jumped up from the bench. "You found him?"

The girl looked at her funny. "Well, like, yeah." She looked back at Lorraine. "I thought you were the one who wanted to see him."

"No, Cinderella here needs to see him," Lorraine said, tossing her thumb toward Kate. "She's having a major heart attack at the moment."

The girl looked Kate up and down.

"She doesn't look like she's having any kind of heart attack to me."

"Trust me, sweetie," Lorraine said. "In a few years you're going to remember this conversation, and you'll know exactly what I'm talking about."

"Whatever," the girl said. She motioned to her friend, and they both skated off.

"Thank you," Kate called after them.

Then the panic set in.

Oh God. Oh God. Oh God.

Tony was right behind them.

Kate grabbed the picture, picked up the hem of her dress, and ran across the path to the same place she'd been standing when he first saw her.

She placed the painting on top of the waist-high concrete fence, propping the painting carefully against the black iron railing. After hurriedly raking her fingers through her hair, she smoothed out her dress as best she could and stood up straight.

"How do I look?" she called out to Lorraine.

"Do you want the truth? Or do you want me to lie to you?" Lorraine called back.

"Lie to me," Kate told her.

"You couldn't look any more beautiful."

Lorraine pulled herself up from the bench. She walked across the path and began smoothing a few more wrinkles out of the satin skirt. She picked at a few of the sequins on the bodice, then adjusted both of the dainty pearl t-straps to a perfect position on Kate's shoulders.

After repositioning Kate so she was standing directly beside the Blessed Virgin, she took Kate's left hand and put it on top of the painting. It crossed Kate's mind that the pose was so fitting, she could have been waiting to have her own portrait painted.

Lorraine stepped back, admiring her work and smiling.

Until she looked down at Kate's feet.

She clicked her tongue disapprovingly.

"Baby needs a new pair of shoes."

Baby.

Kate flashed hot all over.

The couple ahead of him stopped walking and waited for Tony to catch up. When he pulled Skyscraper to a stop beside them, the girl pointed ahead.

"When we left, Lorraine was sitting on a park bench just around the curve. That's where you'll find her."

Tony thanked them.

The couple darted off in the opposite direction, in full jogging mode again.

He sat there for a moment.

It was the first time he'd realized where he was.

Just around the curve.

Tony laughed.

How ironic.

Just around the curve was where he first saw Kate.

He snapped the reins, urging Skyscraper forward.

He was still chuckling to himself.

Until they rounded the curve.

Tony stopped chuckling.

The last thing he expected was exactly what he found.

Kate, standing beside the Blessed Virgin.

Wearing his wedding dress.

And a pair of—what—Nikes?

It didn't matter.

She was the most beautiful thing he'd ever seen.

This woman is *my destiny.*

Kate's heart almost stopped when Tony rounded the curve. The look on his face was more than just perplexed. He looked shocked. As if he couldn't quite believe what he was seeing.

Kate squared her shoulders when he pulled on the reins, bringing his mount to a stop a short distance away from her. The second his shiny black boots hit the ground, she knew she'd never stop fantasizing about this man as long as she lived.

He walked up and stopped in front of her.

My Italian on a stallion, Kate thought.

He unsnapped his chin strap and took off his helmet.

Mercy.

He was everything she wanted—all she'd ever need.

His sexy grin caught her off guard.

"I don't know how to tell you this," he said, "but you and I were destined to be together."

"That has to be the corniest pickup line I've ever heard," Kate told him.

"But aren't you interested in why a guy would be willing to make a complete fool of himself with a statement like that one?"

"Yes," Kate said. "Today, I am definitely interested in why you would make a statement like that one."

"I love you, Kate," he said, "with all my heart."

"I love you even more," Kate told him.

Tony leaned forward, cupped her face, and kissed her.

"Bravo! Bravo! Bravo!"

Then came loud clapping.

"Let me guess," Tony said laughing, "Lorraine?"

"Lorraine," Kate said, nodding happily.

She slid her arms around his neck and kissed Tony again.

CHAPTER 17

❧

One year later

The Petrocelli family has been waiting for this wedding to take place for the last twenty years."

Joey Caborelli said this as he panned the video camera Tony had given him for his birthday across the front of the legendary Boathouse in Central Park.

"We're here at the Lake Room this evening, outside in the garden that overlooks Central Park Lake. Behind those closed French doors is where the wedding will take place." He aimed the camera toward the doors and said, "Tony Petrocelli first met Kate Anderson here in Central Park. Today, they'll be getting married here."

Joey turned the camera back to the large crowd milling about the garden. "As you can see, many of the guests have already arrived. While we're waiting for the ceremony to begin, let's go interview some of the family members and give them the opportunity to record a special message for Tony and Kate."

Mama Gina, dressed in a lovely aqua-colored floor-length gown with a matching sequined camisole, smiled happily into the camera. "My heart is so full of love for both of you, words can't even describe what I'm feeling at the moment." She dabbed at the corners of her eyes with a dainty hanky. "Not that the two of you didn't have me worried," she added, shaking her finger sternly at the camera. "Especially after Kate came to the restaurant and Nonna didn't know who she was."

"What did you say?"

The camera switched from Mama Gina to Rosa Petrocelli, standing beside her daughter-in-law and also wearing a floor-length gown, hers a brilliant shade of purple. She turned her silver head in Mama Gina's direction. "Of course, I knew who Kate was. Who said I didn't?"

The camera switched back to Mama Gina for an answer.

Slightly flustered, Mama Gina said a little too sweetly, "Well, if you did know who Kate was that evening, Nonna, it would have been nice if you'd simply told us that."

Back to Rosa. Now, definitely flustered.

"What was there to tell?" Rosa threw her frail hands up in the air. "Mama Mia! Everyone in the family already knew who Kate was. What do you people want from me? Is predicting the future not enough for this crazy family of mine?"

Mama Gina quickly motioned the camera away.

Joey quickly moved on.

"And now," Joey said, "let's have a few words from the bride's side of the family."

Grace Anderson, looking as smart as ever in a pink

satin suit with a string of antique pearls at her throat, was standing beside a man with his hair slicked back in a long ponytail that trailed down his back. He was wearing a tuxedo—with Birkenstock sandals and no socks. The woman standing next to him was clad in a flowing light blue gauze caftan with a gardenia pinned in her long blond hair.

Joey said, "Would you like to say a few words to the happy couple?"

Grace hesitated for a second, then looked into the camera. "Kate and Tony, I love you. I wish you both nothing but a lifetime of happiness together."

"I'm the proud father of the bride," Rob Anderson said into the camera. He put his arm around the woman standing next to him. "This is Kate's beautiful mother, Mystery."

He pulled his wife closer.

They both blew a kiss to the camera.

"We love you, honey," Rob said.

"We only hope you and Tony are as happy as we've always been," Mystery added.

A distinguished-looking man escorting two strikingly beautiful women walked toward the camera. The designer attire that they wore from head to toe denoted their wealth.

Joey kept the camera aimed in their direction.

"Care to say a few words to the bride and groom?"

Margaret Wellington stepped forward first, smiling into the camera. "Have a beautiful life together, Kate and Tony."

Harold stepped forward, his arm around his pretty wife. "Kate, I wish you and Tony every bit as much happiness as Carla has given me."

"Stop gushing, Harry," Carla said, rolling her eyes.

When they walked away, a rather stooped elderly man came up and stuck his wrinkled face in front of the camera. "I just heard your bride is a graduate of Wells College," Solomon Stein said. "Good choice for any Princeton man."

The old man shuffled off, only to be replaced by a heavyset woman wearing a bright orange dress the same color as her hair. She grinned into the camera. "Tony, all I have to say is that I hope you insisted on buying Kate a new pair of shoes to wear with that wedding dress."

Several more people stopped with good wishes.

Soon, the crowd started going inside to be seated.

Joey followed along behind them.

He stopped when he reached the groom.

Tony was standing at the altar.

His father and best man, Mario, stood beside him.

Joey aimed the camera at Tony.

"Any last-minute thoughts for your bride before she walks down the aisle and becomes your wife?"

"Be beautiful," Tony said.

He winked at the camera.

Joey left the groom behind and headed across the room. He walked down a small hallway, then focused the camera lens on a closed door at the end of the hall.

"Behind this closed door," Joey said, "the bride is getting ready. I've been told no man has ever been allowed to film any bride during her last few minutes of freedom. It sure makes you wonder what really goes on behind that closed door."

"I promise, Kate," Alex said as she zipped up the back of Kate's dress, "I'll never say another word about buying off the rack again. If a dress can still look this good, after what this poor dress has been through, I might even send Vera Wang a fan letter myself."

"You? Sending fan letters?" Kate laughed.

Eve giggled. "Motherhood agrees with you, Alex."

Alex frowned at both of them and reached for her son.

When Eve handed the baby back over, Alex licked her fingers and rubbed them over the top of little Johnny's head. "He would have his daddy's cowlick," she fussed. "That's one inherited trait we definitely could have done without."

Kate said, "Let's just hope he inherited John's personality instead of yours."

"*Not* funny," Alex said, and licked her fingers for another swipe at the baby's hair. She groaned when little Johnny spit up on the front of her dress. "See why I was so relieved when you chose these pale yellow bridesmaid dresses?" Alex walked over and grabbed a wipe from her diaper bag. "Baby puke blends right in with pale yellow."

Kate laughed. "Who would have ever believed Alex Graham would be choosing her designer wardrobe based on what blended in with baby puke?"

Alex mumbled something Kate was glad little Johnny was still too young to understand.

Eve walked up behind Kate. She adjusted the gardenia Kate's mother had given Kate as a wedding present and pinned at the back of Kate's elegant French twist.

"Are you nervous, Kate?" Eve asked. "You certainly don't seem nervous."

"Then she's a better woman than I was on my wedding

day," Alex spoke up. "Remember? I'd taken so much Valium the two of you practically had to hold me up at the altar."

Kate looked at herself in the mirror and smiled.

"You know, surprisingly, I'm not nervous at all. But I'm definitely ready to spend two glorious stress-free weeks on Hunter Mountain."

"Tony said he tried to talk you into a trip to the Bahamas," Alex said.

"He did," Kate said. "Trail's End was my choice. I just couldn't imagine spending our honeymoon anywhere else."

"Ah, yes," Alex said. "Where the magic all began."

Kate stuck her tongue out at Alex.

But she smiled at Eve.

"And what about you, sweetie? Are you getting nervous? In just a few more weeks it'll be your turn to walk down the aisle and become Mrs. George Dumond."

"Except my wedding is going to be a small outdoor ceremony," Eve said. "Nothing like this big, wonderful wedding you're having, Kate."

"Are you kidding?" Kate said. "Your wedding is going to be beautiful, Eve. You and George, standing in the gazebo he's building in his backyard for the ceremony? Who wouldn't love a wedding like that?"

Alex said, "I'll sure love a small ceremony after this extravaganza. *Big* doesn't even describe the crowd already gathered outside. The scary thing is that most of them are going to be your relatives, Kate. Forget Queens. The Petrocelli clan will be able to start its own country soon."

Kate laughed. "True. The Petrocellis are definitely not lacking for family members."

"And I still can't believe your parents decided to come," Alex said. "Even fully clothed."

"I have Tony to thank for my parents being here," Kate said. "He's the one who truly talked them into coming when we flew out to California to see them a few months ago. Tony didn't want us married without my parents being present. Thank God they'd tired of their nudist colony experience and moved back into a commune by the time we flew out to see them. I swear I had nightmares about Tony, staring at the ceiling while he asked my father for my hand in marriage."

Alex and Eve both laughed.

"And while we're speaking of miracles," Alex said, "what about Grace making peace with your parents after all these years? You have to be thrilled about that."

"That's truly the best wedding present ever," Kate said. "Gram's even excited I finally signed the papers on the building I'm leasing. Imagine that. Grace Anderson, excited about a two-bit art gallery in Queens, of all places."

"And I do love the name you decided on for your gallery," Eve said.

"The gallery's name was my idea," Alex boasted. "Kate's Attic—simple, but definitely enticing enough to make you come inside and see what treasures Kate has in her shabby-chic gallery."

A knock jerked Kate's head toward the closed door.

Tony's sister, Theresa, peeped inside, and said, "It's almost showtime, ladies. We have about ten minutes before it's time to start down the aisle."

The door closed behind her.

Kate held her arms out.

Alex and Eve stepped forward for a group hug.

All three laughed when little Johnny reached out and patted the ample cleavage exposed by the low bodice of Kate's dress.

"Great," Alex said. "He's going to be a boob man, just like his father."

"He's adorable, is what he is," Eve said, cooing at him.

Alex looked at Kate, then at Eve. "I guess this isn't the best time to bring up the fact that the three of us won't exactly be seeing each other on a regular basis now." She looked at Kate again. "You're moving off to Queens." She looked back at Eve. "You're moving away to Connecticut in a few weeks. I'm starting to feel abandoned."

Kate looked at Eve.

Eve looked at Kate.

Kate reached out and felt Alex's forehead. "Are you sure you're feeling okay, Alex? Being mushy is so not you."

"I was not being mushy!" Alex rolled her eyes. "For once, I was just trying to tell you how much you both mean to me."

"Mushy," Kate and Eve both said, nodding at her.

"Okay!" Alex shifted the baby to her other hip. "Maybe I'm not the same hard-nosed person I used to be. You lose your identity when you've been an executive and you suddenly switch from worrying about board meetings to worrying about nothing but bowel movements."

"Then maybe you should go back to work," Kate suggested.

"Don't worry," Alex said. "I intend to do just that." She smiled and looked down at her son, "Just as soon as Johnny starts kindergarten."

"Well, for what it's worth," Kate said, "even though

I'll be living in Queens I'm still only a taxi ride away, Alex."

"And just because I'm moving to Connecticut doesn't mean I don't intend to be fully involved in my godson's life," Eve spoke up. "That means I expect both of you to keep a spare room ready for me when I make my regular train trips back to New York."

"Stop trying to humor me," Alex said. "You've both made your point. No more mushy."

Kate said, "I wasn't going to bring this up, either, because it does freak me out when I think about it. But have either of you realized what today is? Other than my wedding day?"

Alex shook her head. "Unless it has something to do with Winnie the Pooh and Tigger, Too, don't look at me for an answer."

Eve said, "It's the one-year anniversary of the blackout. I heard it on the news this morning."

"You're kidding me!" Alex gasped.

"No," Eve said, blinking. "I'm serious. I heard it on the news first thing this morning."

Alex looked at Kate.

Kate looked at Alex.

Eve would always be Eve.

And they wouldn't have her any other way.

"I swear Tony and I didn't plan this," Kate said. "Today just happened to be the first available Friday in August that we could reserve the Boathouse. I was concentrating on the day being a Friday, definitely not on the actual date."

"Does Tony know?" Eve asked.

Kate laughed. "I was afraid to mention it to him when

he called me this morning. You have to admit, everything surrounding our entire relationship has been anything but normal from the very beginning. I was afraid if I added one more twist to the mix, it would push him over the edge."

Alex said, "But you also have to admit how amazing it is that one day changed the course of all three of our lives forever. Think about it. When we had breakfast together one year ago today, I was going to let John sign papers with a surrogate agency. Kate had made up her mind she was never going to see Tony again. And Eve was off to meet George, never dreaming she'd finally have to face the snake."

"Ewwww. The snake," Eve said, wrinkling her nose in disgust.

"And look at all three of us now," Kate said, leaning over to kiss her godson on the cheek. "You have a precious son. And Eve and I are going to marry the men of our dreams."

"Wait," Alex said, putting a finger to her forehead. "Madam Alexis is receiving a very important message. I predict . . ."

"STOP!" Kate said before Alex could finish. "Don't you dare tempt fate today, Alex. Not on the anniversary of the blackout. And definitely not before I say my wedding vows. Everyone has worked hard to make this wedding perfect. Something could still go wrong."

Alex looked at Eve.

Eve looked at Kate.

Kate looked back at Alex.

"Don't be silly," Alex said. "What could possibly go

wrong? You're only minutes away from walking down the aisle."

Kate didn't know why, but she still wasn't nervous.

Not when Tony's three nieces threw their rose petals.

Not when Tony's five sisters walked down the aisle.

Not when Eve and Alex followed along after them.

Then the wedding march started.

Kate got nervous.

No. Catatonic.

That was a better word.

Baby's new shoes were definitely glued to the carpet.

She felt her father tug on her arm.

Kate still didn't budge.

"It's time, Kate," he said.

Still, Kate couldn't move.

She couldn't explain it, but she felt as if she were drowning in a huge sea of doubt. Not about her love for Tony. She had no doubts about loving him. But the last twelve months suddenly seemed like nothing but a blur to her.

Especially the last few months.

She'd been busy planning her new gallery.

Tony's work schedule had been crazy.

They really hadn't spent much time together.

Even the time they had spent together lately had been spent with his mother or her grandmother, going over detail after detail after detail of this megamonster of a wedding they were having.

Maybe that was the problem.

Her big sea of doubt was centered around how Tony

really felt about her. Did he really love her? Or had he just been caught up in the famous Petrocelli marriage prediction legend from the very beginning?

Lately, their entire relationship had become about nothing but the wedding. The wedding that was supposed to be in progress at that very moment. The wedding that Gina Petrocelli and Grace Anderson had worked so hard to make absolutely perfect. The wedding where four-hundred-plus guests were patiently waiting behind that closed door for her to come walking down the aisle with a big smile painted on her suddenly scared-to-death face.

Oh God. Oh God. Oh God.

This was not the time to get prewedding jitters.

The wedding march started over again.

"Kate," her father said. "We have to go now."

He reached out to open the door.

Kate grabbed his hand.

"I need to talk to Tony," she said.

"But, honey," he said, patting the hand that was clutching his arm in a death grip. "You can talk to Tony after the ceremony. Everyone is waiting for us."

"No," Kate said. "I need to talk to Tony now!"

The door at the back of the banquet room opened.

Everyone's head turned in that direction.

Tony started grinning from ear to ear.

Until Kate's father peeked around the door.

When Rob motioned for Tony, Tony frowned.

What the hell?

Tony could feel the heat creeping up his neck as he started the long walk to the back of the room.

The music had stopped now.

People were buzzing with conversation.

He glanced at his nervous-looking mother, who now had her hand dramatically over her heart and her lips moving silently in prayer. Grace was glaring at him rather suspiciously. That son of a bitch Harold—whom he still wouldn't mind punching out—had an amused smirk on his face.

The Wellingtons had been on Grace's invitation list.

Rather than start an argument, Tony had kept quiet.

But that didn't mean he had to like the guy.

Tony hurried on down the aisle, trying to ignore the snatches of conversation that were skipping around the room.

"You don't think she's changed her mind, do you?"

"Maybe she fainted."

"Brides do get nervous, you know."

"I bet this wedding cost a damn fortune."

"What a shame if she backs out now."

If she backs out now.

Kate would never do that.

She loved him.

Tony knew that, whether anyone else did or not.

He opened the door and found Kate standing there.

Her face was almost as white as her wedding dress.

She was in his arms before the door closed behind him.

"Baby, what's wrong?" Tony held her close while she sobbed against his shoulder.

He looked over her head at her father for an answer.

Rob only shrugged.

She finally pushed away from him, and said, "I need to hear you say you love me, Tony. Forever kind of love me. I need to hear you say that before I walk down that aisle."

Tony said, "I love you *beyond* forever, Kate."

He leaned forward and kissed her for reassurance.

"You're positive?" she asked, when he stepped back.

"Beyond positive," Tony told her.

"Even though I've just messed up our beautiful wedding ceremony? Even though my makeup is a mess now? Even though your mother and my grandmother are definitely going to kill me? You do still love me?"

"Beyond completely," Tony said, and grinned.

"Okay," Kate said. "That's all I needed to know."

"Does that mean you're ready to marry me now?"

"Beyond ready," Kate assured him.

Tony leaned forward and kissed Kate again.

The wedding march started up again.

The door at the back of the banquet room opened.

Everyone's head turned in that direction.

This time, Kate walked through the door.

She smiled when she heard the oohing and aahing.

But Kate only had eyes for Tony.

He was standing at the altar, a big grin on his face.

She loved this man.

Madly.

Truly.

Deeply.

Kate stopped walking when they reached the altar.

Her father stepped back and handed her over.

Tony reached out and took her hand.

Kate proudly stepped up beside the man she loved.

"You do look beautiful in that dress," Tony whispered.

Kate whispered back, "Why, thank you. This really cute cop I met in Central Park bought it for me."

"Maybe the two of you were destined to be together."

"Definitely," Kate said, and squeezed Tony's hand.

About the Author

Candy Halliday would win a gold medal if the Olympic committee recognized multitasking as a sport. In addition to being a wife, mother, and grandmother, Candy works a day job and pens her romantic comedies by night. Her books have been published in six different countries around the world. Candy lives in the Piedmont of North Carolina with her husband, a schnauzer named Millie, and an impossible cat named Flash. Never too busy to hear from readers, she can be reached via e-mail at her homepage www.candyhalliday.com.

More
Candy Halliday!

Please turn this page

for a preview of

Your Bed or Mine?

available in mass market

August 2006.

CHAPTER 1

Zada Clark didn't miss the frown on her divorce attorney's face as she hurried up the courthouse steps. Known around Chicago for her killer instinct in the courtroom, Angie Naylon was attractive, she was smart, and she looked the way a successful attorney should look in her man-tailored gray business suit, and with her auburn hair cut fashionably short in a no-nonsense style.

Had Angie not also been an old college friend, the disapproving frown would have intimidated Zada. Having personally held Angie's head out of the toilet back in their college days, however, served as a pretty good equalizer.

Still frowning, Angie looked her up and down when Zada reached the top of the steps. "Are you kidding me, Zada? This is your idea of a mousy-looking outfit for the judge's benefit?"

"No," Zada said stubbornly. "This is my idea of an eat-your-heart-out outfit for *Rick's* benefit. I want him to get his last good look at what he lost when he walked out on me."

"And how shallow is that?" Angie said in disgust.

"Today," said Zada, "shallow suits me just fine."

"Obviously," Angie snipped when two suits and ties walked past, craning their necks around for a second look. She looked back at Zada and said, "Your all-about-me dress certainly leaves nothing to the imagination. And here's another news flash for you. Red is *not* listed on the *mousy* side of the color chart."

"But red *is* listed on a brunette's side of the color chart," Zada argued. "Ask any brunette. It's our signature color."

"It's the *judge's* signature on your property settlement you need to be worried about," Angie said and frowned again. "I warned you this judge was old-school, Zada. That dress blows any chance we had of the judge believing you're the meek and mousy heartbroken housewife who is only asking to keep her home and her poor blind dog."

Angie glared at her again, wheeled around, then pushed through the double-glass front doors and stomped into the courthouse. Zada hurried after her.

"Oh, come on, Angie," Zada pleaded when she finally caught up. "I'm about as mousy as a wolverine, and you know it. You could dress me in a nun's habit, and I'd still look militant."

Angie kept walking.

Zada picked up speed, trying to keep up.

"We still have the poor blind dog hook," Zada mentioned, trying to make amends. "*I'm* the one who's taken care of Simon since Rick walked out on us."

"You keep forgetting Simon is still *Rick's* dog," Angie said. "I told you from the beginning Rick's attorney is going to make a big production over Rick and Simon being injured at O'Hare recovering that explosive device. The dog saved Rick's life. Separating a man from his heroic life-saving dog is not going to be an easy task."

"That's when you bring up the fact that I didn't even know Rick then, but that I was so touched when I heard Simon was blinded in that explosion, *I* visited Simon at the vet's hospital every day and even wrote a children's book about him."

"And Rick's attorney will remind the judge that Rick is one of the top explosive detection dog trainers in the nation," Angie said. "And that he works with dogs on a professional level every day."

"Yes, Rick does," Zada said. "He works at least twelve to fourteen hours every day. I, on the other hand, became Simon's stay-at-home mom once Rick and I were married. The mom who *didn't* walk out and leave Simon behind."

"And Rick's attorney will insist the only reason Rick left Simon behind, is because *Rick* had your house specifically designed so poor, blind Simon *could* function as a normal dog again."

Angie stopped walking and turned around to face her.

"You tell me, Zada. Now that you've blown my strategy and look anything *but* a meek and mousy heartbroken housewife, who do *you* think the judge is going to say deserves Simon and the house?"

"Me," Zada insisted.

Angie groaned and walked off again.

"Angie!" Zada called after her. "*I'm* the one who's made Simon a household name with my *Simon Sees* children's series." When she caught back up again, Zada said, "Be sure and point that out. *Publishers Weekly* and *The*

New York Times have both hailed *Simon Sees* as an inspiration for children with disabilities everywhere. Simon and I even have a national tour of children's hospitals scheduled during Christmas this year."

"How convenient," Angie quipped, "since red *is* your signature color." Her eyes cut sideways for a second. "Take my advice this time, Zada. Wear a different dress for the children's tour."

Angie turned down a corridor.

Zada clipped along behind her in four-inch heels.

At least Angie hadn't said anything about the shoes.

Her sling-back red pumps were as sexy as the dress.

Or maybe Angie just never got *past* the dress.

When they finally reached the designated courtroom, Angie pulled Zada aside and pointed a finger under her nose.

"Keep your militant mouth *shut* for once," Angie said. "I mean it, Zada. I don't want even so much as a peep out of you in that courtroom."

Zada made the zipped-lip motion with her fingers.

"You walk in there and sit down as quickly as possible before the judge notices the lower half of your dress is missing. And it wouldn't hurt to slump a little. Judge Parkins is in his seventies. The way that dress clings to every inch of your body, the old fart could have a heart attack and croak right there on the bench."

"Sit and slump," Zada said. "Got it."

She tried smiling brightly at Angie.

Angie *didn't* smile back.

Fine. Be that way, Zada decided.

Maybe short and clingy wasn't the best choice.

And maybe red wasn't the best color.

But Zada quickly changed her mind when she saw the look on Rick's face when she walked into the courtroom.

He was already seated at one of the tables at the front of the room. With his attorney. And now with an eyes-popped-out expression on his dropped-jaw face.

Zada smiled inwardly.

Screw slumping!

She threw her shoulders back.

She thrust her breasts forward.

She held her head high.

And walked right past her soon-to-be *ex* husband.

Rick was already nervous, but there was no doubt in his mind why his mouth suddenly went dry. Zada always had that effect on him. That feeling of being sucker-punched in the stomach. The kind of feeling that had the power to bring any man to his knees.

Except Rick was done.

No more on his knees, begging Zada to reconsider.

A man's pride could only take so much.

Yes, they'd had one hell of a fight. Yes, they'd both said horrible things to each other. And no, he shouldn't have walked out. Especially when he knew exactly how Zada felt about the "walking out" issue.

Zada's older sister had taken her husband back more times than he could remember; a huge sore spot with Zada. In retrospect, he'd often wondered if that was the main reason he had walked out that day—because he knew exactly how angry walking out would make Zada.

Biggest mistake of my life.

Angry didn't even touch Zada's reaction.

Livid was more like it.

Zada changed the locks on the house the same day.

Zada filed for separation papers two weeks later.

Any chance for a reconciliation had walked right out the door with him. Zada had told him so—in those exact words—during the one and only verbal conversation he'd had with her since the day he left.

After that conversation, their only communication, except through their attorneys, had been brief one-line e-mails. Him confirming every Wednesday he would stop by to see Simon. Her verifying she would make arrangements to be gone for the hour he would be at the house. Six months had passed now, the required separation period in Illinois if both parties agreed to the divorce.

Zada had no intention of backing down.

He had no intention of backing down.

Yet here he was sitting in a court room now, ready to face a judge who would put an end to their marriage, and all he could think about was how good Zada looked in that red dress, and what a damn fool he'd be if he let her go.

Rick was still looking at her, Zada could feel it.

It should have given her immense satisfaction knowing she'd definitely gotten his attention. But as good as she knew she looked in her new red dress, Rick looked ten times better.

The dark-blue suit showed off his tan, and his a-little-longer-than-fashionable hair was still a bit damp and sexy-looking from his morning shower. If she dared look directly at him, she knew his eyes would be a deep, brooding blue today. His eyes always turned darker when he was nervous or angry about something.

Funny, but she'd never even been attracted to blond men before she met Rick. Funny also that the second she met him, her tall, dark, and handsome preference switched to tall, *blond*, and handsome in about two seconds flat.

Of course, his ex-marine finely-honed body hadn't deterred her from quickly switching to the blond side, either. And dear God, if any man had a finely-honed body, it was Rick.

Supposedly thanks to his stupid health food, Zada thought with a pouting frown.

In retrospect, she'd often wondered what the hell she and Rick had been thinking going from a whirlwind romance straight into a marriage. If any two people had ever been total opposites, it was definitely the two of them.

Opposites attract, sure.

But that didn't mean they could live together.

She and Rick had sure proved that point.

In more ways than one.

Rick liked the house kept military-standard neat and tidy. Her idea of daily cleaning was a sweeping glance around the room.

Health-food-nut Rick prayed to the tofu gods who kept him in tip-top physical shape. She was on a first name basis with Ronald McDonald.

Early-to-bed-early-to-rise Rick ran five miles before breakfast every morning. Burning the midnight oil writing meant she rarely got up for breakfast—and *her* idea of exercise was jogging over to the fridge for another Dove ice-cream bar.

Living together had been a total disaster.

The fact that they were both Type-A personalities with extremely limited skills when it came to the art of compromise didn't help matters, either. Zada was surprised they hadn't killed each other the first week after the honeymoon. If the sex hadn't been so fabulous, they probably *would* have killed each other.

Fabulous sex.

Zada quickly dismissed that thought.

Reinforcements zoomed forward to take over.

Mind-boggling sex tapped her on the shoulder.

The twins—*hot and sweaty sex*—whispered in her ear.

Pleasure ran an enticing finger up and down her spine.

Ecstasy did a lively little tap dance just below her belly button.

Zada squirmed uncomfortably in her seat.

She reached for the water pitcher sitting on the table in front of her, poured a glass of water, and took a cool, calming drink. Only then did she chance her first look at Rick.

Dammit!

He was staring right at her.

She still loved him, truly she did.

But there was more to marriage than just great sex.

Damn you, Rick Clark!

Why did you have to walk out on me like that?

"All rise," the bailiff announced.

Angie grabbed her arm, pulling her to her feet.

Zada didn't dare look at Rick again.

But when a sinking feeling hit the pit of her stomach like a wrecking ball, Zada decided "slumping" wasn't going be any problem for her at all.

THE EDITOR'S DIARY

Dear Reader,

Ever meet a tall, dark and sexy stranger and see your destiny? Open those peepers a little bit wider. You won't want to miss a single word or a smoldering gaze from our two Warner Forever titles this November.

To Lady Isobel Macleod from **Amanda Scott's PRINCE OF DANGER**, marriage is a prison and husbands merely irritating encumbrances. Her domineering father and ferocious brother-in-law have proven as much to her. But when she comes upon Sir Michael St. Clair being savagely beaten by vicious strangers, she flies to the lone knight's defense, helps him escape, and flees with him into the rugged Highlands and beyond to Scotland's misty Isles. Alone under the stars with the man whose tenderness astonishes her, Isobel ponders her long-held prejudices. But as their relentless enemy pursues them, she faces a new danger—surrendering her freedom to this fearless yet gentle man . . . and linking her fate to the mysterious treasure that stirs mankind's greed and imagination to this very day. *Affaire de Coeur* raves "Amanda Scott is a master." This one is her best yet, so pick up a copy today.

Do you ever crave stability not passion? Kate Anderson from **Candy Halliday's MR. DESTINY** can relate. She's always wanted a stable marriage to a corporate attorney—no earth-shaking passion necessary. And she's finally found it. Never mind that their sex life consists of discussions in his therapist's office. But when a tall, dark and sexy patrol cop takes one look at her in Central Park and announces that he's her destiny, Kate just laughs. Officer Anthony Petrocelli's grandmother has always told him he would meet a beautiful blond with green eyes in Central Park when he was thirty-six and marry her. Now that he's met that stunning blond in the Park while thirty-six, he can't help but laugh. He wants to take Kate home to his family and disprove their silly prediction and Kate agrees. But after a little time with Anthony, sensible Kate can't help but wonder if stability is overrated. Maybe an unpredictable cop is just what she never knew she needed. RomanceReviewsMag.com raves Candy Halliday's last book was "fun…good reading and plenty of hot sex. What more can a woman ask for?"

To find out more about Warner Forever, these titles, and the authors, visit us at www.warnerforever.com.

With warmest wishes,

Karen Kosztolnyik

Karen Kosztolnyik, Senior Editor

P.S. With a dash of magic and spoonful of spice, next month's books will be twice as nice: Shari Anton weaves the enchanting and passionate tale of two headstrong lovers at cross purposes brought together by a spell fashioned centuries ago in MIDNIGHT MAGIC; and Kelley St. John delivers the steamy and hilarious story of a woman who creates alibis for a living and the sexy childhood friend she can't bear to come clean to in GOOD GIRLS DON'T.

Want to know more about romances at Warner Books and Warner Forever? Get the scoop online!

WARNER'S ROMANCE HOMEPAGE

Visit us at www.warnerforever.com for all the latest news, reviews, and chapter excerpts!

NEW AND UPCOMING TITLES

Each month we feature our new titles and reader favorites.

CONTESTS AND GIVEAWAYS

We give away galleys, autographed copies, and all kinds of fun stuff.

AUTHOR INFO

You'll find bios, articles, and links to personal Web sites for all your favorite authors—and so much more!

THE BUZZ

Sign up for our monthly romance newsletter, and be the first to read all about it!